Finding Sophie

Laura Lovett

FINDING SOPHIE

Author Photographer:
Rose Moyer, www.littlelaughs.com

Cover Designer: Corey Brennan, ELEVATE Design
www.elevate.design

Interior Formatting: Marla Thompson, Edgeofwater Designs
edgeofwater.com

Editor: Sheryl Khanna

ISBN: 978-1-77374-003-4 (sc)
ISBN: 978-1-77374-004-1 (hc)
ISBN: 978-1-77374-005-8 (e)

Praise for *Losing Cadence*

"Intensely riveting, spine-chilling, and highly suspenseful!"

~ *What's Better than Books? Book Blog*

"*Losing Cadence* draws you in and then flings you down the rabbit hole...it accelerates from page one and doesn't slow down. And just when you think there might be a happy ending, Lovett springs an unforeseen twist that will leave you racing towards the finish. Brace yourself for a villain you can't help but love to hate."

~ S.L. Reid, author of the *Evera Dark Trilogy*

"Just when you think you can't hang onto your seat any tighter, Lovett spins yet another twist into the plot of this gripping thriller. Romance, action, intrigue–it's all here in fast-paced, white-knuckle abundance. *Losing Cadence* is a whirlwind ride that readers won't soon forget."

~ Candace Allan, author of *Text Me, Love Mom: Two Girls, Two Boys, One Empty Nest*

"A suspenseful, intelligent adventure exploring passion and obsession, compassion and self-preservation, through a carefully composed, engrossing narrative."

~ Denene Derksen, author of *Dancing With Fire: Two Women Who Fall Out of the Ordinary*

"Forget any other suspense novel you have read in the past...RUN to buy, borrow or steal Laura Lovett's *Losing Cadence*! My breath was held, my heart was stopped, my mind was blown. I cannot wait for what comes next!"

~ Lana Shupe, Book Seller

Praise for *Finding Sophie*

"Lovett brilliantly raises demons while tugging at your heartstrings, and then sets you on a journey that melts together good versus evil versus love…leading to a destination that is both surprising and heartbreaking."

~ S.L. Reid, author of the *Evera Dark Trilogy*

"A thoroughly energizing read! These two spirited heroines grabbed my attention and had me cheering them on into the wee hours of the morning! I couldn't put this sure-fire bestseller down!"

~ Dr. Philip Love, author of *The Indiscretions of Others*

Dedication

THIS NOVEL IS DEDICATED to my three loving children: Nicholas (age 12), Matthew (age 9) and Cadence (age 7). They made it easier to write about Sophie and Cale in this novel. I thank them for giving me "mommy time" to write, and I promise that they can read this when they are at least sixteen! I see much creativity and artistic talent emerging in each of them, and I hope that I inspire them to follow their dreams.

Acknowledgements

I WOULD LIKE TO DEEPLY THANK my editor, publicist and friend, Sheryl Khanna, who has helped me every step of the way (literally, as several of our meetings were walking the hills of our community). Sheryl helped improve the novel by being constructive and honest, yet at the same time kind and supportive. From nixing my "too far-fetched" use of a submarine in the final chapters to bringing up my spirits whenever I received a tough review, Sheryl has been an amazing key to launching this book.

I would also like to thank *New York Times* Best Selling Author, Laura Munson, whom I learned so much from at the Haven Writing Retreat on her beautiful ranch in Montana in June 2016. Laura was a key mentor as I began working on this novel, teaching me to "show, not tell," and about the power of the scene. I also thank my fellow writers at this retreat, who provided support, input and critique to help me improve as a writer.

Also instrumental to this project were the other writers I met along the way, who cheered me on as we encouraged one another's progress. These writers include: Cindy Skogen (AKA S.L. Reid, author of the *Evera Dark* Trilogy), Tammy Rebere (author of an upcoming memoir), Susanne Clark (author of *Dishing Love Daily – And Other Secret Ingredients*) and Philip Love (author of *The Indiscretions of Others*).

Special thanks as well to my dear friend, Indra Singh, who hosted me at her beautiful acreage on Salt Spring Island, British

Columbia in July 2016, where I wrote the final chapters of this novel. And to my running friend, Shari Visvanathan, for her constant enthusiasm for this sequel.

I would also like to thank my five beta readers, who provided a constructive review and extensive feedback to help improve my final draft. In addition to my writer friends, Cindy Skogen and Tammy Rebere, these beta readers included: my sister, Kathleen Hambley, whose mastery of the English language and analytical eye helped me very much; my sister, Sharon Barrett, for her edits and encouragement from the inception of the first book and through this sequel; and my friend, Susan Burrows, who has recommended and bought more of *Losing Cadence* than anyone!

This project required a lot more research than *Losing Cadence*, and I owe a special thank you to my team and external experts who answered my questions to make this story as believable as possible. Thank you to Manya Singh for her research on third-degree burn scars and show choirs (yes, an unlikely combination!). Thank you to Bob Hill for his expertise on luxury yachts, having sold them for many years in Florida; and thank you to Susan Burrows for introducing me to Bob. Thank you to Mike Sorsdahl, my colleague and a former commanding officer in the Navy, for answering my many questions about ships, yachts, lifeboats, nautical miles, etc.! And thank you to Owen Rau for answering my questions about helicopters, including layout, navigation systems and functionality. I had fun naming some of my characters after you!

A special thank you to Corey Brennan of Elevate Design for the stunning cover art, which beautifully complements *Losing Cadence* and captures the essence of this novel. And to my talented niece, Rosie Moyer of mindspinmedia.com, who created the book trailer that perfectly depicts *Losing Cadence* and the beginning of this sequel.

Once a book is written, the work is only just beginning. I have had an amazing team help me with the ongoing marketing of *Losing Cadence* and the launch of this sequel. In addition to my publicist, Sheryl Khanna, I have had help with social media, website design and marketing from Madyson Huck, April Dyrda, Raelynn Deschner, Jessilyn Yuhas and Jaimie Murphy.

I would also like to thank my late friend, Melodie Becker, for her amazing eye for detail when proofreading *Losing Cadence*, as well as her encouragement on the sequel. Mel left us far too young, but I feel her spirit in my life and feel lucky to have had her as a close friend.

Finally, I would like to thank my husband of nineteen years, Scott Lovett. There are many words to describe his role in this project, among them: loving, patient, helpful, encouraging, steady, generous, and so many more. Thank you, Scott, for taking the kids to movies and outings to give me blocks of power writing time. Without you, I would never have finished this novel on time.

Chapter One

RICHARD SAT IN HIS villa in the Bahamas, the warm ocean breeze and sounds of the lapping waves coming through the large, open doors of the massive deck. He was fixated not on the magnificent view, but on his computer screen that was livestreaming his daughter's twelfth birthday party. He felt the adrenaline coursing through his veins as he knew his time was drawing near. He saw her beautiful smile, her sweet face.

"Happy birthday, dear Sophie. Happy birthday to you!" played through the speaker. Sophie took a deep breath, focusing intently on the twelve candles on what appeared to be a yellow cake decorated with pink flowers. She blew with great effort, ten of the twelve candles smoking in defeat, as her friends joked about the two she'd missed. He ached to be there with his family, in Christian's place, where he belonged.

The cameras were his companions; they helped him be part of Sophie's life. He was there for all major events through that small eye nestled so inconspicuously that most top agents wouldn't be able to uncover it. Leo, the ex-CIA agent who helped him in the dark days after Cadence left him to die in the fire, was a genius at this gig. The hideous scars from the third-degree burns on his face and body were a constant reminder of that day; for years, he had wished it had been his last. But in Richard's world there was always a plan, then another, and another one after that. Richard had backup upon backup, which saved his life when a guard who was stationed nearby arrived just in time to save Richard from being burned alive or bleeding out from the deep stab wound in his chest. That knife had only been an inch from puncturing his pulmonary artery. The heat of the fire felt as though it was tearing apart his soul, or what was left of it. The thick, dark smoke engulfed his body, and he felt the sharp, throbbing pain of the wound in his chest as he tried to breathe.

He recalled those final moments on that burning deck. "Let me die," Richard whispered.

"Not a chance," Leo responded, dragging Richard's body away from the burning log home, then wrapping his chest in what felt like a tight bandage. He didn't remember anything after that as he passed out from the pain before being driven quickly away in an ATV through the dense Oregon forest.

He was brought back from those dark memories by the live video of his Cadence putting her arm around Sophie. Sophie smiled, her expression reminding him so much of his own, her eyes and hair giving away the secret of who her real father was. Yet she had her mother's beautifully shaped lips and nose, set perfectly on her porcelain skin. How he longed to put his arms around them both. Yearned for the warmth of their arms around him. Ached every day and every night for their love.

Just then Christian came between them and Richard turned away from the video, his hands making tight fists and his breath quickening. He couldn't bear to watch anymore, and stormed out of the room as the recording continued. He would watch more of his wife and daughter later, as was his daily ritual.

As he walked outside the villa and onto the soft, white sandy private beach, he breathed deeply to calm the rage that seeing Christian always caused. Soon, he promised himself. Soon this torture would come to an end and he could have what belonged to him.

Chapter Two

After everyone finished their cake, I sat down and looked at my twelve-year-old daughter, smiling in awe at how much she'd grown. No longer a child, Sophie was beginning to show the early curves and height of her impending teenage years. Her strawberry blonde hair hung in long, soft curls for her party. Her green eyes took on a darker or lighter color depending on the clothing she wore. Today they were bright, picking up the vibrant shade of her green and pink patterned top, with a black skirt topping her long, lean legs. She stood five-foot-two, only four inches from my height. Sophie's beautiful lips sparkled with pink lip gloss. High pitched girls' laughter filled our dining room, which smelled of sugary sweetness intermixed with the last remnants of smoke from her twelve smoldering candles.

I was startled out of my thoughts by a warm hand on my shoulder, as Christian sat down beside me and whispered in my ear, "Our girl's growing up fast."

"I know. Yet it seems like forever ago that she was a baby," I said. Just then our nine-year-old son Cale came running up to his sister as she was cutting the cake, eager to devour his piece. He grinned as he tickled his big sister, Sophie yelping in return

Unlike his sister's pale features, Cale had inherited Christian's dark brown curls and soft brown eyes. I smiled at how lucky I was to have these two beautiful, healthy children. And I felt such immense love for my husband, reaching for and squeezing his hand. I felt at peace on this February day marking a dozen years since I gave birth to Sophie Maria here in New York.

Like an unwanted mosquito, the thought I was hoping to avoid began buzzing around in my mind. It nagged at me until it forced itself to be acknowledged. Richard and the last note he'd sent when Sophie was born; his declaration that when she was old enough to understand that he was her real father, he would no longer keep his distance. I shuddered at the thought. Yet I knew the time had come to share this with Sophie. Perhaps we should have donc so earlier? I'd agonized over whether to tell her at age ten when she had learned the facts of life. Was she old enough back then to take in the truth about her biological father? No, she was still too innocent at age ten, and same with age eleven, we had reasoned.

Yet I knew I was taking a risk by waiting. If Richard had decided to surface and tell Sophie he was her father before I did, Sophie would be traumatized. Yet I wanted her to believe for as long as possible that Christian was her birth father. Sophie would have the rest of her life to live with the truth. But age twelve felt like the right time; waiting any longer would be wrong. Christian and I agreed that it needed to happen now. Partly because we believed in honesty, and felt that Sophie deserved the truth. But also, because we needed Sophie to be aware that Richard was likely still out there and the risk of abduction was one we had to address openly. Knowing the truth would allow us to build precautions as Sophie became more independent in her teenage years.

That night I awoke in the early hours of the morning, anxious thoughts bringing my mind to wakeful worry. Christian was sleeping soundly, his arm draped over my side, his deep, steady breaths maintaining a peaceful rhythm. I gently placed his arm onto the bed, and quietly made my way to Sophie's bedroom. She slept deeply, the blanket pulled to her chin as was her habit since she was a child. I stood in the hall outside her bedroom and silently cried for her last night of living without the truth … the truth of the crazy and unbelievable yet real story of how Sophie was brought into this world.

The following day, a cloudy Sunday afternoon, Sophie, Christian and I sat together in the living room of our New York City apartment. We had arranged for Cale to go to a friend's house to give us privacy. I sat beside Sophie on the pale blue couch, and Christian sat kitty-corner on a blue and green checkered armchair.

"Mom, dad, this is weird," she said, brows furrowed. "What's wrong?" she asked, knowing when I said we had to talk that something serious was coming.

"Sophie, we need to tell you something. You … your …" my voice cracked as my tears came quickly. Christian handed me a tissue, his calm gaze a comfort as the emotions shook through me. I struggled to find the words to tell our daughter the truth. I felt my hands shaking.

"What your mom and I need to tell you is that I'm your dad in every way possible, but I'm not your biological father," Christian explained.

"What? That can't be true!" Sophie exclaimed, as if willing us to be wrong.

"Oh, Sophie, it *is* true," I whispered through my tears. "It's a long story, but one that we feel you need to know," I said, stroking her back, the tears welling in her eyes too.

"Why didn't you tell me sooner?" she asked, a small tear slipping down her rosy cheek.

"We wanted to wait until you were old enough to understand, as it was an unusual situation," Christian explained, knowing I was having a hard time holding myself together.

"But how come I've never met him?" Sophie asked, curiosity overriding her shock.

"Because … cause he's not mentally well, Sophie," I carefully explained. "He disappeared before you were born, and he's wanted by the police."

"What?" Sophie exclaimed, her eyes wide with shock, as she brushed another tear from her cheek. I hugged her small waist as I passed her a tissue.

"This is hard to say, Sophie, but you need to understand. Your father was my boyfriend in twelfth grade, and we only dated for a few months. But ten years later, when I was engaged to your dad," I said, my voice cracking with a flood of emotions, "he abducted me and forced me to … to marry him," I whispered, tears falling onto my white pants.

Sophie's face was a mix of shock and sadness as she absorbed this unexpected story. "How … how did you get away?" Sophie stammered.

"With great courage," said Christian, before I could reply. "Your mom was braver than you could ever imagine in getting away from him after being there for over three months." The pride was clear in Christian's voice, yet he was coming very close to portraying Richard as a monster, which he was, but I was hoping to soften this message for Sophie's sake.

"Mom, was I born then?" Sophie asked.

"No, I was only just pregnant by the time I escaped," I replied. "Christian has been in your life from the time I found out that I was expecting you," I said, gently stroking her back.

"I remember seeing you in the very first ultrasound, honey. It was just like you were mine. Not once have I ever thought of you any other way," Christian said, leaning forwards and reaching out to touch Sophie's hand.

"What is his name?" Sophie asked.

"Richard. Richard White," I answered, trembling as I said the name out loud that I had avoided in this home, as if it were a profanity.

"Where is he now?" Sophie asked, curiosity curbing her tears.

"Nobody knows," I answered. "He was very wealthy and was able to disappear. But he really wanted a child and I believe he might try to come back into our lives." The pain etched in my voice as I explained this possibility. I knew Richard's level of persistence in getting what he wanted, and nothing would surprise me.

"So, we need to be vigilant and careful, Sophie," Christian said. "As I can't let him take you, or your mom again."

"Wow," Sophie whispered. "This seems so unreal. Would

he … *hurt* me?"

I swallowed, a lump had formed in my throat from the pain of this conversation. This was a delicate balance between honesty and not wanting to portray Richard as a complete monster so that Sophie lived in fear. But we needed to be realistic. "No, I don't believe he'd hurt either of us," I said. "He's mentally ill and obsessive, but he does, in his own way, love us." The word love felt strange on my tongue. But it was his perception, regardless of how anyone else defined love. I truly believe he did what he did for love, but was dangerously lost as to the true meaning of the word.

"What does he look like?"

I tried to find the right words to answer her valid question. "He has green eyes, like yours ... and blonde hair, similar to yours. And he's tall, about six-foot-two. He was my boyfriend a long time ago, and he was handsome and brilliant. He had a lot of good qualities, but I knew he wasn't right for me. He became very possessive and I felt that I needed to break up with him. But I want you to know, he did have good qualities; it wasn't all bad until he abducted me ten years later and I knew just how mentally sick he was," I explained, seeing her absorb every word, as many questions filled her young mind.

"Oh, mom, this is so *weird*," Sophie said.

"I know, Sophie, but we want you to know the truth. Your dad and I love you very much and we wanted to raise you, as you are a part of me. And you have the good parts of Richard in you, too. You're intelligent and attractive, just like he was. You're athletic and confident, just like him. You don't have *any* of his dark qualities." I felt her shudder at the word "dark."

"Do you have any photos?" she asked.

"I don't have any, but the lead agent on the case has some that he will share with you when he briefs you further this week," I explained. I noticed her eyes widen at mention of a briefing with the FBI, and added, "We just need you to understand how to take the right precautions to stay safe."

"What if . . . what if he tries to take me away?" she asked, the fear palpable in her young voice.

"Oh, Sophie, don't worry. That's why we live in this secure building and that's why we don't let you go out on your own. As you get older, we will need you to be very cautious. Until Richard is caught, we cannot risk him trying to take you."

"Exactly, we need you to be very aware of your surroundings, and to know what Richard White looks like in case he does turn up," added Christian. "Your mom and I could have changed our identities after this all happened, but we wanted to live as normal lives as possible. We made the decision that we couldn't spend our lives hiding, and the fact that it's been over twelve years is a good sign. Chances are he's gone forever, or at least we hope."

"Wait a second," said Sophie, her eyes looking distant as she focused on a thought. "I wonder if that was him?" she said.

I felt my body tense. "What?"

"It was last spring," Sophie began. She had always loved to sing, so we'd put her in voice lessons from the time she was four. Her talent continued to flourish and last year she had won the role of Dorothy in her school's musical theater production of *The Wizard of Oz.* She practiced every moment she could, and we were very proud of her. Her voice was sweet and pure, carrying the music with grace and passion.

Sophie explained how she was at a rehearsal after school and was singing *Somewhere Over the Rainbow.* "There were only a few parents near the front, and Mr. Jones and Mrs. Kramer were taking notes," Sophie said. "Then my eye caught someone entering the back of the theater, a tall guy in a long, black coat, who sat in the very back row. I thought it was somebody's parent. But when I finished the song, my teachers and the cast clapped, but what caught my eye was that man in the back standing and clapping. He clapped well past the others, then sat back down as the teachers turned around to look at him."

"Oh my God," I whispered, certain it was him.

"After we finished another song, my friend Lucy and I went to use the bathroom and when we passed the man in the coat, he said, 'You're a talented singer.' I shivered as he struck me as very unusual, wearing a long coat like that on a spring evening, as well as large sunglasses and a baseball cap. He was also covering his chin with his hand, so that we saw only a portion of his face, which looked scarred. I said thanks and Lucy asked him if he was someone's parent," she explained.

"And what did he say?" Christian asked, visibly anxious.

"He said 'Yes,' then his cell phone rang and he turned away from us to take the call and Lucy and I went to the bathroom. We both thought he was odd and he gave us the creeps, but when we went back into the theater he was gone," she concluded.

"You never told us this," I said.

"I didn't think much about it as we went back to practice and I forgot about him," Sophie said. "I'm sorry, now I wish I had," she added.

"God, why can't he leave us alone?" asked Christian, looking angry, and running his fingers through his dark curls as he sighed with frustration, shaking his head.

"It may not have even been him, honey," I said, not really

believing my own words, which were meant to calm the anxiety we all felt. "And if it was him, he didn't try to take you or appear again, thank God," I added.

"But I wouldn't put it past that madman," said Christian. "We'll need to talk to Jack Kent about adding security detail again," he added, shaking his head.

"I know," I whispered. "Give me a minute." I stood and went down the hall into the master bedroom. I opened the shiny Cherrywood jewelry box that sat on my dresser. The top layer where my necklaces and earrings were kept pulled out, and underneath is where I kept my most private keepsakes and memories. There sat a pale pink envelope addressed to Cadence Weaverly. I had moved it out of Sophie's small keepsake chest and into here when she was six-years-old and curious enough to examine its contents. I grabbed it and walked back into the living room, touched by the loving way Christian had moved beside Sophie and was holding her hand and speaking softly to her.

"I have something I feel you should see," I said, sitting next to Sophie and handing her the letter. "This was the very last time I heard from him. I've saved this for when you were old enough to understand," I added.

She cautiously opened the envelope, pulling out and unfolding the pale pink paper. She read the letter slowly out loud, pained curiosity clear on her pretty face.

"Dear Cadence,

It has taken me this long to put into words what I have been feeling. Your betrayal hurt more than the stab wound and burns that I endured that day. I would rather have died knowing you loved me, than lived on knowing you left me to die. As fate would have it, I survived and am trying to forgive you for the sake of our daughter. Sophie is beautiful and I cannot thank you enough for bringing her into this world.

I can see that you are happy – that he has taken the role of loving husband and father. I would give anything to have you and Sophie as my own. But I know taking you would lead to the same outcome – you constantly trying to escape from me. I have decided that until Sophie is old enough to understand that I am her real father, I will keep my distance. But when that time comes, she will know who I am and how much I love her.

I will look in on you two from time to time to make sure you are doing well, and I will put money aside in an account for Sophie so she never has to worry about money for the rest of her life.

Cadence, despite what you did to me, I cannot stop loving you and our daughter. I hope before I meet Sophie one day that you will explain to her who I am and the fact that I wanted her more than anything and would never hurt her. Please don't portray me as a monster but as a husband and father who deeply loves his two ladies.

Love Always to you both,
Richard

As I watched the tears spill from my daughter's eyes, I wondered if I had made a mistake in sharing Richard's letter.

But Christian and I had discussed this too, and decided it was best to be transparent. I had even wanted to keep the letter from Christian when I first received it, but it was burning a hole in my mind as I thought of it constantly. It was as though its secret existence allowed Richard to have a place in our home. So, I shared it with Christian, his eyes filling with tears of anger and fear for this man who would never be fully gone. Although there was nothing any of us, including the FBI agents on the case, could do to track it, the information was confirmation that Richard was alive.

Sophie swallowed hard as she wiped her tears with the tissues I passed her, then looked from me to Christian and back again. "Mom, what *happened* to him?" she asked.

"Oh, Sophie. He hurt and killed many people as he tried to keep me as his prisoner. I eventually gave up trying to escape, as I knew there was no way out without risking more lives. But a very brave woman, Maria, whom your middle name honors, was also being held and she was not going to let us remain prisoners. She had the courage to stab Richard, then set his house on fire so we could escape," I said, the words sounding foreign even to me, as if this were a movie that was so far-fetched it couldn't really have happened.

"But he *still* got away?" she asked.

"I honestly don't know how. There weren't any security guards around, and he was bleeding and the fire was all around him. Someone must have arrived just in time. Thankfully, Maria and I were able to escape and call for help, but I still have terrible nightmares," I said, my voice quivering.

"Oh, mom," she said, hugging me tightly as we cried with both sadness and fear.

Chapter Three

RICHARD LOOKED AT THE scene on his screen of his wife and daughter hugging. Yes, his time was drawing near. She now knew Cadence's side of the story, but she also needed to hear his. To hear how fiercely he loved Cadence and Sophie, and how the only reason he still breathed was because of them.

There were many times when he wanted to take his own life, to end the constant, relentless voices in his head. Angry voices telling him that he wasn't loved and didn't deserve to be here. Telling him how badly he'd fucked up, how he'd stupidly missed the key detail of checking for the note that Cadence had planted in her flute, which led to her escape. How he hadn't seen through her lie about it being broken, and fell into her trap of sending it to a flute technician who called the cops. If he'd been more vigilant, that note would have never left his property and they would still be together as a family. Of that he was sure.

He also hated that miserable voice from the past; the one

that would pull the curtains open to reveal memories from his childhood that he yearned to forget. He saw himself at Sophie's age, walking into his house with his math exam in hand, proud of his ninety-eight percent. His father was always working, and Richard dared not interrupt him in his large office with those double French doors that remained tightly shut. But on that day one of the doors was open and Richard saw his father sitting with his hands covering his face. His father was a tall man, with graying hair and a matching, neatly groomed beard. Always dressed professionally, he had never seen his father in casual clothing.

Hesitantly, he walked towards the door, peering into the dimly lit office. "Father?" he asked, with trepidation. He was never allowed to use the word dad, as that was slang according to his parents. His father looked up suddenly, eyes bloodshot and furious. "You know not to interrupt me, *ever*!" he yelled.

"I just … I just saw the door open and wanted to tell you about my, um, math exam," he stammered.

"Speak properly! I didn't raise an imbecile," his father shot back.

"Here's my math exam," Richard said, his hand shaking as he passed the stapled sheets to his father, who grabbed them forcefully, nearly ripping the exam. "Not only do you interrupt me, but you do so over something like *this*?" he asked, a look of pure disgust in his gray eyes. He shook his head, scowling at his twelve-year-old son.

"I just thought, you'd be … pleased," Richard said, trying

to hold off the hot tears

that threatened to release.

"GET OUT!" his father yelled, crumbling the exam into a tight ball, and throwing it at Richard's face. "I *never* want to see a grade that's less than perfect from my son," he added, turning his chair back towards his desk as Richard quickly left, gently closing the door behind him. The hot tears flowed as he ran upstairs and locked himself in his bedroom and curled up crying in his closet, careful not to make a sound as his parents had no tolerance for tears. *Cry baby*, said the nasty voice in his head, over and over. *Cry baby, cry baby, cry baby ...*

The memory mercifully faded and he was brought back to the present. He would not be like his father. No way. He yearned to praise and encourage Sophie. He was already so proud of his little girl, and it took everything in him not to run up to her, pick her up and hold her tightly in his arms each time he watched her from a distance. He remembered the time in the theater when he was so moved by her beautiful singing, and ached to hold her when she spoke to him as he sat at the back of the theater. He knew that even his willpower, which was as strong as steel, may not last when she returned from the bathroom, so he abruptly left.

Over the past twelve years, there had been other times when he was near Sophie, but he was extremely careful knowing that security personnel were always around. Whether it was at school, on field trips, or shopping, he'd remain hidden in the background, sometimes even relying on binoculars. But he knew his time in New York needed to be limited due to the high risk of being seen, so about seventy-five percent of his time was spent in the Bahamas.

He turned off the video feed as he could not stand to see Christian hugging *his* daughter. He went to the bathroom, and as he washed his hands he stared at the man looking back at him in the mirror. The horrible scars on half of his face had only slightly faded over the past twelve years, from fiery red to a dark brown color. They covered the entire right side of his face, from his chin to his forehead, including part of his nose. What had once been a face he considered handsome, was now half the face of a monster; his scars raised and leathery in texture, despite several plastic surgeries. The inherent challenge, his plastic surgeon explained, was that the extent of burns on his body didn't allow for a large enough patch of healthy skin to repair his facial scars.

He ran two fingers over the surface of what had once been his smooth arm covered in soft hair, now a rough, uneven patchwork. His arms and legs were a myriad of shades ranging from dark to pale yellow, to pale white. Multiple plastic surgeries to repair the worst of the burn scars only marginally helped his appearance. The scar on his right elbow joint was the most problematic, because he could not easily bend his arm, which required even further surgeries. All this from the torture he endured so many years ago.

"Cadence, how could you let this happen to me?" he asked into the empty bathroom.

Silence.

"I would have given you and Sophie the perfect life, and so many of our potential years together have now been wasted."

The voice spoke in return, as if another being was standing beside him. *She doesn't love*

you. Neither of them love you. You look like a monster,

and your money can't buy their love.

"Shut up! They *will* love me. Sophie is my flesh and blood and ties me to Cadence for life. Nothing can change that!"

Will they really accept a monster into their lives?

The voice was relentless. He knew it all too well.

"They will have no choice," he said, turning off the light and slamming the bathroom door, trying in vain to escape the evil voice that was part of his every day.

Chapter Four

I WATCHED AS SOPHIE nervously fiddled with her bracelet as she sat across from Agent Kent, who'd been a steady fixture on the case for the past twelve years.

"Thanks so much for meeting with us, Jack," I said, grateful for how he looked at her with compassion, his blue eyes steady and calming, framed by his dark, salt and pepper hair. Christian and I sat on either side of Sophie, there to support her through this briefing process.

"I know this news must not have been easy, Sophie," Jack said. He was genuine and calm in his approach, in contrast to Sophie who was nervously twitching her leg and playing with her fingernails. "But it's safer if you know the situation so that you can be aware and careful in your daily life. Like your parents explained, Richard White is unpredictable and could surface again. In my whole career, I've never seen a case like this, which is why I've put off retiring for as long as I can to see this case get solved," he said with a warm and reassuring smile. "I've made it my personal mission to put Richard White behind bars where he belongs."

"Do you think he'd try to take me and my mom?" Sophie asked, focused intently on Agent Kent for an honest answer.

"I think it's possible, but it's difficult to say. If you assume that it's in the realm of possibility, and take all the necessary precautions, the likelihood is very low. Unlike before, he is a known entity now and has had to go into hiding to avoid arrest. It would be extremely difficult for him to abduct either of you now, and if it did happen we're be much better equipped to find you. But I'm here to tell you what you need to do, Sophie, to make sure this never happens."

"Okay, I'll do whatever's needed," Sophie calmly responded, locking eyes with Agent Kent so he knew she was serious. I was proud of her bravery and resiliency, as I knew the news about Richard had been difficult to process. It was still very fresh for Sophie, having only learned about her biological father's existence a few days earlier.

"First things first, security is key. With the additional sighting at the theater last year, we need to increase security so that we can keep you safe and maximize the chance of catching him. Whenever you're out, whether it's with your parents or on your own, having security with you is critical. We thought we could avoid this, but given how close he got to you, we cannot risk you being on your own. This building and your private school are both safe; he cannot get into either and both are completely aware of this threat. But beyond these places, you will always need a security detail and you need to keep an eye on where they are, in case there's a sighting. I'm still stunned that he had the nerve to show up at your theater practice. We're surprised that he'd take that type of risk, and we've increased our measures accordingly," he repeated, looking saddened yet determined.

"Where do you think he lives?" Sophie asked.

"It's hard to say, but most likely out of the country. His face was all over national media for quite some time, and the case gained so much attention that he'd be hard pressed not to be recognized. He has the means to live anywhere he wants, and travel here as often as he wants. But like I said, it's risky for him to be here, so if I had to guess I'd say he's rarely nearby."

"Should I tell my friends?" Sophie asked, having discussed this with us as well. She was torn between feeling embarrassed, yet knowing that she needed support around her should he surface again. I felt sad for her, as she explained how she worried her friends may not want to be around her knowing there was potentially a crazy man following her.

"It depends on the situation, but I recommend that your close friends be made aware. The more eyes the better, in case he's nearby. The best outcome would be to catch him and be done with this once and for all. But until that happens, we all need to be very vigilant," he said, his voice calm yet firm. "We have a GPS tracking app in all your cell phones. But we can't rely on phones alone, so we're also going to attach these GPS tracking devices to your jackets and school bags and belts so that we always have a way of knowing where you are."

"Okay," Sophie said, taking this all in while trying to hide her level of shock at the extremity of the situation.

Agent Kent went on to explain more of the security protocol, and when he left we all felt drained. We went out for Italian as a family, still electing to keep Cale innocent about our scenario, at least until he was a year or two older and could better comprehend that his sister had another father, who happened to be a wanted criminal.

That evening, as I was getting ready for bed, I heard a faint sound from Sophie's bedroom. I walked quietly, my slippered feet landing softly on the dark hardwood, and stood outside of her door. She was sobbing. I felt tears sting my eyes as I opened her door. She was curled up on her bed crying more intensely than I'd ever seen her cry before. I lay down beside her and hugged her tightly, trying to comfort her and not lose control by sobbing myself.

"Why, mom? Why would he want to hurt us?" she cried.

"Oh, Sophie, he would never hurt you or me, he just wants to have us in his life. And he … he never will if I can help it," I said as confidently as I could.

"I just wish they could catch him."

"So do I, Sophie. So do I …"

Chapter Five

RICHARD WOKE UP IN a cold sweat, tears coating his rough, scarred cheeks. His sobs must have woken him from the nightmare. Each night would bring its own terrors: the fire, losing Cadence, his childhood. Each nightmare equally horrible.

This particular dream was so real that he swore he was there, with his parents, at their lake home, on that sunny August day when his mother had a nervous breakdown. He could still picture the high log ceilings, the pristine lake view, and the trees that were too tall to see the tops of. This place was large, but to a boy of nine it looked colossal.

He walked into the kitchen, looking for a drink, only to find his mother with her hands in a pot of water that was coming to a boil. She was moaning in pain as the water became hotter, her brown hair disheveled as it hung limply down her white housecoat.

Richard was shocked and stood still for a moment, then

lunged forwards grabbing his mother's arms. "Mother, don't!" he pleaded.

Just then his father entered the kitchen. "Constance?" he roared, as his son pulled at his mother's arms, which stubbornly refused to leave the nearly boiling water. His father leaped forwards and pushed Richard out of the way, causing Richard to fall over and knock down a nearby bar stool. He yanked his wife away from the scalding water, her hands a deep red, but not yet blistering. "What the hell are you doing, you crazy bitch?" he screamed, as Richard maneuvered into the corner of the kitchen, shaking with fear.

"I can't go on like this, Alexander," she whispered. "I can't feel anymore. I hate ... *being*," she said, staring at her red hands.

"I give you all of this ... and you hate 'being'?" he yelled. "You're a madwoman. Crazier than I thought. One hundred screws loose. And our son has half of your fucked up genes! Good God, I might as well check him into the psych ward along with you," he yelled, the rage boiling over much like the water that now bubbled in the stainless steel pot.

"Alexander, please ... this has nothing to do with Richard," she begged. "It's me. I can't *feel*, you've taken away my ability to *feel* anything," she said, bowing her head in defeat. Richard wished he could escape, but was too terrified to move. He'd learned the hard way to disappear when his father was in a rage.

"You can't *feel* anything, Constance? And you blame me? Well, feel *this*," he yelled, as he grabbed the glistening metal handle of the boiling pot, and threw the now boiling water on her, which also splashed across the floor, hitting Richard's leg, making him involuntarily scream, which was nothing in comparison to his mother's painful shrieks.

"So, you do *feel*, after all," his father stated with vile confidence, and then left.

"Mother, are you okay?" Richard asked, as he crawled towards her as she lay on the floor in agony, blistered red skin appearing wherever her housecoat didn't offer protection. "Can I get you some ice?"

"I'm … fine. Please go," she said in a weak voice.

Richard didn't tell his mother about his pain, his burns. It wasn't worth it. He wanted to call the police, but he knew better. The one time he had tried that, there was hell to pay for many months, especially for his mother.

As the scene of this painful dream finally faded, he was left with a feeling of gratitude that his daughter would never have to face the pain that he'd endured growing up. That his Cadence would never be treated as his mother was. He was not the monster his father was. He may look like a monster now, but he *wasn't* one. He deserved to be the father and husband he was destined to be. He had suffered long enough.

Chapter Six

"I'M SO EXCITED WE won!" Sophie exclaimed, grinning widely as we sat around the kitchen table having deep dish pepperoni pizza for dinner. Her show choir had won the regional competition and were going to compete nationally next month. She passed the forms to us, which outlined the dates, costs and required paperwork. "It'll be so much fun to go to San Diego! Can we stay longer and go to Disneyland?" she asked, looking from me to Christian and back again, her green eyes filled with excitement and anticipation.

Christian glanced at the dates, his dark eyebrows furrowed. "Oh, honey, I wish we could, but the symphony plays twice that week … I just can't make it work this time. But your mom and Cale should go," Christian replied, glancing over apologetically towards me, and squeezing my hand under the table. True, my career was flexible as a part-time private flute teacher and music composer, which I'd begun to do more seriously last year. I was able to work around the kids' schedules, and appreciated not being tied to a full-time job.

I felt my heart sink thinking about going to San Diego without Christian. I felt as though part of me would be missing if I went for almost a week without being near him. Ever since the abduction I had a difficult time when we were apart for any more than a couple of days. My nightmares would intensify and I'd find myself in an increasingly anxious state of mind. My tired mind would then convince me that I was being watched, and I would constantly look over my shoulder. It was a vicious cycle between lack of sleep and paranoia, each making the other worse.

"Mom, don't look so sad, we'll still have fun!" Sophie said.

"Yeah, I can be the dad of the family," Cale added. "I can do the rollercoasters now … the ones I couldn't do when we went last time!" We'd gone to Disneyland as a family, three years earlier when Cale was six and Sophie nine.

"Of course, you can, Cale. We'll have a great time!" I said, trying to sound as cheerful as possible. My children both grinned widely, as they figured out it would be thirty-five more sleeps until the trip.

It was six weeks ago that Sophie learned about Richard, and life was starting to feel somewhat normal again since her security briefings were over, and she had explained the situation to her closest friends, and we to their parents. She realized that they were still her friends, and everyone appreciated knowing that security was on hand.

Sophie finally seemed to run out of what seemed like an endless stream of questions about Richard and my time with him, both in high school and during the abduction. I tried to be honest, yet not share every vivid detail; it was as if I was reliving the trauma when I explained things, and I didn't want Sophie to feel my pain. She knew what she needed to know, and I tried to balance the horrible side of Richard with his good points. To instill in her that he *did* have positive qualities, however shadowed they were by his lack of respect for life and freedom.

Sophie also got used to faithfully having her cell phone fully charged and on her, as well as always carrying her handbag or school bag, which each had built in GPS trackers. She even had a removable, small rectangular tracker that she placed on either her belt or bra strap, depending on what activities she had that day. The key point the FBI emphasized was that she always needed a tracker on her body, and one that she carried with her, so that she could be found if something happened; an abductor would likely assume there was only one, not two trackers.

I had a similar scenario, with a tracker in my Kate Spade purse, as well as a detachable one I clipped onto my bra each day. Even at night I'd clip it onto my pajamas, knowing that the last time I was taken was when I was asleep. I felt most vulnerable at night, especially when Christian and I were apart.

I asked my typical question as Sophie headed out of our apartment for school: "Got your trackers, honey?"

"Yep, mom. It's so weird to know they can track our every move. So much for privacy," she said, smiling weakly.

"Sophie, I'd much rather give up privacy than live the alternative," I said. Of that I was sure.

Chapter Seven

RICHARD STOOD ON THE upper deck of his newest purchase, a superyacht that he had spent the last few years researching and then having custom built. This beauty, which he named the Great White, stretched three hundred and fifty-two feet in length. It boasted fifteen spacious staterooms, and included a ten-meter pool and twelve-person hot tub. He went to great lengths to have his identity kept one-hundred percent confidential, brokering the purchase through his right-hand man, Leo. He had hired Leo, an ex-CIA agent, after he and Cadence had come back from that debacle in Jamaica and he knew he couldn't fully trust the competence of his existing security team. Leo was carefully chosen, and was only days away from starting on Richard's security team when Richard fled with Cadence and Maria from his California mansion after the FBI had zeroed in on its location. He had called Leo from the helicopter flight to his log home in the deep woods of Oregon, and luckily Leo arrived within minutes of Richard perishing in that fire. Or perhaps that was unlucky, the nasty voice in Richard's head reminded him yet again.

"Mr. White, is everything okay?" Leo's deep voice asked from the other side of the upper living room, which occupied most of the upper deck along with Richard's office. Plush white armchairs and sofas, with light blue accent pillows scattered on them, lined this opulent room. Its dark hardwood gleamed beautifully, not a scratch upon it.

"Yes, Leo, I was just thinking," Richard said, coming back to the present.

"Are you happy with the final product, sir?" asked Leo, leaning against one of the white pillars at the entrance to this grand room. Leo was forty-three years old, lean and muscular with red hair, steel blue eyes, and fair skin. He was divorced and estranged from his ex-wife and their teenage daughter, although he sent them money regularly. Leo seemed content being single and was the most loyal employee Richard had ever hired. He trusted Leo like nobody before, and paid him royally for his commitment. But it wasn't just the money that kept Leo loyal, it was the challenge of protecting one of the most wanted men in America.

"I'm ecstatic. This yacht is stunning, Leo. Just stunning. It will serve me well," he said, nodding his head as he smiled at his second-in-command.

"Great. You'll meet your crew tomorrow and set out next week," Leo said. He was glad to be Richard's protector over the last twelve years. Leo had a tough ending to his CIA career, feeling bitter and resentful towards the agency. He was done with that type of bureaucratic bullshit, and tired of being called "rogue" and "rebellious." Sure, he had attitude and confidence, but he'd had enough of being boxed in and passed over for the promotions he deserved. He knew he was smart and a damn fine agent. He always delivered, and it was their loss when they cut him loose. Words like "unfit" and "disrespectful" still rang in his ears when he thought of how the agency described him, which was pure bullshit.

Leo was also cynical about women. Just like his ex-wife, Cynthia, Cadence had been ruthlessly unfair. There was no doubt how much Richard loved that woman. And sure, she loved someone else, but to leave him the way she did was horrific. Seeing the nasty scars on his boss every day made Leo angry at how unfair life was, and it motivated Leo to do everything in his power to protect his employer.

"I'm going to do one more walk through and unpack more of my things," Richard said, "and I hope your state room is to your liking."

"Absolutely, sir. This is beyond any boat I've ever experienced. Hell, it may as well be called a cruise ship," he said, smiling widely, in awe of his employer's ability to have accumulated and used such vast amounts of money, all unbeknownst to the authorities. Yes, Richard was brilliant, but so was he; they made a killer team. Leo grinned, heading down the hall to his room to crack open a scotch.

Richard climbed down two flights of stairs to the master suite. The many windows allowed for a panoramic ocean view. The large, four poster bed beckoned with warmth and comfort. There was also a sitting room with a fireplace, and a lovely hot tub on a private deck. He walked through the decadent master bathroom, elegantly tiled with the finest pale blue marble. He closed his eyes and tried to imagine Cadence, just as he remembered her twelve years ago, in a bubble bath back in their home.

He walked out of the master suite and down the hall to Sophie's room. Its décor was carefully chosen with her favorite colors and items he knew she would love, for he knew his daughter all too well … from her favorite berry lip gloss, to the song list on her iPod, it was all here for her. There was a shelf lined with books she loved and those she was likely to love. He had imagined reading her favorite stories to her so many times, and soon it would become a reality. Although she was growing up, she was still his child and he would relish every moment with her to make up for those lost twelve years.

Alongside the bookshelf was a desk for Sophie's schoolwork. He had also built a practice room with acoustics made to help her lovely voice sing like a bird. Richard breathed deeply, smelling the newness of this beautiful yacht, intermixed with the scent of the lovely pale pink roses adorning his daughter's room.

He would be the best husband and father he could possibly be. Of that he was sure. He had known this since he was a child. He would be everything his father was not when it came to his own family. He had made more money than he ever thought possible, being driven from an early age to build wealth to control his fate. One of the only things he appreciated from his parents was that they constantly told him that he was superior to other kids, and his spare time had been spent learning about money instead of slacking off playing video games and watching TV. From an early age he was trading stocks, and could vividly remember his father screaming at him when, after ten weeks of straight gains, he lost a few hundred dollars. His relationship with money was a strong, deliberate one that was built into mastery over many years and several very successful businesses. He had developed a strong intuition for when to buy and sell businesses, coupled with a sharp analytical ability.

But money was only one small positive part of the education his father had provided. A memory came unwittingly into his mind, awakening the emotions he preferred to be buried. He was thirteen years old. With puberty upon him, he was very curious about women. He had once seen his father looking at a Penthouse magazine when walking past the open door of his den, which was declared out of bounds to his son and wife. His den had a lounge type feel, with dark brown leather furnishings, including a big sectional, reclining couch, and a massive TV. There was a long, dark gray granite covered bar, a pool table, a dart board, and a poker table. Although his parents never had friends over, nor had friends period, this place cried for parties.

Richard knew his father was away and decided to see if the Penthouse magazines were still in this mysterious room. Curiosity overcame the strong fear he had of his father. He slowly entered the dark room. It was nine in the evening and his father wasn't due back from his business trip until the next afternoon. Rather than turn on the light fully, he used the dimmer switch to cloak the room in just enough light to find his way around. He searched the most likely location, a magazine rack beside one of the reclining chairs. Only business magazines like Forbes, The Economist and Fortune were in the pile. But he wasn't ready to give up yet, no matter how terrified he felt.

He walked over to the bar, moving quietly despite knowing that his mother never came to this part of the house. He opened one drawer to find bar utensils and cutlery. The next contained dishcloths and napkins. The third … Penthouse, Hustler and other magazines, a pile of voluptuous breasts awaiting his curious eyes. He took one of the Hustlers, dated three months earlier, and closed the drawer behind him. He sat at the end of the large sectional, flipping carefully through the intriguing photos. Were breasts this large even real?

Just then he heard a giggling voice coming down the hall, as well as the easily recognizable and fear inducing tone of his father. Before he could even think of hiding, his father rounded the corner and spotted Richard. "What the fuck are *you* doing here?" he asked with a tone of pure hatred, as if his son were nothing more than a fly to be squashed.

"Oh, he's cute!" said a woman, stumbling into the room behind him. Her blonde hair was teased, and hung in a giant mane down her bare back. Her low-cut, red dress was so tight it barely contained her large breasts that threatened their escape. "Nice to meet you, kid," she said cheerfully. "I'm Twyla." Richard could smell her sweet perfume as its vapors circulated the room.

"Nice to, um, meet you, ma'am," Richard said, shaking with fear and shock.

"So, you broke into my personal space and found my stash of reading materials, son?" asked his father, smiling yet with an ominous tone in his voice.

Richard pushed the magazine aside. "I'm sorry, father. I was just … curious. I'll leave now." He began to stand up just as his father lurched forwards and pushed him back onto the couch.

"You aren't going anywhere! I'll give you a better lesson in porn than any of those magazines. And not a word of this to your mother," he threatened. Richard wondered if his mother had heard his father and Twyla come in, but doubted it as she spent most of her days locked in her bedroom, which was in another wing of their sprawling home.

"No, I really should go, father," Richard pleaded, deeply regretting ever coming into this freaky room.

"Twyla, take off your dress, now!" his father demanded.

"Alex, not in front of—"

"Now, you whore!" He yanked down the zipper that hugged tightly down the small of her back, and the red dress was on the floor in seconds. Underneath she wore a black bra and G-string. He proceeded to unfasten the lacy bra as she protested.

Richard gasped as her large breasts bounded out of their cups. "Now this is porn!" his father chuckled. "Come and feel these beauties, son," he said, more a demand than a question.

"No, father, I don't—"

"NOW!"

"Alex! He's just a boy!" Twyla pleaded. Was she a prostitute? A girlfriend? His father was always working. How would he have time for a girlfriend? She must be a prostitute. She looked and smelled and acted like the few he'd seen in movies.

"A *boy* doesn't come searching in out-of-bounds rooms for porn, Twyla," he rebutted, squeezing her left breast roughly.

"I didn't mean to, father. I'll never come in here again," Richard continued pleading, more scared than he could ever remember being around his father. And that said a lot, as there were many times when he was terrified ... terrified for himself and for his mother.

"You're not leaving until you feel these legends," his father said.

Richard knew that tone. There was no negotiating. No compromising. And the punishment afterwards, which was inevitable, would be even more severe if he kept resisting. He slowly stood and walked towards Twyla and his father. He saw his father's hand let go, so he followed suit and placed a hand gently on her breast.

"Both hands, son," ordered his father.

Richard awkwardly touched the other breast.

"Squeeze those tits!" his father demanded. "Don't be a pansy!"

Richard obliged, but was careful not to be rough as he squeezed Twyla's breasts just enough so his father could tell that he had obeyed. They felt warm and rubbery to his touch.

"Good job, kid," said Twyla. "You have a natural touch," she added, obviously trying to calm Richard, as he felt hot tears building, and could feel his hands shaking.

"Now sit down and get educated," his father demanded.

"But, can't I go? I won't tell mother," he said, his voice shaky despite his best efforts.

"Not until we're done, boy." And with that he watched as his father had sex with this woman, who was clearly a prostitute given how she acted and reacted. Clearly, she felt at home with his father and didn't mind being groped and ridden like an animal. And all in his own house with his mother sleeping upstairs in the other wing. Richard had never felt more disgusted or appalled by his father, and would rather have taken another beating than endure that hour in that dark cave with the two of them. A thirteen-year-old spectator, his eyes losing their innocence and faith in the world.

Richard came back into the present, detesting that memory.

Whenever it came he tried to replace it with his many memories of making love to his wife. His Cadence. He thought he could feel the moment Sophie was conceived. It was different than the other times. He felt that Cadence may actually have enjoyed him. Them. And he knew she could feel that again, she would just need time. And patience. But both of those had ran out prematurely, and now twelve more years were lost.

Whenever he felt that intense ache for Cadence, he would open the digital file of their wedding photos and flip through the images of the two of them on White Island. They were an attractive couple. He looked handsome, his skin smooth without scars. She looked so beautiful, despite the redness in her eyes and the fear in their light blue depths. He could still feel her breasts, so natural and soft in his hands. Unlike Twyla's monstrous ones that had felt so wrong in his young hands.

This time would be different. There would be nowhere for Cadence to run. They would be his. Sophie. Cadence. His family. Out in the open sea. Away from the eyes and ears of the world. Making up for all those lost years. Finally, all his.

Chapter Eight

I PULLED THE ZIPPER closed on my red suitcase, and jumped when Christian suddenly hugged me from behind as I stood in our bedroom. The sun shone through the windows as I looked around our comfy bed and all the things that made our place home. Our wedding photo hung on the wall; we both looked so happy and in love.

"Sorry to startle you, lovey," he said, delicately kissing my earlobe.

"Oh, Christian … I wish you were coming," I said, having avoided saying that too often in the days leading up to the San Diego trip. I didn't want him to feel guilty. His career was important to him. To us. And the orchestra needed him, their prized cellist.

"Me too, Cadence. Me too. But you three will have fun, I know it. There's nothing to worry about, security will be strong and the time will fly. I couldn't be prouder of our Sophie."

"Me too," I said, planting a kiss on his lips. He smelled of the musky cologne he always wore, a scent that made me feel at home and loved. We hugged tightly.

Sophie bounded into the room. "You guys ready?" she chirped, followed by Cale, who was vibrating with excitement. We were flying directly to San Diego from New York City, staying two nights there, followed by three nights near Disneyland. Five days away from Christian was more than enough, yet I was looking forward to watching the competition and spending some fun filled days with the kids.

Christian drove us to the airport, where two security guards, Adam Brown and Drew Walters, met us at the American Airlines terminal. They were both traveling with us and trading off shifts so we would have 24/7 protection. Being in public places like Disneyland and Sea World required a more elaborate security protocol. We had received two detailed briefings in the past week leading up to our trip. We told Cale that we would have a security team with us, and rather than explain that Sophie's biological father was the threat, we said it was my ex-boyfriend who had stalked me in the past and had recently been sighted. Cale's eyes were wide as he asked question after question.

"Mom, why would he want to hurt you? Does he have a gun? How big is he?"

"Oh, Cale," I patiently explained, "when you're older I can explain more, but for now you just need to know what he looks like, and that he could turn up on our trip. But our security team is great, so you don't have to worry. You know the plan if you spot him in any of the parks, at our hotel or Sophie's performance?"

"Yep, for sure, mom. My cell phone will always be in my

pocket." He felt his pocket proudly, happy to finally have his own cell phone after nagging for one the last year as his friends were all getting them. We resisted, not wanting our boy to grow up too fast. But reality, and security, now dictated he needed to be able to call for help immediately if a threat ever presented itself.

"I'm proud of you, Cale. You're brave and fast and smart. But don't worry, chances are very low that you'll ever need to make that type of call," I said, even though he seemed more excited about his bravery than worried about an actual threat.

The flight went smoothly, and as we landed on the tarmac in San Diego I squeezed each of my children's hands. Cale smiled at me, his brown eyes and hair reminding me so much of Christian's. And Sophie, my beautiful Sophie, who I wished didn't remind me of Richard, but whose face I loved with all my heart. I was so very proud to be accompanying my young, talented star.

The weather was perfect as we stepped out of the terminal, sunny but not scorching hot. Our two security guards were with us in a large black Chevy Tahoe SUV; they sat in the front, while the kids and I sat in the spacious back row. The ride was smooth and it didn't take long to arrive at the hotel; a beautiful Marriott located at the San Diego Marina District.

When we checked into our room, I opened the curtains to the window overlooking the marina. We were on the twelfth floor, and the view was outstanding. I could see yachts in the harbor, sailboats on the sea. Couples were strolling along the boardwalk. Sophie and Cale stood beside me, excited about exploring what would be their home for a few days. "This place is awesome!" Sophie exclaimed.

"It rocks!" Cale added.

"So glad you two like it. There were so many hotels to choose from. Do you want to go for a swim in the pool before dinner?" I asked, having already given the heads up to security that this was very likely to happen.

"Yeah!" they said in unison. Although they sometimes fought, as siblings do, they generally got along well. The best music was their laughter when they made jokes that cracked each other up.

We went for a swim in the large pool, as our security guard, Drew, sat in a lounger observing us through his sunglasses. It was taking me some time to get used to being watched again, but given the increased risk level I knew it was necessary. Drew was a serious guy, mid-thirties, muscular, with dark brown hair cut in a short, military style. He was also quiet and observant, qualities I appreciated in security personnel.

I scanned the other guests at the large pool, with busy, white loungers surrounding it. Older men and women whose dark skin was tough from years of laying in the sun. Happy couples. Families. No sign of Richard; although, I always seemed to sense him around. I never felt fully out of his eye. His reach. I felt as though he was giving me this time, these last twelve years, but he wasn't done with me yet. For that reason, I was never fully able to relax. I was always vigilant and aware of my surroundings. Aware of anything unusual. Anyone who made me nervous, or stared at me or my children for too long. But at this pool, in San Diego on a sunny Tuesday afternoon, nobody seemed out of place. Water suddenly splashed my face, and I yelped as Cale laughed. "Gotcha! Now see if you can get me!" he dared, swimming quickly away like a fish. And with that I tried to push my thoughts aside and play pool games with my kids.

Sophie's performance was the next day. She stepped out of the bathroom looking lovely in her outfit; a sequin pale blue and white top with a matching skirt that flared out. She needed to wear her hair in a curly ponytail, so she had been using her curling iron and asked me to help. As I rolled pieces of her soft, strawberry blonde hair, I felt as I had hundreds of times before … Thank God, I had her. I'd been so close to not having her. But in every way, she was normal and clearly a part of me. I couldn't imagine our family without her.

"How does this look?" she asked, as she applied her eye shadow, a task I normally did for her competitions and shows, but I was too busy curling her hair.

"Lovely, sweetheart," I said. "Maybe a bit more of the blue in the crease. It's always tougher to see from stage so err on the side of a tad more," I explained, as I wrapped yet another tendril of long, soft hair around the hot rod.

"Do you think he will be there?" she asked, her voice hesitant, yet curious.

"It's always possible, but let's hope not. If he is, he would be doing it just to see you. I know he'd never hurt you, Sophie. You know that, right?" I asked, as I had many times before. I felt that I needed to emphasize that although Richard was a monster, he would never hurt her. I truly believed that.

"Yeah, I know, mom. It's just still so weird to me. When I perform now I always scan the audience and wonder. It creeps me out that he could be there," she said, her eyes gazing down at her hands, which were nervously playing in her lap.

"Well, think of it this way, if he is, there's a greater chance that our security team will catch him. These guys are really on top of things."

"True. You always find the silver lining, mom," she said as she turned and smiled. "Can you help me with my blush? I'm not good at this makeup stuff."

The theater lights dimmed as the national show choir competition began. The first choir was from Boston, the boys and girls dressed in sailor outfits and doing a great rendition of *What Shall We Do with the Drunken Sailor.* Next was a choir from Los Angeles singing *A Whole New World* in vibrantly colored genie costumes. Third up was Sophie's choir, walking proudly onto the bleachers in their glittery outfits, the boys with their sequin bow ties, ready to perform an energetic version of *When You Wish Upon a Star.* I wondered if he was here, as I tried to focus on my talented daughter and squeezed my son's hand.

Chapter Nine

RICHARD SMILED AS HE took in the scene before him. His talented, beautiful Sophie up on stage, making him the proudest father ever. She had so much enthusiasm and was a natural, her curled ponytail flying from side to side as she moved to the music with the other kids.

His eyes moved from the stage to his Cadence, seated many rows ahead, her arm around the boy. Richard was in the sound box, the only way he could risk being there. Leo had paid off the sound technicians, and Richard was able to come in very early, dressed as a technician. The security guards would not see him in the dark booth or think to look for him there.

"These two guys really seem on the ball, boss," Leo had explained. "But not as smart as us," he added with a smug smile. What would Richard do without Leo? Every time that thought entered his mind, he made sure to add ten thousand dollars more to Leo's annual bonus.

Richard felt the adrenaline, which had been building for weeks, making him hyper aware. He could almost feel the softness of Cadence's hair in his hands, as he stared at her from behind. She wore her hair shorter now, falling just to the top of her shoulders. It was still beautiful but he would prefer it long again. He saw her lovely hand, those delicate fingers, moving on her son's shoulder. She loved that boy, there was no doubt about that. He only wished he was the father. Damn Christian for taking what should have been his.

As their number came to an end, and applause broke out, Richard resisted the urge to stand up and clap. He was bursting with pride and anticipation. Twelve long, painful years were coming to an end. He had learned to be patient, but it had not been easy counting down thousands of days.

Richard was overjoyed for Sophie as her choir won first place in the competition. He zoomed in on her smiling face with his camera, smiling widely himself in response. Once everyone left the theater, Leo sent him a text saying that it was safe to leave. He put on a hat and glasses so that as little as possible of his scarred face would show, and left the theater for his new home.

After a celebratory dinner with the rest of the choir, we went back to the hotel. The kids wanted to go for an evening swim, so we headed down to the pool. It looked beautiful lit up in the evening, and I knew the hot tub would feel wonderful.

As the hot water enveloped me, it felt even better than I'd imagined. Cale turned on the jets, which worked their magic on my tense shoulders. A few minutes later we were joined by an older gentleman, probably in his early sixties with short white hair and tanned skin. He seemed friendly.

"Nice to meet you, ma'am," he said. "I'm Peter."

"I'm Cadence, nice to meet you too, Peter," I replied. "And these are my children, Sophie and Cale."

They both shook Peter's hand. He asked them each how old they were and in what grades, and what they liked to do, which made me think he might be a grandfather.

"Nice hotel. I'm spending a night here while they do some work on my yacht," Peter explained. "I could've stayed on it, but sometimes it's nice to be on dry land!"

"You actually have a yacht!" exclaimed Cale. "How big is it?"

"Cale! Don't be nosey," I scolded.

"Not at all, curiosity is what made me my money," he said, a warm smile on his face. "Asking the questions others are afraid to, that's how my company grew into so many new product lines over the years. And here I am, retired and loving my life sailing around the world," he explained. "So, to answer your question, my yacht is *very* large. Too large for me alone, so I have my lovely girlfriend, Jessica, along for the ride," he smiled. I wondered if Jessica was a lot younger than Peter.

"Is there a pool on it?" Sophie asked.

"Oh, yes, a refreshing little pool," he answered. "I swim laps in there every day." How could one do laps in a "little" pool, I mused, knowing that it was bigger than he was letting on.

"One day I want to go on a yacht, mom," said Cale.

"One day, sweetheart. Maybe you'll even have one of your own," I said.

"You never know!" Peter said. "I would never have guessed that I'd have a yacht one day. I came from small town beginnings.

Worked hard to build my companies, which make manufacturing tools and equipment for automobile factories. You could do the same, kid. The American dream," he smiled.

"I wanna be a pilot," said Cale with confidence. "A pilot with a yacht!"

"I'm a pilot. I got my license so that I could fly as I was tired of the hassles of airports, especially for short flights. I'm gettin' a bit old for longer solo flights, but it's certainly worth flying shorter stretches to save time," he said. "Maybe one day you will own a yacht with a helipad like mine, and fly your own helicopter on and off!"

"That'd be great!" exclaimed my wide-eyed son, in awe of this man and his yacht.

Our friendly conversation continued, with Cale and Sophie alternating asking questions to Peter. I felt myself relaxing for the first time since we set foot in the airport. I could see Adam, who'd just taken the night shift over from Drew, out of the corner of my eye. He smiled from a distance, sitting discreetly behind at a patio table. I felt safe.

"Would you like a tour, kids?" asked Peter. "I'd be happy to show y'all what a yacht looks like. And you could have a swim too, if you wanted. We don't leave port until the day after tomorrow. Jessica wanted to do some shopping. She's quite a princess so needs her breaks from the open sea!" he laughed.

"I'd love a tour!" said Cale.

"Yeah, me too!" exclaimed Sophie.

"I'll have to check with … check our schedule," I said, almost slipping about our security detail. "We're going to do Sea World tomorrow, but if the kids want to spend some time on your yacht before or after, it'll probably work," I said, smiling at

Peter. He reminded me of my father: happy, chatty, and friendly. I'd hoped my parents could have met us here, but they were in Europe on an extended retirement vacation. One of many, as they were making the most of their retirement years by seeing as many parts of the world as they possibly could.

"I will write my number down for you, ma'am. The name's Peter McLaughlan. You can give me a ring tomorrow morning and let me know if you want to stop by. And your mister is of course welcome, too," he added politely.

"He's back in New York. He's a cellist with the New York Philharmonic. Sophie had a show choir competition here, but he couldn't get away this week with too many performances and practices," I explained.

"Well, wish I could meet him. You sure have a talented family. I'd be honored to give you a tour if you can fit it in. I'd better get dried off as I'm more wrinkly than usual from all this water, which is *very* wrinkly, even for an old guy," he chuckled.

I smiled at his self-deprecating humor. "Okay, I'll be in touch either way, Peter. And thanks for your offer of hospitality," I said, smiling back at him.

Peter climbed out carefully, and wrapped a towel around himself. He fished inside a small black waist bag he'd brought, and pulled out a pen and small pad of paper, on which he wrote his name and number and left it tucked under our towels. Once he was gone, the kids began to beg.

"Mom, please!" pleaded Cale. "When will we *ever* get this chance again?"

"Yeah, mom, *please*," Sophie added, in her sweetest voice.

"I'll chat with Adam tonight, but I'm sure it'll be fine," I said. To be honest, I was as curious as they were to see what this grandiose yacht looked like.

We went back to our room, Adam a safe distance behind. When the kids were inside, I turned around and got Adam's attention. He hurried over, after checking that nobody else was in the hallway.

"Adam, a gentleman named Peter McLaughlan invited the kids and me to see his yacht tomorrow. He seemed like a very nice man. The kids are keen to see it, and go for a swim in the pool, maybe before or after Sea World? But I wanted to run it by you and Drew before making any final plans. His name and number are on this paper," I said, handing him the note. I knew that what seemed innocent still needed to be vetted by our security team.

"That should be fine, Cadence. We'll just need to run a background check and, to be safe, both of us will need to accompany you."

"Oh, I don't want to inconvenience you. I know you two trade-off shifts," I said.

"Not at all, Cadence. It really isn't a problem, provided the guy's history is clean. Let me check into it tonight and then we can firm up a plan first thing tomorrow morning."

"Sounds good, Adam," I said.

"Okay, Cadence. Have a good night."

"You, too."

That night one of my nightmares came again. This one was on

White Island. I was running down the white sandy beach in my wedding gown, and Richard was chasing me. He was on fire, literally, and I could hear his painful screams.

"Cadence! Don't leave me!" he pleaded. I turned to look back at him, tripped on my gown, and fell flat on the beach. I tried to stand up, but my arms and legs wouldn't let me. They were numb and I couldn't move. I was trapped.

Richard was suddenly upon me, falling on top of me, flames and all. "Help!" I screamed, as my dress caught fire.

"You're never leaving me!" he roared, as we were entangled in a mass of flames.

"Help!" I struggled with all my might to pull away, to roll out the flames, but couldn't get free.

"If *I* die, *you* die with me!"

"Mom! *Mom*! Are you okay?" Sophie asked, as I came back to reality, drenched in sweat and tears.

"Just a … dream," I said, my breathing quick and shallow. "Sorry to wake you, sweetheart," I added. I reached for a tissue from the bedside table.

"Oh, mom, I'm so sorry for your nightmares," she said, having unfortunately experienced these before. "I wish he'd never taken you."

She embraced me, and I felt my breath even out.

"I love you, Sophie. We're safe, honey. Safe from him."

Chapter Ten

THE NEXT DAY WAS bright and sunny, not a cloud in the sky, as I pulled open the heavy, white hotel drapes. My nightmare seemed like a distant memory, and the kids' laughter made me smile. I loved when they got along and played together. I checked my cell and there was a text from Adam saying that the background check on Peter McLaughlan came back clean. Indeed, he fit the description I gave and owned a large yacht. He had kids and grandkids, and was married and divorced twice, and currently in a two-year common-law relationship. To err on the side of caution, both Adam and Drew would accompany us, with Drew arriving earlier to check things out, and Adam driving us there. Adam asked that I give Peter a call to let him know we'd be there by 10:00 a.m. He also included Peter's number in the text, which I dialed.

"Hello," answered Peter's jovial voice.

"Hi, Peter, it's Cadence Davidson from the hot tub at the

hotel last night."

"Oh, good morning, Mrs. Davidson! So, you can make it?"

"Yes, absolutely. The kids are excited. Is 10:00 a.m. okay?"

"For sure! Do you have a pen? I'll give you directions as there are quite a few yachts here today."

I carefully wrote out his directions on a hotel notepad. "We can only stay about an hour, as we have a big day planned at Sea World."

"That's fine. Enough time to show you around. Remember to bring their swimsuits. They'll have time for a short swim after the tour. You as well, if you'd like."

"I think I'll stay dry, but the kids would love that," I said. It all felt very relaxed and I smiled, feeling at peace and safe, despite the need for two security guards on this trip.

The kids and I ordered room service for breakfast, enjoying French toast, fruit and a delightful latte for myself. I put on cream colored capris and a teal colored, short-sleeved top for the day, along with a floppy, brown sunhat and my sunglasses. My hair was pulled back into a small ponytail to keep myself as cool as possible, as it was supposed to be a hot day. The kids wore shorts and t-shirts, with their swimsuits underneath. "Make sure to pack underwear, you two!" I said, as we put the items we'd need for both the swim (including towels), and Sea World in a backpack. Sophie asked me to braid her hair, which I quickly did, while at the same time reminding Cale to put on his hat.

I dialed Christian from the SUV on the way to the yacht, but he didn't answer. I realized that he had an early practice that day. He'd texted earlier, wishing us a great day. I texted back saying that we loved him and were headed to visit a yacht and then to Sea World. I added how great the security was and how safe I felt, despite missing him.

Adam got us there within twenty minutes and parked in a lot about a ten-minute walk from the port. The yachts and sailboats were plentiful, lined up neatly on the calm water, waiting to be free in the vast ocean.

"His is docked at the very end," explained Adam. "Drew said it's bigger than any he's ever seen," he chuckled. "I'm curious myself, but I need to keep a good distance behind. If you keep walking straight then hang a left, it's the largest one by far. You can't miss it."

"Thanks, Adam. We appreciate all you're doing for us," I said.

"My pleasure. Now go have fun! I'll meet you right here in an hour," he said. "And remember to check the time as we'll start to worry if you're longer than seventy-five minutes," he added.

"Sure thing," I replied, as the kids bounded happily ahead, eagerly anticipating the yacht tour.

We walked past about ten or so yachts, some quiet, others bustling with workers and owners.

"Mom, look at that!" exclaimed Cale, his eyes bulging and mouth wide open with awe, as he pointed to a massive, gleaming white yacht at the very end. I counted five levels.

"Oh my God," I involuntarily uttered.

"Wow, it's gigantic!" added Sophie.

"It looks like a cruise ship!" I said. We'd all stopped, the three of us gawking at this monstrous ship. The word boat or yacht didn't do this vessel justice. The words *Great White* were written on the back, in dark gray, contrasted with the shiny white of the ship.

"Great White is a type of shark, right mom?" asked Cale, grasping my hand in anticipation.

"Yes, that's right, Cale," I said, awestruck by all I was taking in.

"There's Mr. McLaughlan!" exclaimed Sophie, as she grasped my other hand and pulled us forwards for our adventure. He climbed down the stairs onto the dock, and rushed towards us.

"Welcome," he said. "So glad you found it!"

"Peter, this is a truly amazing ship," I said.

"Why, thank you," he grinned. "We have no time to waste, so ladies first," he gestured us ahead. "We're going to head up these stairs and begin the grand tour!" he said, as Sophie took the lead, and I followed, holding Cale's hand, which vibrated with excitement.

We climbed a staircase and began our tour. The first room we entered was a luxurious lounge type setting, with multiple sofas and comfy chairs, as well as a beautiful marble bar with eight white leather bar stools. Ocean blue colored accent cushions sat on the lovely white furniture. Everything looked new.

"This is amazing," exclaimed Sophie. "It looks so new, how long have you had it?"

"Oh, not too long, honey. But we have great cleaners as well," he smiled back. "This is where we relax after a hard day at sea."

Sophie and Cale plopped down into the soft seats to test them out. "Like sitting in a cloud," said Cale, his smile wide.

"Now I know your time is tight, so let me show you a few more key spots and then get you to the pool. Follow me to the upper living room." We followed him through a hall and up another three staircases, passing several doors.

"Whoa! This is huge!" said Sophie, staring around the beautiful room, with a row of large windows looking onto the ocean. An ornate crystal sculpture with tones of blue was the showpiece of the room. "That's so pretty," she added, looking up at it in awe.

"Ah, that's called the *shining beauty*, meant to depict the beauty of a woman," he explained, nodding with a wide smile. "Now let's move back down to the most important room, the kitchen," he laughed.

The kitchen was outfitted with restaurant grade appliances, made of gleaming stainless steel, with ample work surfaces. Through a door we entered into a dining area with a panel of windows and a magnificent view. The table had eight dining chairs and a glistening glass surface. Cale put his hand down on it as he stared out the windows. "Cale, please don't touch! We don't want to mark Mr. McLaughlan's table."

"Oh, no, don't worry about that. We don't live like it's a museum. And please, call me Peter," he said, leading us through an archway that opened into a large wine cellar. Hundreds of bottles lined the walls, along with built in fridges for the whites. I smiled, thinking how I'd love one of these in our place back in New York.

"'Wine makes daily living easier, less hurried with fewer tensions and more tolerance,'" Peter recited. "One of my favorite quotes by Benjamin Franklin."

"I can see that! With a wine room like *this*, in a yacht *this* spectacular, you must really enjoy life," I said.

"That we do," he smiled back.

"Now here's the formal dining room," he said, leading us through another archway into a gorgeous room with a table for ten, a stunning rectangular crystal chandelier, and three sculptures built into large, lit up nooks in the wall. The sculptures depicted marine life, each carved from different stone. One looked like a squid, the next was a starfish and the third a seahorse … the craftsmanship and colors were stunning. Before I could look further we were whisked down another flight of stairs leading to the pool deck, which was glorious.

"Yay!" said Cale. "I can't wait to jump in there." He pointed at the long, rectangular pool, which was surrounded by four large white loungers. Situated at the end of it was a hot tub that looked like it could easily fit twelve or more people. He led us behind the pool, and showed us a wonderful cedar sauna.

"So, are you kids ready for a swim?" he asked, smiling broadly.

"Oh, yeah!" they replied in unison.

"The change room is back here, near the sauna."

The kids ran inside, nearly tripping over one another with excitement. Peter and I were alone, a gentle breeze blowing in from the ocean. "Thank you so much for hosting us," I said, deeply breathing in the salty air.

"My pleasure. Now, what can I get you to drink?"

"Iced tea would be nice," I said.

"I do a fine Bloody Mary, you know," he chuckled.

"Too early for that," I turned and smiled.

"And for those beautiful children?"

"Lemonade, please."

"Consider it done. Now go relax and make yourself at home."

I walked to the edge of the pool deck, leaned on the railing and savored the feeling of the sun warming my skin. I took a few deep breaths, feeling safe and relaxed.

Chapter Eleven

RICHARD GAZED DOWN THROUGH the window of his office, situated on the uppermost deck of the yacht, just below the bridge. It was surreal to finally see her here. She stood on his deck, their deck, looking at the ocean. He could feel the adrenaline pumping throughout his body. The anticipation was electrifying. And not only would he have his wife back, but he would finally get to hold his beautiful daughter.

He watched as the children jumped into the pool and started to splash each other. Cadence sat on a lounger beside the pool, smiling at her children. He wished it was singular – only one child – his Sophie. But there were now two, with Cale being the wrinkle in his plan. He agonized for months over the decision of whether or not to take Cale. He had made up his mind but doubt was creeping back in.

There was a knock on the door, and Leo entered. "Everything is working perfectly, boss," he said.

"That's what I want to hear. But Leo, I'm doubting my decision about Cale," he said, running a finger over one of the bigger scars etched on his forearm, its rough surface so familiar. Cale would be a constant reminder of Christian, Richard thought bitterly. But if Cale was taken from Cadence, he feared that she would be too broken to enjoy the rest of their lives together.

"I know it's a tough one, but it's too late to change the plan now. He would be able to relay too much about this yacht, not to mention it would greatly shorten the timeline of when the police know they're missing."

"I know. And I know it would make Cadence and Sophie's adjustment even more difficult if he's not here," he said, staring down at the kids who were now hanging onto the pool edge near their mother. He could tell how close the three of them were. Soon to be four. "Let's go ahead with the plan. It's almost time," he said.

"Good, the staff are all aboard and Captain Jeffries is ready to set sail when you give the word. And we should get notice any time now about the two security guards," Leo added, pacing the office with anxious anticipation. This plan required a team that was extremely creative, clever and experienced. Not only months, but years had been spent fleshing out the details of how to outsmart the FBI. The superyacht turned out to be the most flexible option, allowing them to be off the radar, so to speak, and constantly on the move. Cutting edge radar deflectors had been installed to make the yacht extremely stealth to radar. In addition, radar jamming capabilities were added to further avoid detection once they were out at sea. It had just been a matter of time before Cadence and Sophie were at a seaside location where they could be taken, and Richard was grateful that time had finally arrived.

His team had hacked into the cell phones and e-mail accounts of the two security guards who were on the trip. He had two of the best hackers hired from China, who had formerly worked in intelligence then left to pursue more lucrative private careers. He also had a highly skilled hitman, named Sergei, who was meticulous and efficient; he refused to work with anyone else. "The only person I can trust one hundred percent is me," Sergei had stated when Richard first interviewed him. It was Sergei who would be taking out the two security guards, and the timing was absolutely key. If one caught onto the other being taken out the whole plan could crumble. But Richard had solid trust in Sergei, and didn't doubt that this plan would be executed flawlessly.

Just then Leo's cell phone rang. "Leo here. Roger that. I'll let the boss know," he ended the call. "Adam and Drew have been taken care of, and Sergei has their phones."

"Excellent. Let's leave port ASAP."

"Okay, boss, I'm on the final checks." Leo quickly left the office.

Richard walked to the window once more, looking down at Cadence. His intense longing for her had been with him every day, but today he felt as though he couldn't wait another minute. She was now within his reach. Within his full control. And his Sophie was so close to finally meeting her real father. He would be the father he had always wished his own would be.

He watched as Peter escorted the children, followed by Cadence, into the change room. Peter closed the door, and locked it as per the plan. Richard swallowed, knowing there was now no turning back. He wished there was another way, a less traumatic one than beginning their new lives locked in a change room. He closed his eyes, his fists tight as he recalled how his father had locked him up more than once. And now here he was, locking up his own wife and daughter. But soon they would know they were not in harm's way, unlike Richard's childhood, to which his mind wandered back …

As Richard continued through his teenage years, his father became increasingly more abusive. Richard remembered going through a growth spurt at age fifteen, when he never seemed to get enough food. One night he woke up with hunger pangs at 2:00 a.m. and headed quietly down to the kitchen. He opened the door to the huge walk-in pantry and grabbed a box of cereal. He heard voices and froze. It was the familiar giggle of one of the countless women his father had brought home to screw, under the very roof where his wife and son were sleeping upstairs.

Ever since the incident in his father's private room, he knew to keep as far away as possible from that part of the house at night, in hopes of never having another such encounter. But here he was in the pantry knowing there was no way out without having to face his father, who could range from cold to cruel, depending on how drunk he was.

He assumed his father would immediately know someone was in the pantry, given that the kitchen and pantry lights were on, but instead he heard giggles and groans.

"Right here, right now!" demanded the woman's shrill voice.

There was the sound of a chair falling over, and then a pan crashing to the floor. Why did his father have absolutely no discretion? His mother was increasingly depressed and had to spend two separate weeks in the hospital lately. Why couldn't his father keep his many affairs away from their home? Richard squeezed his hands into tight fists, wanting to punch his father in the face. He longed to hear his father's nose break, causing pain right back at the man who had inflicted so much upon him since he was a toddler.

Minutes later the sounds stopped, and Richard listened intently for their footsteps so he'd know when the path back to his room was clear. Suddenly the pantry door swung wide open and there stood his father, naked. His father's initial shock turned quickly to rage.

"What the fuck are *you* doing here?" he yelled.

Richard looked down, trying to avoid staring at his drunk and naked father.

"I was getting a snack and didn't want to … interrupt you," he said, his voice shaky.

"Oh, likely story. You wanted free porn, you little pervert!" he chuckled, a malicious edge to his voice.

"No, I didn't. I was here before you came home," he explained as calmly as he could.

"You were here before I *came*," sneered his father, "and it was a damn fine one with my gorgeous Charlize," he added.

"Father, may I go back to bed?"

"I thought you were hungry. Wasn't that your reason for being down here?"

"Yes, but I … I can wait until morning," he said.

"Are you saying that Charlize and I made you lose your fucking appetite? Now I'm insulted," he said, roughly grabbing Richard by the arm and pulling him into the kitchen. Charlize was lying naked on the table, her large breasts spilling over as she lay on her side and smiled up at them both. Her black hair was long, and her makeup garish.

"Nice to meet you, kid!" she giggled.

'Um, you too," stammered Richard.

"He thinks we're sickening, Charlize," Richard's father smirked.

"That's not very nice," she said, with only a hint of her smile remaining.

"I didn't say that," said Richard.

"Well, we took away your appetite, didn't we?"

"I'm just tired, father. May I please be excused?" he begged.

"I'd rather you stay and get your appetite back," he ordered, shoving Richard back into the pantry. Richard was now big enough to fight back, but he knew that his father's rage knew no limits. Fear overtook his own anger as he stood at the back of the pantry shaking. "There's plenty of food ready for when you aren't so sickened by your father. Have a good night," he said, locking the pantry door behind him. There was a reason every single door in this house could be locked from the outside, Richard thought. It was one of the many methods his father used to punish Richard and his mother. Richard eventually fell asleep on the hard, cold wooden floor. As the hours passed before the horrified housekeeper let him out, he thought and dreamed about how one day he would kill this man … and how he might do it.

His memory was interrupted by Leo, who had come into the office to get the final okay to leave port.

"Yes, let's go," Richard said with certainty.

Peter entered the room as Leo left to let the captain know that it was time. "Sir, they're locked in the change room. Any minute now they're going to realize that, so I'd suggest I speak through the intercom so they don't panic when they feel this vessel moving." Although Peter could put emotion aside, as he had to for his entire criminal career, he felt some degree of remorse for this woman and her children. In the end though, the money Richard paid was outstanding and would set him up quite nicely for the rest of his life. Whatever moral decisions Richard wanted to make were not Peter's concern. But he did want the transition to be as smooth as they could make it for this unsuspecting woman and her nice kids. Panic would not help anyone.

"Yes, please go ahead," Richard said, feeling almost robotic as the steps they had rehearsed so many times in the past weeks played out.

"Okay," Peter said, pressing the intercom on the wall next to Richard's desk. "Hello, Mrs. Davidson?" he asked. Richard cringed every time he heard her last name.

"Hello?" asked Cadence, sounding confused.

"You and the kids need to stay calm," Peter explained.

"What do you mean?" she asked, clearly anxious.

"The door is locked, but you're safe," said Peter. "There's no need to panic," he added.

"What? We need to leave, right away!" she demanded. The children's questioning voices could be heard in the background. There was the sound of her banging on the door, working hard to open it.

"I'm afraid that's not possible, ma'am," said Peter. "We're leaving port, but you will be safe and only temporarily locked in that change room."

"I'm calling the police," Cadence declared. Sounds of shuffling came through the speaker, along with her kids asking what was happening in panicked voices. "Where's my phone?"

she screamed. "You took it?"

"We have your phone, you won't need it. We have Sophie's as well," answered Peter.

"Bring our phones back, now!" she screamed.

"Stay calm. You and your children are safe. I will come back on the speaker once we've left port," said Peter, ending the conversation.

Richard stared at the intercom, a torrent of emotions swirling in his mind. Anticipation. Elation. Conquest. At last, they were here and there was no turning back. No escaping. He felt the movement, subtle at first and then very solid under his feet. The yacht was backing its massive body into the ocean, pulling away from the ugliness of reality and into the world Richard had meticulously created for his family.

Chapter Twelve

I HELD SOPHIE AND Cale tightly to me, comforting them as best I could. We sat on the cream colored, cushioned bench of the change room. Glistening wood-paneled walls held towel hooks around us. I was trying not to break into sobs as I felt my children trembling in my arms.

I *knew* it was Richard. There was no other explanation. He'd lured us into this trap and now we were clearly headed out to sea. I felt the power of this mighty yacht coursing through the water, sure of itself and its path, pulling us further and further from our lives and freedom.

"I'm so scared, mom!" cried Sophie. "Why would that man do this to us?" she asked.

"Yeah, mom, why would he take us away?" Cale added, his body trembling in my arms as I looked down into his tear-filled eyes. I rubbed his shaking back with one hand, and held Sophie with the other.

There was no point covering up what I knew was happening. I had to be honest, as we only had each other. "I think he's working for Richard White," I said, certain that my words were being monitored through the intercom system.

Sophie gasped, "Oh my God, mom."

"Who?" asked Cale. It was the one question that I desperately wanted to avoid answering. Now I would have to tell Cale about his sister's biological father under these terrifying conditions. There was no avoiding it.

"Cale, remember when we were being briefed by the FBI about that ex-boyfriend of mine who might stalk me again and why we needed security?"

"Yes," he said, staring into my eyes.

"Well, there's more to the story. We didn't want to scare you, but you need to know the truth of what's happening," I said gently. "Richard White is a man who abducted mommy a long time ago, before I was married to daddy. He held me hostage, but I escaped," I whispered, conscious of the virtual ears lurking around us. "He forced me to marry him and I had Sophie in my tummy when I escaped," I explained in language that he could understand. "He's Sophie's birth father."

"But daddy's her father!" declared Cale, his small brown eyebrows frowning with outrage at the audacity of my claim.

"No, Cale," said Sophie calmly. "Richard White is my *biological* father. I've never met him and I only learned about him this year. The police could not catch him, as he's really good at hiding. He has lots of money and this fancy yacht is probably his," she said, mature beyond her years.

"But why would he want to take us away?" Cale asked, his innocent voice sounding bewildered.

"He probably wants us to be a family," I answered, fear and anger vying for prominence in my mind. "He doesn't understand that you can't force people to be a family," I added, speaking louder in the hopes that he could hear me. But my courage was short-lived as I shuddered in fear, knowing we were moving quickly into the open sea given the intensity of the engines beneath us.

"Will he hurt us?" Cale whispered, my heart breaking at this question.

"No, Cale. He won't hurt us. I promise that I'll keep you safe," I said, not knowing what to expect, but certain I would protect my kids with my life if that's what it took.

"Hello again, ma'am," Peter's voice came through the intercom. "I will be down in a few minutes to let you out," he said, a statement not requiring a reply. After all, I had nothing to say. This feeling was all too familiar, from twelve years ago. Anger coursed through me, as I hoped and prayed that Adam and Drew were able to act quickly … unless, oh my God, I hoped they were not hurt.

I had to think quickly. "Try to be as calm as you can, kids. He can't take us far without help being on its way." I thought about the GPS trackers in our cell phones, but knowing Richard, these would have already been disabled. Sophie and I also had trackers attached to our bras, for which I was grateful. Surely the FBI would be following us already.

Just then the door opened and Peter stood there smiling, as if we weren't being abducted, as if this was just another happy day at sea. "I'm going to show you to your rooms now," he explained.

"You liar," I hissed, holding Sophie and Cale protectively.

"I'm sorry, ma'am, but I'm just following the boss's orders. I apologize for the little white lies yesterday and today, but you're safe here, I promise," he added, as if this assertion could make up for the horrible crime he'd just committed.

"Safe? With *Richard White*? You don't understand how wrong this is. We have the best security and FBI agents tracking us. You *won't* get away with this," I said, looking him squarely in the eye.

"Nothing I can do, ma'am. Just doing my job. You can ask the boss any questions you have later," he added, deferring his part of the responsibility for abducting us. "Now follow me, I think you're gonna like your rooms!"

Chapter Thirteen

We went down one flight of stairs and were led along a hallway. Peter opened the first door and said, "Ladies first," as he motioned us inside. I held each of my children's hands, not wanting to let go of them. This was a large room, with a double bed, two bedside tables, a bookshelf lined with books and boxes, and a desk. "This is Cale's room," Peter explained.

Cale looked terrified, eyes wide as he looked around at this foreign room. I gave his hand a squeeze. "We don't plan to stay here long, and while we're here my children will stay with me at all times," I asserted. "And is your name even Peter?"

"Yes, ma'am, Peter's my name, although not a McLaughlan. You definitely seem like a woman who knows what she wants; I can see why you and the boss are such a good match," he said with a smile.

"They are *not* a match! My dad is her match," Sophie said in an icy tone, crossing her arms as she glared at Peter.

"And you, dear, *definitely* take after him," he said, continuing to remain calm and cheerful.

I shook my head in anger as he showed us Cale's en suite, which had a sparkling white tub, shower, and marble sink. I doubted it had ever been used.

He led us back through the hall, and into the room next door, stating that this was Sophie's suite. Her room was bigger than Cale's, with a queen size canopy bed, a vanity stocked with silver brushes, creams and perfumes. There was also a fully stocked bookshelf, with a desk beside it, and a large bouquet of pale pink roses fragrantly sitting on top. Unlike Cale's more basic bathroom, Sophie's was much larger, with a corner jetted tub and a large rain shower. It boasted double sinks, with various toiletries and hair products arranged on the counter. She looked surprised as she picked up a tube of berry lip gloss from the cosmetics organizer. "This is my favorite lip gloss. How did he know?" she asked, looking unnerved as she turned towards me.

Once again, a shiver of déjà vu ran through my body. "I don't know, Sophie," I said. "I'm sorry this is happening," I added softly, knowing Peter was observing and likely to report our reactions back to Richard. Or even more likely was that we were under video surveillance. I cringed at the thought, as I scanned the ceiling looking for cameras.

Sophie's suite also had a walk-in closet, which was already stocked with clothes. I shivered from the memory of my own fully stocked closet twelve years earlier. But I somehow felt calmer, less panicked than I did back then, as I had to remain strong for my kids. And perhaps because I'd experienced this violation of my privacy before, the shock factor was lower.

"Mom, why is there so much stuff here? How long does he

expect us to stay?" she asked.

"We're not staying for long," I said, looking Peter squarely in the eye as I continued to squeeze both Sophie and Cale's hands. "So, you won't need all these things," I added. Peter remained calm and cheerful, not responding to my tone of indignation.

"And through this door is Sophie's music room," he said, opening a door to a beautiful room with a panel of windows overlooking the ocean. There was a sofa, an armchair, a music stand and a shelf lined with music. There was what looked like a professional recording system with a microphone. Another large bouquet of pink roses sat on a table beside the sofa, giving off a subtle, sweet smell. Sophie and Cale both stared at a large, framed photograph of Sophie as Dorothy in *The Wizard of Oz* last year.

"This is so weird, mom," her voice trailed off as she looked around.

"I know, it's unnerving." I shot another sharp look at Peter, who was gesturing us back into Sophie's room. It brought back memories of the music room Richard had waiting for me in his mansion when he abducted me. I hadn't yet seen a flute for me, and wondered if he would avoid having one around given the note I planted in my last one twelve years earlier.

"I'm going to need you three to change into some new clothes, which are sitting on that armchair in the corner. There's a bag to put the clothes you're wearing in. We need *everything* off, and there's a fresh change of clothing for each of you. Oh, and be sure to put your GPS tracking devices in the bag as well," he instructed.

I froze. Was he just saying this to find out if we had tracking devices? "What are you talking about?" I asked, doing my best to show a look of confused annoyance rather than my mounting fear.

"Ma'am, you know what I'm talking about. There's a GPS device in your clothing and Sophie's. They've been blocked, but we still need to examine the physical devices."

I swallowed, torrents of fear coursing through me as I realized that our chances of being followed had greatly dwindled. Of course, Richard would have a highly experienced team handling our abduction, which would've been much more challenging than when he stole me from my life twelve years ago. But what if he was just saying these devices were blocked, but they really needed them in order to deactivate them? Just in case we were being duped, we had to hold onto them as long as we could. "You're crazy! The only tracking device was in my cell phone, which you stole, Peter," I stated with confidence.

"Ma'am, don't make this more difficult than it needs to be. I can do a search right now of you three, but I doubt you'd want me to do that, and I know Mr. White wouldn't be happy with me touching his ladies."

I cringed at the words "his ladies," even more so than imagining Peter's hands going anywhere near us. I could sense both Sophie and Cale were terrified. "We'll get changed, just give us some privacy," I said, taking a step further back into the room while holding Cale's and Sophie's hands.

"Alright, but you know the deal," he said firmly, and closed the door. Gone was his jovial manner in place of a no-nonsense tone.

"Mom, I don't want him to touch me," Sophie exclaimed.

"He won't, Sophie; I won't let him," I answered, once again scanning the walls and ceiling for cameras. There didn't seem to be any. “But we will hide the trackers, Sophie,” I whispered in her ear. “So, let’s change and then hide them wherever we can,” I said in the quietest whisper I could. Sure, Richard’s people would eventually find them in here, but in case these devices were still tracking, I wanted to buy as much time as I possibly could.

“Mom, I’m scared,” Cale whispered, as he tugged off his shirt. I helped pull it off, then hugged his soft chest to me.

“It’ll be okay, Cale. Nobody will hurt us and we’ll get off this yacht soon.”

“I hope so,” he said, stripping down to his underwear, then pulling out the clothing in the

bag meant for him. “There’s even underwear in here … that’s weird,” he said.

“I know, sweetheart, but I’m sure they’ll fit so you might as well replace yours.” Indeed, everything fit perfectly, right down to Cale’s navy blue Polo shirt, tan shorts, and brown leather sandals.

Sophie and I undressed in the bathroom, underwear and all, and changed into the outfits that were sitting on the chair. Mine was a pale blue, cotton, knee-length sundress, with a cream-colored bra and panties. Sophie’s was a pale pink sundress, with a pink bra and underwear, in the same brand I had been buying for her. He was just as meticulous as he’d been before, I thought.

“I’m so freaked out,” said Sophie, as I unclipped the tracking devices from our bras.

“Try not to worry. The FBI will find us. I know they will. And Richard White won’t hurt us, he just wants a family and is very sick in his head,” I explained, bending down to hug them.

"Almost ready in there?" asked Peter through the closed door.

"Just need a couple of minutes!" I yelled. Sophie and I then scanned the room, and walked into the music room looking for the most creative option for each tracker. We ended up placing Sophie's inside one of the many music books, and mine under the inside lining of the jewelry box. As I lifted the soft velvet lining, I couldn't help but notice the array of necklaces, bracelets and earrings for Sophie. Only twelve years old, with more precious gemstones than most women have in their lifetime. Typical Richard, I thought.

"Remember, Richard White is not normal. We need to be safe and remember that help is coming. We can't upset him too much as I don't know what he's like now. I will protect you two, I promise. I love you both so much," I said. "And so does your dad. He'll do everything he can to get us back home soon," I added. Tears welled up in all of our eyes at the mention of Christian. I was so angry at Richard that I could explode, but tried to continue remaining calm.

I opened the door and stood before Peter, handing him the bag with a look of disgust. "Here you go," I said.

"I want those devices, so they'd better be in there," he said.

"Whatever we had on us is in the bag," I answered, my voice equally assertive.

"Okay, I'll trust you for now. Mr. White has requested that you and Sophie come to the upper living room to meet him. The boy can make himself comfortable in his room until lunch," he directed.

"Cale is coming with us. I'm not leaving him," I stated. Cale looked up at me with wide eyes, then fearfully back at Peter.

"There's nothing to be afraid of, Cale. Mr. White just wants a private meeting with the ladies before he meets you. You're a big boy, won't you be fine on your own?"

"Peter, he's only nine. He's in a strange place. I don't want him alone," I answered on behalf of my son, anger rising in my veins.

"Fine, I will stay with him, but that's the only way this will work. The boss insists on meeting Cale after he has spoken with you and Sophie," he said, his voice firm.

"Mom, I'm fine in my room. But I don't want this man with me," he said, firmer and more maturely than I would've expected from my nine-year-old son.

I paused, debating whether to fight this further, but feeling in my gut that I wasn't going to get my way anyway. I had to choose my battles carefully, as I knew there would be many.

"We'll be back as soon as we can," I said, hugging Cale tightly.

"It'll be okay," Sophie added, clinging to her brother as though she'd never let go.

"Come along now, ladies," Peter said, closing and locking Cale's door behind us.

As we ascended the gleaming hardwood stairs, I felt waves of panic for what lay ahead. *Please*, I silently prayed. *Please* let help arrive soon.

Chapter Fourteen

When we arrived at the upper living room, Peter gestured for us to go in first. I scanned the room looking for Richard, but he was nowhere in sight.

"Take a seat wherever you'd like," said Peter.

Sophie and I sat side-by-side on a plush white sofa. She grabbed my hand tightly, and I could feel the cold, clamminess of our combined nervousness.

"Can I get you anything to drink?" Peter asked.

"No, thanks," we said, almost in unison.

"Alright, the boss should be in momentarily." And with that, Peter quickly left the room.

"Mom, I'm scared," whispered Sophie.

"Me too, but be strong, Sophie … we'll get through this."

We both flinched when a tall form suddenly entered the room wearing a strange white mask that covered half of his face; it reminded me of The Phantom of the Opera. He paused and stared at us, and the familiarity of those intense green eyes took me back twelve years.

The rest of him was almost fully covered with a white turtle neck, tan khaki pants, and a white glove on his right hand. He slowly moved forwards, and I felt Sophie grasp my hand tighter. This moment was surreal, and I could hear nothing in this vast room except our quick breathing.

"My two beautiful ladies," he said, sitting directly across from us in a white armchair, moving the blue accent pillow aside as he sat. "Forgive me for hiding half of my face, but I don't want my scars to scare my darling, Sophie," he said, staring intently at his daughter, then back at me.

Before I could think of a response, Sophie said, "You may be my father, but you don't own me. You can't … can't just steal us from our lives like this."

He leaned forwards. "My dearest daughter, Sophie. I love you so much. I missed your childhood and I've sacrificed so much in this world to finally have my family back. You've had twelve years of your childhood without me, and now it's my turn to be with the two ladies I love most," he said.

"You don't even know me!" declared Sophie. "And I already have a dad I love very much," she added. I could feel her trembling despite trying to appear brave.

"And you will grow to love me, too, Sophie," he said. "We are a lot alike, you and I. I've watched you grow up from a distance. I'm so proud of you," he said, clearly emotional about finally being across from Sophie. "Your mother did a great job raising you so far." He leaned forwards as he stared at me through his white mask.

"Then why abduct us, Richard? Why put us through this?"

I asked, staring at this strange man. "You can do the right thing and let us go. *Please*, just let us go."

"Cadence, my love, I *did* let you go … for twelve whole years. I lost my family, and almost died not only from the burns and stabbing, but also from the emotional pain of watching you slip into another life with our daughter. Sophie is *ours*, not *his*."

"I'm not yours!" said Sophie, leaning forwards for emphasis. "And mom's not *yours* either! You can't do this. People can't be owned. It's wrong," she said, as hot tears fell from her eyes. The same green eyes as Richard's, which I could make out looking intensely at us through his white mask. Although I could sense Richard's anger growing, I was proud of Sophie's courage in standing up to him.

Richard stood up abruptly. "You're *mine*! You're my flesh and blood, Sophie, and I'm tied to your mother for life. She has been my soul mate since I first laid eyes on her twenty-two years ago. Despite what she did to me, I forgive and love her more than ever. This is our beautiful new home at sea where we can finally be a family. And I've allowed your brother to be part of our family, as I know how much you both would miss him," he said.

"Allowed? Richard, you didn't *allow* any of this … you forced this," I said. "There's still time to turn around, take us back and do the right thing," I said, trying to remain as calm as possible. I knew from experience that anger just bred more anger with Richard.

"That's *not* going to happen," he said. "It has taken me years to build this life on the sea for us, and we're going to live it. Haven't you hurt me enough, Cadence? Wasn't leaving me to bleed and burn enough punishment for a lifetime?"

"I thought you were dead when we left that house. I didn't know Maria would stab you, and we ran for our lives from the fire," I said, trying to calm his anger. "I'm sorry you suffered, Richard," I added, which was true. To see only half of his face was unnerving; he must be significantly scarred to be wearing this mask the first time he met Sophie.

"If you're truly sorry, you will allow yourself to love me, Cadence," he said in a calm voice. "And you will encourage our daughter to love me, too."

"You're crazy," Sophie said. "You can't force people to love each other."

"I cannot force you, but I have years to wait patiently for it to happen," he said, as he stood up and walked towards us. "I want to hug you both," he said.

Sophie flew off the sofa and backed away. "Don't come near me!"

Richard moved in beside me, and as I stood he pulled me back down and into his arms. I struggled to get up, but the more I did, the tighter he held me.

"Let her go!" cried Sophie, moving closer to us. Little did Sophie know that Richard would not be told what to do nor when to do it. Being as persistent as she was, Sophie came around to the front of the sofa and tried to pull Richard's right arm off of me. In an instant, he released that arm from me and used it to pull her into the embrace. "Stop!" she yelled.

"My two loves. My beauties," he said, as we squirmed in his vise-like embrace. "At last I have my family where we belong … together."

Chapter Fifteen

RICHARD'S SUFFOCATING EMBRACE FELT like it would never end. Finally, he responded to our cues and let us pull away. I shuffled over on the sofa, but Sophie abruptly stood and backed away, glaring angrily at Richard.

"You're crazy," she said, her voice calm and icy. "We're not a family, no matter what you think!"

I knew Richard well, despite the dozen years that had passed. I could see his fists clenching, and hear his breath quickening. I felt the familiar fear of anticipating his rage, but at the same time was sure he wouldn't harm us. But would he threaten Christian as he had when he abducted me twelve years earlier? I trembled at the thought. It would be significantly more inhumane if he threatened Christian's life in front of Sophie and Cale. No, he wouldn't … I hoped.

Richard sighed deeply, and I could tell that he was consciously relaxing his hands and calming down his building rage. "Sophie,

I know you're a loving, wonderful girl. You may think you hate me, but over time you will realize just how much you and I are alike. And I'm willing to wait for as long as it takes for that day to happen."

"It will *never* happen," Sophie declared. "I hate you!" And she stormed across the living room, brushing against the ornate crystal sculpture, positioned so beautifully to catch the sunlight in an array of prismatic colors.

I stood, ready to chase after Sophie, but felt Richard's gloved hand grasp my arm, pulling me back onto the plush sofa. "There's nowhere for her to go. She just needs time," he said, as Sophie paused at the entrance, looking back to see if I was following.

"I need to go to her, she's scared," I said, struggling to pull away from his grasp on my arm.

"Let my mom go!" yelled Sophie.

"She's my wife," Richard replied in his deep, commanding voice.

"I am not," I stated, quietly but firmly.

"I never signed any divorce papers, so your marriage to *him* was never legal. And besides, it's a moot point as we're together now to focus on our future, not the past. We need to discuss what our life will be like here. I won't let your mother go until you come back here and treat me with respect, Sophie," he scolded.

"Richard, please," I pleaded.

"I *mean* it; we can stay here all day, but I will *not* be told what to do. I'm through with being the outsider and you will listen to and respect me." His voice had a force to it that brought a shiver through me. I could tell he was serious. Yet Sophie was stubborn, too. But was she as stubborn as Richard?

To the outside observer, apart from the unusual mask, the three of us on this luxury yacht would seem like any wealthy family having an everyday squabble with their teenage daughter. Yet to us it was the beginning of a long, arduous nightmare. A battle of the wills.

Sophie stood still for a moment, seeming to contemplate our situation. "Fine," Sophie said, walking back towards us. I could see tears rolling down her cheeks. "Please let go of my mom, I hate when you hold onto her like that," she said, sitting down on the armchair where Richard had first sat, directly across from us.

Richard slowly released my arm, and as I made eye contact with Sophie, I couldn't hold back my tears. One step worse than my own fear during the last abduction was seeing my daughter's terror.

"I know this is going to be difficult for you both," Richard began, "but I need you to know that I love you both with all my heart. You are my queen and my princess, and I won't lose you ever again. I know it will take time to feel like a family, but that's acceptable since we're in this for the long haul."

"But what about my school, and my choir … and my friends?" cried Sophie.

"Those are the sacrifices needed for us to be a family again. But I will make it up to you, Sophie. You will continue to develop your beautiful voice in the studio I built for you. And once you're eighteen you will be able to build friendships again in college."

"Noooo!" cried Sophie, her sobs intensifying.

"Richard, you can't do this. You can't hold these kids and me captive on a boat. It's cruel and—"

"This superyacht is *cruel*?" he asked, stretching out the word cruel, while shaking his head. "The *Great White* is one of the grandest yachts ever built. I promise you that Sophie will have life experiences and see parts of the world she would never have otherwise. This will be a key part of her education and she will learn all I have to teach her," he went on, describing his one-sided plan.

"Don't I have any say?" Sophie cried. "You're a dictator and a criminal to do this to us."

"Sophie, I am *not* those things. But I do know what's best for us."

"You do not. You don't know me. You don't know Cale. You just think you do," she said. Her grief was mixed with anger and defiance as she sat across from her father, two sets of green eyes glaring at one another.

"I know enough, Sophie. I've watched you grow up. I've been with you all along, through your good and bad times," he said.

"Richard, spying on us from a distance doesn't count," I said.

"I was closer than you think. I had a place in your home. I was able to observe your dinner table. To hear you describe your days. To hear about your successes. To feel for you on your tough days."

I tried not to focus on my growing nausea, nor the tightening in my chest from his disturbing explanation. Was he completely delusional now? "Richard, you couldn't have spied in our apartment. Security would never have let—"

"Cadence, *don't* underestimate me," he interrupted. "I watched through a tiny camera mounted over your kitchen table, and another in your living room."

"There are *no* cameras in our apartment, Richard. FBI agents secured our place. There was no way you could've gotten away with installing cameras."

"Oh yes, they were tiny and a new technology that was built in a way that only top agents could find if they looked carefully. Your agents only examined that apartment *before* you moved in. Their error was not examining the place regularly." He looked from me to Sophie and back again as he calmly delivered this disturbing explanation. "The molding on the walls allowed for implanting the devices in a way that you could only see them if you knew exactly what you were looking for."

"I don't believe you. Prove it," said Sophie, finally gaining composure through her tears. I did believe Richard, unfortunately, having seen firsthand what he was capable of during my abduction twelve years earlier. But Sophie was as stubborn and defiant as Richard, and would need to witness what Richard was capable of in order to believe him.

"Alright, I will show you in my office," he stood and motioned for us to follow. "It's on the other side of this deck." I gave Sophie a quick hug, then followed Richard with my arm around her shoulder, trying my best to comfort her. The shock and fear shook through my body, with anger threatening to explode through my every pore. I could sense similar emotions in my daughter, and felt powerless with Richard in full control.

I paused briefly and whispered to Sophie, "Everything will be okay, honey."

"I'm not sure about that, mom," she whispered back.

I swallowed hard, not knowing what to say, but hoping she was wrong.

Chapter Sixteen

RICHARD WALKED ENERGETICALLY THROUGH the living room, and ushered us through a set of gleaming wooden double doors, which led into an office with windows on three sides and sliding doors opening onto an outside deck. The pool was in full view below us. His office was breathtaking with its nearly panoramic ocean view. On his large desk was a laptop and two external monitors. Situated on the left were two framed photographs: one from our "wedding" twelve years earlier on Richard's private island, the other last year's school photo of Sophie.

"How did you get my school picture?" Sophie asked, as he turned on his laptop.

"I had one of my hackers get into the photography company's Web site; it literally took minutes." He smiled at the photo, and reached out to put his arm around Sophie, but she backed away immediately.

"That's so illegal," she said, shaking her head and locking

eyes with her father.

"True, it's illegal. But is it fundamentally wrong? I don't believe it's wrong when the intention is a good one. I believe it's right for a father who loves his daughter to proudly display her photo. And there's absolutely nothing wrong with wanting to be a part of his daughter's life."

I knew there was no point arguing, but Sophie didn't know Richard well enough to understand this yet.

Sophie took a deep breath, then began. "It's one thing stealing my photo without permission, it's another forcing my mom to marry you. That's crazy illegal *and* plain wrong," said Sophie, shaking her head as she stared at the wedding photo of Richard and me standing amidst the tropical background of White Island. My smile appeared forced, with anxiety evident on my pale face.

"Ah, Sophie, you are too young to understand the extent of love I have for your mother. That's a story I will share with you another time," he said, wise to avoid this debate.

"But you're right, Sophie," I said, despite my better judgment. "Abduction is completely illegal, no matter what emotions are behind it." Richard turned and looked into my eyes. I could see a mixture of rage and love in their green depths; the pull and tug of the two emotions at play in his complex brain.

"I won't bother responding to that, Cadence. Instead, I'm going to prove what Sophie asked me to. Would either of you like to take a seat?" he asked, motioning towards two chairs at the side of the room.

"No, thanks," we both said, almost in unison.

"Okay, here we go." He flipped on one of the external monitors, and then opened a folder on his laptop that said, "My

Family." There were dozens of subfolders labeled by month and year. He opened a file to reveal an image of our kitchen table at dinnertime. He pressed play and turned up the volume.

"I'm so excited we won! It'll be so much fun to go to San Diego! Can we stay longer and go to Disneyland?" Sophie was in full view, her expression displaying excitement and anticipation. I was also in the video, as well as Cale seated across the table. Oh, Cale, I thought, anxious to get back to him as soon as I could.

The camera angle didn't show a clear picture of Christian. It showed more of his back, although part of his face was sometimes in view when he turned to speak to the kids. The picture and sound were clear enough that it brought me back to that moment. I shuddered at this extreme violation of our privacy.

Sophie and I were silent as we watched our private family discussion unfold on Richard's laptop. Feelings of intrusion washed over me, followed by panic over what intimate family moments Richard may have witnessed over the years.

"How could you violate our privacy like this?" I asked, trying to control myself from screaming and slapping his face. I could sense equally strong emotions brewing in Sophie, who stood on my other side.

"Yeah, this is crazy. You're a spy, Mr. White," she declared.

"Sophie, don't call me that. Dad would be ideal, though I know that's premature."

"I will *never* call you *dad*. I already have a dad," she said.

"Well, father will have to do then."

"Richard, don't push this," I said.

Sophie was furious but didn't reply, just rolled her eyes.

"Please don't do that, Sophie. The only reason I had eyes on your home was because I didn't want to miss out on knowing my daughter, that's all. My other option was to take you back sooner, but the timing wasn't right until now. And I think you've had a good upbringing and education in your first twelve years, which I thank your mother for," he said, locking eyes with me.

"Then why pull her away from all of that, Richard? Don't you see how traumatic this will be?"

"Sophie is resilient. We're all resilient. Sure, it will be a tough transition but I know it's the right thing, and she will settle in eventually. This is all based on love," he added.

"Love is about *trust*, Richard. It's about giving people the freedom to love you back. You haven't given us any choice, and you've breached our private life in an unforgivable way," I added, watching his gloved and non-gloved hand form into fists.

"Cadence, I have the right to love my daughter. Sophie's my flesh and blood. You ripped her away from me, but I had every right to be part of her life. I was forced to live in hiding, while you built another family. I had no say for twelve years. The cameras were my only way to be part of your lives. You may not forgive me, but I wouldn't change a thing about the videos. They helped me survive."

Feelings of pity flooded me, yet anger and violation held strong. I recalled the confusing emotions from twelve years ago, and even back from when we'd dated. There was a small part of my heart that felt sad for Richard. Sad that he continued to hang on to someone who didn't love him, and continued to persevere down a painful and illegal path.

To live twelve years focused on us, watching Christian raise his daughter from a distance, told me that Richard was sicker than he'd ever been. I didn't know what to say or do; I wanted to run but there was nowhere we could run to. I hoped and prayed we were being tracked and that this nightmare would soon be over.

"Richard, you may have clever security and a plan to evade capture, but we have excellent agents on the case and security guards with us who are not going to let you get away with this," I said, trying to assert whatever control I could, and also wanting to calm Sophie who was once again crying and shaking.

"You underestimate me, Cadence," he said, flipping to his Internet browser and searching for "Breaking News San Diego." The first few links were headlines that took my breath away:

> *Breaking News: Two men found shot dead among yachts at the Fifth Avenue Landing Marina in San Diego*
>
> *Murder on the Marina: Police on the hunt for shooter*
>
> *Yacht owner terrorized after discovering floating body*

"No!" I screamed, as he clicked on the first link, showing the story along with a photo of a body bag surrounded by police and paramedics, with tape partitioning the crime scene in front of the familiar row of yachts we had walked by this morning. The words blurred through my tears as I gripped Sophie's hand:

> *At 10:25 a.m. police were called to San Diego's Fifth Avenue Landing Marina, where a yacht owner discovered a body in the water next to his vessel. The body, appearing to be a man in his thirties, is yet to be identified, and had been shot twice in the head.*

Upon a search of the area, police discovered a second body on the deck of another yacht. This was also a man, yet to be identified, who was shot both in the head and chest. The FBI is now involved in this investigation.

The owner of one of the other yachts at this port, Sylvia Stanton, described the unfolding scene as terrifying. "This is a peaceful place and the yacht community has never witnessed this type of crime here. San Diego is a relaxing port, and a city we love. Now we're terrified and can't wait to pull away. I thought I heard a bang shortly after ten, but it didn't sound like a gun so I imagine it had a silencer. I hope the police catch the killer soon."

"Adam and Drew didn't deserve to be killed!" I cried. "They were protecting us. How could you do this?"

"It had to be done, and they didn't see it coming or feel a thing. Sergei was efficient, and I couldn't risk either of them getting away. I'll admit that they were skilled, but they were still no match for my team," he added. His confident tone made me want to strangle him.

"You're a monster!" cried Sophie, pulling at my hand as she raced from Richard's office. "I can't stand being in the same room as a murderer," she said. I felt the same, and was on the verge of vomiting. I instinctively followed Sophie as she entered the living room, and ran towards the exit, only to be met by a man with red hair and fair skin who blocked the door.

"Not so fast, Mrs. White."

"Let us through!" I demanded.

"But what about introductions? Finally, we get to meet. I'm Leo."

Chapter Seventeen

RICHARD SAT AT HIS desk, his feet anchored to the floor. Though he wanted to chase after Cadence and Sophie, it wasn't necessary as there was nowhere for them to go. He had them in his full control.

He could hardly believe he had them back. Finally! His two beautiful ladies. His family. Minus the boy, whom he would have to tolerate. But seeing the boy by the pool brought flashbacks to the boy he once was. He heard the voice, the condescending, nasty voice in his head, whispering to him.

They think you are a monster. You think this is an adjustment period, but they are never going to love you. It's too late. You should've taken them back when Sophie was a baby, so she would know no other father.

"No, this was the best way to do it. And I will earn their love," he whispered back into the empty office.

You think you know how to be a father? Where did you learn about what a good father is? Certainly not from your own, who was a deranged lunatic. And your mother a mentally unstable, sorry excuse for a mother. How can you possibly think you can be any better than those you learned from?

"Shut up," Richard said. "Shut the fuck up."

His words triggered a memory of his father saying those exact words to him. As much as he didn't want to remember, the images and sound of his father's menacing voice filled his mind, and he was brought back to his sixteenth birthday.

His father had insisted on a dinner at one of the fanciest restaurants in Boston. What was unusual was that he insisted that Richard's mother, Constance, come as well. She had been spending almost all of her time in her bedroom after falling into a depression. Richard had tried everything to cheer her up, but she remained solemn.

He overheard his father yelling at her from down the hall. "I had my secretary make a reservation at Blancos, and you're coming, Constance. I'm tired of you being a slug in this house, and our son is turning sixteen. You can't miss his birthday dinner."

Richard strained to hear, but couldn't make out his mother's quiet response.

"It's all in your head, woman. You need a higher dose of your happy pills; I will call your psychiatrist back. Our kid needs a mother."

It was quiet and then BANG. It sounded like his father had punched the wall, but he didn't hear a scream from his mother. Before she would have screamed, but now it was as if his father had snuffed out all of her remaining emotion.

"Fuck you, Constance. You're coming even if I have to drag your skinny, wilted body there. Now get in the bloody shower and clean yourself up. Our reservation is for 6:30. And do yourself a favor, wear some perfume; you smell like a rotting corpse from being cooped up in here all the time."

Their door flew open and Richard quickly turned so as to look like he was walking towards his room. He was a nervous wreck after having heard yet another argument between his parents. Thankfully, they were less frequent than they had been in his younger years, but when they did happen his father was increasingly cruel.

"Ah, it's the birthday boy. I was just getting your mother organized. You know how she takes hours to freshen up," he said with a fake smile.

"If she's tired I don't mind it just being the two of us," Richard offered.

"Not going to happen. We're going as a family and that's that. When I turned sixteen it was a big deal in my family, so we're going to have the best meal in town tonight for yours. Suit and tie please, son. I'm going down to my office to finish up some work. Can you check on your mother's progress in the next hour? I hate being late."

"Okay, father." Richard went into his room and closed his door. He sat on the bed, his face in his hands, and let his tears fall. His tears were far fewer than they used to be; he felt as though he had used most of his lifelong supply of tears by this point. He hated living in this house. His father didn't like him to spend any time with friends or in outside activities, so his time outside of school was spent trading stocks. School came easy, so Richard would finish his homework quickly then find himself reading about business and analyzing various business strategies.

He knew he would never be like his father. He would be much more successful, not only in business but in marriage. He would treat his wife like a queen, and choose someone he respected. He hated seeing the disrespect his father bestowed upon his mother. It took every ounce of his willpower to refrain from punching his father in the face.

Richard put on his suit and looked at himself in the mirror. His acne was starting to subside, and he liked the way he looked. His blond hair was full, and contrasted well with his green eyes. Better looking than his piggish father, he thought. Then he heard a voice.

"What?" Richard asked, sure there was someone behind him. But when he turned there was nobody in his bedroom.

You're lame. You don't have any friends. No girl is going to notice you, acne or not.

"Shut up!" Richard said. "I am going to make something big of myself and have any woman that I want. You wait and see."

I'll believe it when I see it.

"Shut the fuck up!" Richard said, and stormed out of his bedroom, slamming the door behind him. He leaned against the wall in the hall beside his room, the sleek hardwood floor cold beneath his feet. The realism of the voice freaked him out. It seemed so authentic, so malicious. He forced himself to take a few deep breaths, knowing it would disturb his mother to see him upset on his birthday.

He walked to the end of the long hallway and knocked gently on her bedroom door. He no longer thought of this as his parents' bedroom, as his father was often away, with another woman in the basement, or in the guest room. There was no love left between his parents, and he wondered if there had ever been any.

There was no answer, so he knocked again. "Mother?"

A few seconds passed. Still no response. He turned the knob, and the door slowly opened. The room had a stale, dank odor with a faint tinge of pharmaceuticals in the air. Almost like a hospital smell. The bed was unmade but empty. The en suite door was closed, so Richard quickly walked to it and knocked. "Mother, are you in there?"

No response.

"Father told me to check on you as we have to leave in an hour," he said, a feeling of dread building in his stomach.

No response.

Richard slowly opened the door. His mother lay slumped on the floor, with bright red blood soaking into the white bathmat on which she lay. Three half emptied pill bottles were scattered around her.

"Mother!" Richard screamed, kneeling beside her. He instinctively felt for a pulse, and found a weak one. Where was the blood coming from? He checked her arm, which lay beside the blood, and saw a diagonal slice near her wrist. The cut continued to bleed, but luckily it didn't seem to have sliced through the main artery of her wrist; the ulnar artery, Richard randomly remembered from biology class. Regardless, he needed to stop the bleeding, and grabbed a towel from the rack above the toilet. He knelt and tied it around his mother's wrist. He then ran back into the room to call 9-1-1, nearly colliding with his father.

"I heard you scream. What's going on?"

"Mother needs help. I'm calling an ambulance."

"Wait a second, until I check her," his father ordered,

running into the bathroom. "Fucking hell, Constance!" he yelled. Richard watched as his father bent down to examine the scene. He saw his father feel for a pulse too.

"She needs help right away," Richard said.

"She'll be fine. I don't want to draw attention to how fucked up this family is. She will come to, and I will get her into the psych ward where she belongs."

"She could die! I need to call 9-1-1," Richard protested.

"She's not going to die, this has happened before," his father said, standing to face Richard, his demeanor as nonchalant as if this were an everyday event.

"We can't risk it. Her pulse is weak. I'm going to call," Richard said, running for the phone beside his mother's bed. As he reached for the receiver, he felt his father's hand grab his right arm, pulling it back.

"You're not calling anyone, boy," his father commanded.

"Yes, I am," Richard retorted.

"Over my dead body," said his father, now grabbing both of Richard's arms and looking up into his eyes. Yes, Richard was now two inches taller than his father, and stronger from daily weight lifting over the past six months in their basement gym.

Richard filled with a rage that he had never before experienced. It felt red hot and permeated his every cell with anger towards this man. At his family. At his life. He grabbed his father's upper arms and gripped tightly with all the force he had. The red rage shot through him as he held on hard while his father struggled to free himself. "I'm not listening to your bullshit anymore!" he screamed, and threw his father to the ground. He landed hard.

Richard then ran to the phone and dialed 9-1-1. Ring …

"Don't you dare!" shouted his father, struggling to stand.

"Yes, this is an emergency. My mother has cut herself and took some pills," he stated, as his father's eyes looked like they would bulge out of their sockets. His skin was bright red, and his mouth was gaping as he watched his son defy him. "Okay, thank you." Richard hung up the phone, and faced his father who was coming at him in a fit of fury.

"You son of a bitch," his father roared.

"How dare you call my mother a bitch," Richard replied, meeting his father head on for a physical fight.

"And you're a worthless sack of shit just like her, boy," his father shouted, growing increasingly redder and shaking in a crazed frenzy.

"She's a better person in every way compared to the repulsive creature that you are," Richard said, not comprehending that he'd actually said these words. Richard braced for the physical attack that was imminent, wondering if he did indeed have the strength to fend off this madman. But suddenly Richard's father froze, and reached for his head.

"Ow," he whimpered. He looked at Richard and it was as if he was trying to focus, but was having trouble. Richard noticed his left eyelid slightly droop.

"My head," he whispered.

"Serves you right, you abusive animal," Richard said.

His father then buckled and crashed to the floor.

Had his father had a heart attack? Richard couldn't be bothered to check his pulse, and instead rushed back to the bathroom to check on his mother, who was still unconscious but thankfully had a slightly stronger pulse since he'd tied the towel tightly around her wrist.

"You'll be okay, mother. Your life will be better now."

The doorbell rang three times in succession, and he raced downstairs to the double doors of the mansion to let in the paramedics. Both of Richard's parents were rushed to the hospital, one alive and the other dead upon arrival. For once Richard's prayers were answered, as he watched his father's dead body being covered. A sweet sixteenth birthday indeed, Richard thought.

Chapter Eighteen

LEO EXTENDED HIS HAND towards me as he stood blocking our way out of the living room. He was a few inches taller than me, lean and muscular in a short sleeved white shirt. His blue eyes were intense and piercing as they stared back at mine. I could smell his musky cologne, and hear his deep, rhythmic breaths.

"Another of Richard's criminals," I replied, refusing to shake his hand.

"Well, now, I wasn't the one who tried to murder and then burn him alive, which is defined as criminal in my books," he said. I immediately detested this man, who gave off an aura of hypocritical righteousness.

"I wasn't the one who stabbed him and set the fire," I retorted, "but I did run for my life as I was being held captive by a murderer."

"He may be a murderer, but anyone he's killed has deserved nothing less. The boss is fiercely loyal, and I'm glad I was there to save his life. If it wasn't for me he would've burned to death. I'll never forget what he's been through and my job is to protect him with my life," Leo concluded.

"Now can you please let us pass, I need to see my son," I said, refusing give him the satisfaction of responding to his rant.

"Peter messaged me and wants to speak with you first."

I cringed, knowing the conversation that was coming. "Please, can I just see how Cale is doing first?

"Peter checked on him ten minutes ago. He's just fine, watching a movie in his room," he said, almost mocking me for fretting about my son. My dislike for Leo intensified.

"You seem like a control freak," stated Sophie, eyeing him with distrust, her eyes red from crying.

"I guess that's one way of describing my job," he replied, staring down at Sophie. "I ensure that Mr. White is fully protected, and that nothing goes wrong like it did twelve years ago. And yes, dear, that means complete control over all the moving parts," he said. Cocky bastard, I thought.

Just as I was about to try and push by, Peter came up behind Leo. "Howdy ladies. We need to talk," he ordered, gesturing Leo to move us back into the living room.

"I really want to check on my son, Peter. Please," I asked, trying to plead with him. Movie or not, I knew Cale was scared.

"Have a seat for a few minutes, then you can see your son," Peter said. It was not a question but a command. Sophie and I looked at one another and knew we didn't have a choice. We quickly walked back into the living room and sat on the nearest sofa. There were two armchairs across from us; Peter took one, while Leo stood behind the second, staring at me and then Sophie. Leo gave me the chills, and I instinctively grabbed Sophie's hand.

"Mrs. White, we need to get on the same page here," stated Peter. "I asked you to put everything that was on your person, and Sophie's, in the bag. And you deliberately defied that order."

"I don't know what you're talking about, and don't treat me like a child," I said, trying to echo the same level of authority. "And I'm not Mrs. White, I'm Mrs. Davidson," I added.

"Firstly, you *are* Mrs. White to us. You were married to the boss, and divorce papers were never issued," Peter contorted.

"I was unwillingly married, so divorce papers were never needed considering the marriage was not legal."

"That's not how we see it. But besides that, you purposely hid the two tracking devices. But rest assured, it didn't take the team long to find them. There's not much you can hide on this yacht, as we know every nook and cranny. The point of the matter is that you'd best not to defy our orders," Peter stated with a militaristic tone.

"Don't speak to my mom like that," said Sophie, her green eyes glaring from one man to the other, reminding me so much of Richard.

"Honey, if your mom breaks the rules she will be reprimanded. And so will you," added Leo. "What happened twelve years ago is *not* going to repeat itself here under our watch. Life will be calm and orderly, not a game of cat and mouse as it was before when the boss almost died."

"This is illegal. You have kidnapped us and cannot seriously expect us to act like a happy family," I said. "This is completely wrong, and you're brainwashed to believe it's okay to do this to me and my children."

"This girl is also Mr. White's child. The resemblance is

unmistakable, not only in looks but in personality," Peter chuckled, nodding as he looked across at Sophie. "The boss has a say in her life, too," he added.

"The way I see it, you have two choices. You can make this difficult or smooth, it's up to you," said Leo, smugly leaning on the back of the armchair as he looked down on us.

"I don't think the word 'choice' even comes into play here," I replied. "You know where I stand; we're being held against our will and I'll do whatever I can to protect my children."

"You're not making this easy," Peter said. "To reiterate, there's nowhere to run or hide, and the entire staff have been with the boss for years now. Loyalty is strong in this crew, and there's no way you can talk or write or message your way out of here. The GPS signals on all of your devices were disabled well before we set sail, and the FBI is only now scrambling to figure out what happened. We've also deactivated our signals, so there's no way to track us. We'll be just one of the thousands of boats in the international waters, armed with the latest technology to allow us to remain hidden and avoid any unwanted encounters. When we gas up it will only be for that purpose, and at very select ports. Rest assured that you will be well hidden at those times." Peter leaned forwards and looked directly at me, then at Sophie, as we stared back in disbelief. "Hopefully you can now understand that efforts to escape are not only a complete waste of energy, but will also make for tension between us."

I sat silently. Hopelessness threatened to consume me like it did twelve years ago, but I sensed Sophie boiling with anger beside me. "You'd better not treat us like this, as my *father* wouldn't appreciate how you're talking to me and my mom," said Sophie.

I winced as she referred to Richard as her "father" and a feeling of foreboding crept over me.

"Sophie, we're just having a direct and honest conversation," said Peter.

"To me it sounds scary and rude," replied Sophie.

"You haven't seen our rude sides yet," laughed Leo, his thin lips curved into an arrogant grin. "This is nothing."

"I will make sure my father knows exactly how you're treating us, so you'd better be nice," said Sophie, in her most authoritative twelve-year-old tough girl voice. I was proud of her for defending us, while I tried not to scream or cry. The last abduction seemed impossible to escape from, but this time it was so much worse. I couldn't imagine how we'd ever escape if the FBI couldn't track us. Our lives at sea flashed in my mind: years of cruising the world at the hands of Richard and these controlling, militaristic men. Cale and Sophie's remaining childhood in captivity. Tears escaped as I thought of never seeing Christian again, and what he must be feeling right now having lost all three of us.

"We're nice people, Sophie," said Peter. "So long as you're all nice to us, we'll be nice to you" he added, eyeing me with a warning look as he spoke.

"Yep, we can be friends or not, but hiding things is not the best way to start a friendship. Can we start over?" asked Leo. I was revolted that he could even think of using the word friendship.

"We'll never be friends with you guys," said Sophie. "Anyone who makes my mom cry will never be a friend."

I wiped away the tears that I hadn't even realized were running down my face. Peter pulled a tissue from a box on a side table, and handed it to me.

"We don't mean to make her cry," said Peter, clearly trying to sound empathetic. "Mrs. White, do you want to see Cale now?"

"Yes," I said through my tears.

"I want to speak to my father," Sophie demanded.

"Sophie, I think you should stick with me for now," I said.

"No, mom, I really want to talk to him," she said, squeezing my hand, and I knew she was wise beyond her years and had her reasons. If anyone could influence Richard, it would be Sophie.

"Okay, but don't be long, Cale will want to see you, and I'll be worried," I said. "And be careful not to anger him, he has a temper," I whispered, knowing that Leo and Richard were listening to our exchange.

Sophie stood and turned towards Richard's office.

"I'll check to see if the boss is okay with you popping by," said Leo, heading in the same direction.

"I don't need a chaperone or an appointment to talk with my own father," Sophie said, walking faster to get ahead of Leo.

A battle of the wills ensued, as Leo sped up as well, with both of them arriving at the same time to the double doors leading to Richard's office.

"I need to talk to you … father," Sophie said, knocking on the gleaming, wooden doors.

"Is it a good time for Sophie to come in, boss?" interrupted Leo.

The door opened in response, and Richard stood looking down at his daughter. "It's always a good time, Sophie," he said, beaming with surprise and adoration. "You can leave us, Leo. Please close the door behind you," he added, looking directly at Leo, while gesturing Sophie inside.

Leo looked taken aback. Leo had been Richard's right-hand man for twelve years. The trust between them was rock solid, and this abduction had been years in the planning. Leo felt that he knew what was best for Richard, even more so than Richard himself. He feared that this girl might manipulate his boss, and didn't like it one bit. Daughter or not.

He stormed back into the living room, but Peter had already escorted Cadence to see the boy. He felt an odd feeling of control slipping away from him. It was a feeling he remembered well from his days at the CIA. "There's no way in hell I'm letting these manipulative bitches hurt him again," he muttered, as he stared out of one of the windows towards the endless blue ocean.

Chapter Nineteen

"SOPHIE, DARLING, COME HAVE a seat," said Richard, gesturing for her to sit at one of the dark brown, leather chairs in front of his desk, while he came around to sit facing her. He leaned towards her and stared at Sophie through his strange, white mask.

"Thanks for talking to me," Sophie said, her voice hesitant as she stared back at the same green eyes as hers.

"Any time, Sophie. No matter what I'm doing, I will always make time for you," he said, aching to hold and comfort her, as it pained him to see her bloodshot eyes and tear-streaked cheeks.

"I don't like the way that Leo and Peter speak to mom," she said, getting right to the point. "They're not only rude, but they also make her cry."

"Oh, Sophie, I definitely don't want your mother to be sad. I love her very much. They're just doing their job to protect us, but I will speak with them about this." It pained him to hear these words from his daughter, while it angered him that his team was being this harsh. He knew the abduction would be traumatic, and expected weeks of pushback before their lives became somewhat normal, but he assumed his men would have a bit more patience and diplomacy.

"Thanks … father," she said. Sophie knew that the word "father" was a powerful one that she could use to get through to him. She hated what he was, but sensed that she had more power if she treated him with some respect and kept her cool. Maybe she could even convince him to free them.

"Sophie, I know it seems horrible that I have taken you three away from your lives in New York," he said, seeming to read her mind, "but it's all because of my love for you. And I know we will get along. I can already tell that you and I think alike. I'm going to teach you so much, Sophie. To mentor you and show you the world. I'm so proud of you, and excited to finally be part of your life."

Sophie wanted to argue against his crazy words, to bring up how she had a great life and he was now ruining it, but instead she forced herself to bite her tongue and remain calm. "Can I see your face under that mask?" she asked, curiosity overtaking her.

"I think my face will scare you. Maybe once we've gotten to know each other better," he said.

"No, I want to see it *now* please, father," she said, leaning forwards and looking intently into his eyes, which were bordered by the white solid material of the bizarre mask.

Richard was moved by her sweet, calm voice. He could hardly believe that his daughter was sitting across from him and that they were having a normal conversation. His daughter! His own flesh and blood, right here. His love for her overtook him, and he felt that he had no choice but to do what she asked. To be what she wanted. Not once had his father ever done anything he asked, and now he had the opportunity to be a real father to Sophie.

"Okay, but please don't be scared," he said, reaching to the back of the mask and unclicking the leather strap that held it firmly in place. He slowly pulled it up, feeling the cool air caress his scarred skin.

Sophie stared, not uttering a sound as she took in the face that was before her. Half of his face was covered in a horrible looking patchwork of scars that were a dark, brownish red color. The bumpy surface covered half of his forehead, working its way down to his nose and chin, while the other half, where the mask did not cover, was his normal skin. The contrast was startling, but Sophie didn't feel scared or disgusted. Instead, she felt a mix of curiosity and sympathy.

"I'm sorry this happened to you," she whispered. She forgot for a moment that this man was their abductor, a crazy man who had stolen her mom not once, but twice, and was now ripping her and Cale's lives away. Instead, she felt sorry for this badly scarred man who was trying so hard to gain their love.

"Me, too," he replied. "You're not scared to see this?" he asked.

"No, just sad that your face was scarred so badly. It must've hurt a lot." Sophie could not stop staring.

"It sure did, Sophie, but not as much as losing your mother did. Losing Cadence was worse than being burned alive. I don't ever want to feel that pain again."

Sophie didn't know how to respond. Hearing him speak about her mother like this felt weird. Instead, she used the opportunity to bring the conversation back to the situation at hand. "Father, I'm scared. Those men are creepy and I'm worried about what's going to happen."

"Sophie, *I'm* in control of this yacht. There's no need to be scared. Please know you can come to me any time. You're my number one priority and I want you to feel safe and secure at all times in your new home." He reached for her hands, unable to resist the urge to comfort his daughter. Sophie flinched, but did not pull away. He smiled as he gently squeezed her soft, young hands, comforting her as best he could. "Sophie, I'm the luckiest father in the world," he said. "And I will make sure you're the happiest daughter in the world." He smiled again, half of his smile straining against the rough, leathery scar tissue.

Sophie stared into his eyes, trying not to be distracted by his hideous scars. This was all like a dream; it was surreal to be sitting across from Richard, to feel his hands squeezing hers. A pang of sadness overtook her as she felt disloyal to her real dad. Christian was the best dad in the world, and there was no way this strange man could ever come close or replace him. But she was going to use his adoration for her to her advantage to try and help her family get out of this terrible mess. "I know you want what's best, father, but we're all so scared. I don't know that holding us captive will ever feel like being a real family," Sophie said, taking after Richard's confident nature.

"Well, Sophie, let's give it a try." He squeezed her hands once more, then gently let go, leaning back into his chair. "I'm going to walk you back to your room now, and speak with my men."

"Okay," she said, watching intently as Richard gently placed the mask back on his face and used both hands to buckle the strap with ease. He motioned her to stand, and opened the office doors ushering her into the living room. Leo was sitting on an armchair near his office, and stood abruptly when they entered.

"Leo, I'm going to walk Sophie back to her room, and then I'd like to have a brief meeting with you and Peter," he said, his voice confident and commanding.

Leo looked taken aback, his blue eyes concerned but respectful. "Okay, boss, I'll get Peter and we'll be in your office in ten," he said. He then looked Sophie in the eye, the slightest glare showing through. Sophie fully glared back as she followed her father past Leo and through the living room.

"I'd like to see my brother," Sophie said, as Richard walked closely behind her.

"Alright, I will take you there, darling. Ladies first," he added, motioning her down the gleaming, hardwood stairs. The staterooms were two floors down. He brought her to Cale's door and said, "Your mother is in there with him. Lunch will be served in half an hour. I will have Peter show you the way to the dining room then," he said, smiling down at her.

"Okay," Sophie replied, reaching for the handle as her father disappeared down the hall.

Chapter Twenty

SOPHIE OPENED THE DOOR to see Cale and me sitting on his bed. I was comforting him as he had indeed been terrified when I had arrived back at his room. He'd tried to maintain a brave face for Peter, but as soon as I entered, he broke into sobs asking if he'd ever get to see his dad again.

Sophie rushed over and sat on the other side of Cale, and put an arm around her little brother, reaching for my hand with her free one.

"I'm glad you're back," said Cale.

"I'm okay, and we *will* get through this," Sophie said, bringing her voice to a confident whisper, knowing full well we were being recorded. "He trusts me. I can get through to him," she said, leaning as close to us as possible, creating a cocoon of love and protection amidst our unpredictable future at sea.

"Oh, Sophie … Cale … I'm so sorry this is happening," I said, my voice cracking with emotion. "But we need to be strong. I don't trust Leo one bit," I added, involuntarily shaking as I pictured his steel blue eyes glaring at me. I knew that he detested me before we even met; the feeling was mutual. I didn't like Peter, either, but something about Leo gave me the chills.

"I told him that Leo and Peter scared us, mom. He's going to talk to them," Sophie whispered directly into my ear.

"Oh, Sophie, thank you ... you're so brave and I know that Richard won't hurt you, and he'll make sure those men don't either," I said, trying to convince myself. Richard was insane, of that I had no doubt. But men who would willingly abduct children as part of their job scared me just as much, if not more, for they didn't love Sophie and me as Richard did.

"He wants us to join him for lunch in half an hour. He will get to meet Cale too," Sophie explained.

"Well, we don't really have a choice and we need to eat. I think the FBI will find us soon, as they know which port we left from, so it shouldn't be long before they zero in on this yacht," I said, trying to sound confident for my children. Yet as I said the words I felt doubt creeping in. For Richard was brilliant and strategic, and no doubt was already completely off the radar.

Richard entered his office and sank into the leather chair behind his desk, closing his eyes and taking a deep breath to try and calm his turbulent feelings. He had spent so much time with Leo and Peter, masterminding this whole sequence of events. And things had gone flawlessly, except for the fact that his daughter and Cadence were terrified. Leo and Peter needed to treat them with respect; they were his ladies. Leo especially seemed to be walking a fine line, and Richard needed to ensure Leo did not overstep. His thoughts were suddenly interrupted as Leo and Peter entered his office.

"Take a seat," Richard said, staring at the two men from behind his desk. Leo sat in the chair where Sophie had been sitting, and Peter sat in the one beside it. The air smelled of leather and Leo's musky cologne.

"I'd say it's time for some scotch to toast how seamlessly this all went down," said Peter, his eyes glowing with victory.

"Not quite yet," said Richard. "I need to make sure you two understand that Cadence and Sophie mean the world to me. They're terrified and you need to treat them with respect," he said, looking at Peter's shocked face, then locking eyes with Leo.

"Boss, with all due respect, we need to remain in control here. We're not risk free and they'll do anything they can to cast doubt and poke holes in our system in order to escape," said Leo.

Richard took a deep breath, continuing to stare at Leo. "We *will* remain in control, Leo, but we will *not* be tyrants who terrify my ladies," Richard said, his tone brooking no argument. "The way you spoke to Cadence is not acceptable, Leo. She's my wife and not some prisoner."

Leo's pale skin reddened, looking more like his hair, while his hands clenched into fists at his sides. They were manipulating Richard and he wouldn't stand for it! "I need to remind you, boss, that Cadence left you to burn in that fire. She's not to be trusted," he added, looking away from Richard's penetrating, green eyes.

Richard stood up, glaring down at Leo. "I don't need to be

reminded of that!" he roared. "Every damn day I'm reminded of it when I look at my face! And there's nowhere they can go. I need you to be civil and kind to my wife and daughter, Leo. Is that clear?"

There was a moment of silence as Leo tried to slow his rapid breathing and control the rage he felt boiling inside. "Yes, sir," he finally said, knowing when his boss was serious. He had seen enough of Richard's temper to know when to shut up. But it was hard to watch Richard being played this way.

"And you, Peter, are you clear on this?" Richard asked, seeing Peter also looking red and rattled.

"Yes, indeed, sir," Peter said.

"Now please leave me be to collect my thoughts as lunch will be shortly. Can you get them in fifteen minutes, Peter?"

"Yes, but don't you want to include the boy as well?"

Richard's heart sank as the reality of having to meet the boy sunk in. He was growing to regret his decision to include him. "Yes, I suppose we do need to feed him," Richard replied.

Leo and Peter left, and Richard practiced the breathing technique that he had worked so hard on these last few years. He knew that his anger was a beast to be tamed, and breathing was one of the only ways to tame it. Getting to six breaths a minute; four seconds in, five seconds out, then one second pause and repeat. Eyes closed, seated comfortably, working to release his tense shoulders. Unclench his fists. Release the tension in his forehead.

Yet despite being in the present moment, he couldn't control the ugly thought that pushed its way into his mind: What about the boy? Christian's boy. Part of the package. He had to show him kindness, and perhaps even grow to love him. But it would be no easy feat. He hadn't even met the boy, yet just thinking of him brought back his boyhood memories and the dreaded voice …

You won't be able to treat the boy any different than your own father treated you. You're a monster just like he was.

"No, I'm nothing like he was," Richard whispered back, willing his deep breaths to continue, to snuff out the relentless voice.

You're everything he was, and worse. He never abducted children. He never killed people.

"I did everything I had to for love. And love is what differentiates me from him," Richard spoke calmly into the empty office.

Love is reciprocal. Nobody loves you, and you can't force them to. Even your own parents didn't love you.

And with that heartless statement, Richard was plummeted back into the scene when he lost his father and only had what was left of his mother. He was in the emergency room, his father's dead body lying in a hospital bed. A nurse mumbling words of sympathy, which were incomprehensible to Richard's racing mind.

A doctor came in and spoke about how the brain aneurysm would have taken him suddenly, without the chance to suffer. How sorry he was for Richard's loss, and that he was welcome to come and check in on his mother, who was resting after being treated for her "conditions," which Richard knew to be the self-inflicted cut near her wrist, prescription drug overdose, and blood loss.

"Can I have a few moments to say goodbye to my father?" Richard asked the nurse and doctor.

"Yes of course," they spoke simultaneously, their voices a murmur in his jumbled mind.

When they closed the door, Richard slowly walked to his father's bedside. His tall body lay there, gray hair and beard neatly groomed as always. Gray eyes forever closed. It seemed so surreal, and Richard sat on the side of the hospital bed, looking down into the face he had feared his whole life.

"Father …" he said, barely able to speak. But just as he thought the torrent of emotion he felt inside would bring tears, he instead broke into a grin. He was suddenly overcome with joy. "You can now go where you belong, to rot in hell," Richard said, his voice calm and clear, nodding as he smiled widely. "I only wish I had killed you with my own hands," he added. "And this is for all the times you hurt us, you fucking animal," he added, slapping his father's cold, dead cheek. He spat in his face as a final token of his hatred, then covered his father with the white hospital sheet. He felt a new bounce in his step as he exited the room. A fresh conviction to face the world with a new level of control and so much potential.

—

He was brought back to the present by a knock on his office door. "They're in the dining room, boss," Leo's voice came through. "You ready?"

"As ready as I'll ever be," Richard said, relieved that the hospital door had closed out that final memory of his father. And now he had the opportunity to be what a real father should be.

Chapter Twenty-One

SOPHIE, CALE AND I moved our chairs as close together as possible as we sat on one side of the large, rectangular dining table. There were four place settings atop the gleaming glass surface, two on one side, one at the end and one across. We pulled the one across to our side so that we could sit together, with me in the middle of Cale and Sophie. A man we hadn't yet met, dressed in a formal white server's attire, entered after Peter left.

"Bonjour, it's my pleasure to introduce myself. I'm Pierre, and I will be your server," he said, his French accent polished, and his manners impeccable. He had dark brown hair, a small goatee, and was tall and slender. His smile seemed genuine, yet I sensed he would maintain a clear, professional boundary.

"I'm Cadence. It's nice to meet you, Pierre," I said, knowing there was little point in trying to align the staff to our side; but Sophie had other ideas.

"I'm Sophie, and this is my brother, Cale. I'm sure you

already know that we're being held as prisoners," she said, staring at Pierre, who visibly stepped back, his jaw dropping at the bluntness of Sophie's words.

"Mademoiselle, I know that you are Monsieur White's daughter. I'm merely here to serve you," he added. "May I bring you anything to drink?" he asked, desperately trying to change the subject.

"Do you have soda?" asked Cale, his boyish plea for sugar breaking the ice.

"Oui, monsieur, any type you desire," Pierre answered, the tension in his face relaxing.

"Dr. Pepper, please."

"Absolutely. And you, Mademoiselle Sophie?"

"Prisoner's Pepsi, please," said my quick-witted daughter.

"We have Pepsi," Pierre said, ignoring her jab.

"And water's fine for me, Pierre, thank you," I said, my heart racing as Richard entered the dining room, his mask still catching me by surprise. He observed the three of us seated closely together and walked towards us. As he moved to his seat at the head of the table, he stopped to shake Cale's hand. Cale clung to me, terrified and unwilling to extend a hand towards this strange, tall, masked man.

"It's nice to finally meet you, young man," Richard said. "Don't let my mask scare you, it is less scary than the scars it hides," he explained, attempting to relax the tension permeating the room.

"Don't come near me!" Cale blurted, his voice muffled by my arm. I could feel the warm moisture of his tears, and gave Richard a sharp glance.

"Fair enough. Sophie and Cadence, you both look lovely,"

he said, gently touching each of us on the shoulder, before moving to his place beside Sophie. "I'm so glad that you got Cadence's most beautiful features, Sophie," he smiled. "Yet I love that you take after us both," he added. We tried to ignore his comment, but I saw Sophie wince.

Just then the sunlight caught the large crystal chandelier that hung above us, sending a burst of rainbow colors onto the large table. Richard noticed Sophie look between the light fixture and the rainbow patterns reflecting on the glass surface. "I know you love rainbows, Sophie, so I picked this fixture with you in mind," he explained, looking at his daughter with a proud smile. "And at different times of day it seems to catch the light at different angles, creating the most brilliant patterns."

An uncomfortable silence ensued, broken by Pierre's entrance with our drinks. "What can I get you, Monsieur White?" he asked, as he carefully placed our glasses, and adjusted the place settings to where we chose to sit.

"I will have a glass of our yacht prosecco, as will my wife, as a reunion toast is in order."

"Oui, Monsieur," Pierre said, and scurried off.

"She's not your wife," stated Sophie.

"She's our *dad's* wife," added Cale. Both kids glared at Richard, their fierce love for Christian shining through.

Richard crossed his arms, a gesture I remembered well from when I challenged him twelve years earlier. He looked at Cale, then at Sophie. "Your mother and I were married twelve years ago, on our beautiful island, and I still have the certificate to prove that," he said, in a calm voice.

"Let's not get into all that right now, Richard," I said. "Cale and Sophie are obviously scared and miss their dad very much."

"I understand that it will take some time to get to know and love me. But I can assure you that we will make many amazing memories here together. And over time I will take you on exotic adventures all over the world. Your lives will be so much richer in every way possible," he added, gesturing towards the panel of large windows, showcasing a magnificent view of the vast blue ocean.

"We don't want to be rich, we just want our lives back," said Sophie, staring directly at Richard. I could see her anger growing in direct correlation with the terror evident on her little brother's face.

"Sophie, you will make new friends, and our lives will be wonderful in so many different ways," he said; the argument impossible for either side to win, with both Richard and Sophie being equally stubborn.

"I wanna go home!" interrupted Cale.

"This *is* your home," said Richard.

"No, it's not, and you're a monster," cried Cale, hot tears flowing down his face as he glared at Richard. I hugged him tightly.

"Please, Richard, don't push this; it's all very new and scary for them," I begged, my eyes pleading with his as they stared intently back through his mask.

"Cadence, I'm only telling the truth. The children need to understand and then take the time needed to adjust to their new lives. And let me make myself clear to all three of you," he paused, making eye contact with each of us for effect, "I won't be called a monster or a kidnapper or a criminal or any other vicious name to me or my crew. I don't deserve to be called anything hurtful. I've suffered unimaginably, and I demand respect from all three of you," he stated in the confident, business-like tone I remembered all too well. "Anyone who insults me will take a 'time out' in an isolation room on this yacht. You will learn that it's not worth it to treat me with disrespect," he stated with an unnerving clarity. I shuddered.

"You sound like a prison warden, not a father," stated Sophie. While I was proud of Sophie's quick and wise retorts, I was also nervous that she would soon cross the line with Richard.

"I'm stating the facts, Sophie. I know we will become very close, and I will be the best father ever. But you need to respect me and trust that I have planned what's right for you," he said. I could tell that his delusion was so ingrained that he believed it with every cell in his body. "I love you very much, and the last thing I want is for my ladies to spend any time in the isolation room," he said, looking from me to Sophie and back again, while completely ignoring Cale.

"Cale doesn't belong in there either, Richard. We're scared and your threats don't make this any easier," I said.

"The same rules apply to … to him," Richard said, refusing to make eye contact with Cale, who continued to glare his way, his small body tense at my side.

"His name is Cale," Sophie said.

"When he's ready to shake my hand, and respect me, then I will use his name, my darling," Richard said, his voice softening every time he focused on her.

Sophie sighed, but maintained eye contact with her father, their green eyes identical in color and intensity. The shade of green seemed to darken when they were angry. I remembered that well from twelve years ago. I also remembered Richard's volatile moods, and the tone of his voice when he was serious, which he was now. And I knew that he wouldn't hesitate to lock any of us in the isolation room unless we acted like a happy family. But would he threaten Christian again, as he had so many times before? I cringed at the thought.

"I'm not shaking his hand," Cale whispered.

"That's okay, Cale, but please be respectful," I whispered back.

Pierre entered the room with the prosecco, which was already uncorked. He filled two crystal flutes, placing them in front of Richard and me. "The food will be brought in momentarily. Your favorites, children," he added with a smile as he left.

"I asked for a special children's lunch today: cheeseburgers, chicken fingers and fries, as well as macaroni. I know those are what you often order at restaurants so I thought you would enjoy this as a treat today, as we will normally be eating much healthier," Richard explained, smiling warmly at Sophie.

"Thank you," said Sophie, her voice cool.

"You're very welcome. And for you, Cadence, my love, fresh fish caught this morning, along with a wonderful salad our chef has concocted," he said, leaning forwards to stare closely at me across the table. "You've hardly aged, Cadence," he said. "You look a bit different … your hair used to be so much longer. But your gorgeous blue eyes haven't changed a bit," he observed, lifting his glass. "I'd like to toast our reunion," he said.

I gripped my glass, while at the same time feeling Cale's grasp tighten on my arm. I could not bring myself to toast this madness, and instead rose, pulling Cale up with me. "I need to excuse myself. Where's the bathroom?" I asked Richard, watching as he placed his glass down in defeat.

"Down the hall and to the right," he answered.

"Sophie, we'll be back soon," I said, tugging Cale away from this surreal encounter.

I found the door to the bathroom, and closed it behind Cale and me.

"Mom, I'm so scared of him," Cale said, his big brown eyes looking once again on the verge of tears.

"Oh, Cale. I'm hoping help will come very soon. We just need to be calm and not upset him. I don't want to risk us being put in that isolation room … I couldn't stand you or me or Sophie being locked away," I said, kneeling down to look into his eyes.

"Mom, what if we try to find a lifeboat on here and take it? Would someone find us? We're not too far away from San Diego yet, are we?" Cale asked in quick succession, his young voice serious and calculating.

"Oh, honey … we're too far out to sea to risk that. This yacht moves very quickly. But not as quickly as the FBI or the Navy or the Coast Guard who are hopefully catching up with us."

"Mom, did you really marry him?" Cale asked, confusion clear in his questioning gaze.

"Not because I wanted to, Cale. He stole me away like he's doing to us now, and forced me to marry him," I explained. "Your dad is the man I love, and I escaped to get back to him as soon as I could. Just like we'll do when help comes," I said, hugging him tightly, then gazing around the bathroom, hoping we weren't being recorded. "We should go back now. You must be hungry," I said.

I led Cale back to the dining room, and paused at the archway, seeing Richard and Sophie absorbed in what looked like an intense conversation. Pierre entered with a platter of food, carefully placing plates in front of Richard and Sophie, as Cale and I walked back to our seats.

Sophie looked towards us, smiling down at the chicken fingers and cheeseburger in front of her. In front of Cale was gourmet mac and cheese, with real cheese bubbling at the surface. "Cale, you can have whatever you like. I'll have any of these meals … they all look delicious," she said, trying to lighten the mood.

Mac and cheese, please," said Cale, fork already in hand, as hunger distracted him from the unnerving, masked man across the table.

My salad looked delicious. Sliced fresh fish, delicately seasoned, sat atop beautiful greens, orange pepper, diced cucumber, and a medley of other vegetables.

"I hope you enjoy," said Richard, looking pleased. This will be short-lived, I thought, hoping the time until our rescue would fly by.

The children ate quickly, famished from the ordeal of the past few hours. The prosecco was refreshing and helped to slightly calm my racing mind. I chewed my fish carefully, too anxious to notice the taste or texture. I swallowed it alongside the nervous lump in my throat. How could I be here again? How could we be here? It felt like a dream. My eyes wandered around this surreal scene, taking in the opulent dining room, fixating on the three sculptures sitting in the lit-up nooks in the white wall across from us.

"I bought them because they reminded me of the beauty of my ladies," said Richard, staring through his white mask at the stone carved marine life. "The squid is lithe and energetic, like you ladies often are," he said, smiling at Sophie and me, then back towards the champagne colored creature. "And in contrast, the starfish is beautiful, poised and relaxed, like I hope you will be while enjoying the sunshine on the Great White," he said, staring at the deep red sculpture. "And finally, the seahorse is attentive and engaging, ready for his next adventure," he explained, looking at the deep blue colored, stone seahorse. "He reminds me of exactly how I feel right now," he said, nodding gently as he gazed across at me, then turned towards Sophie. "And I know you will both feel excited about the adventures that will come once we've settled into our lives together."

I felt like the pearl in an oyster: locked in this prison at sea.

Chapter Twenty-Two

"Sophie, you look like you could use some downtime," said Richard, smiling. She had finished most of her meal, as had Cale.

"Yes, it's been tiring," Sophie responded. "Maybe we can have some time alone in our rooms?"

"Great idea. You two can relax, and your mother can get settled in our room," Richard said.

Both kids' jaws dropped as they looked from Richard to me.

"Richard, I'd like to spend some time with the kids; they've been through a lot," I said, jolted into reality by the fact that our reunion was imminent. My optimistic side had hoped rescue would occur before I had to face Richard alone.

"Fair enough, but I *do* want to show you the sunset from our suite," he said. "It's one of the most glorious views from the Great White," he added.

"I want my mom to sleep in my room," said Cale, glaring across the table at Richard.

"I'm afraid that's not possible," answered Richard. "We're a family now, and the parents sleep together in their own room," he added, the three of us flinching at the boldness of the words *family* and *parents.*

"You're *not* our parent!" exclaimed Cale.

"I *am* Sophie's father," he said, glancing only briefly at Cale then back at Sophie and me.

"Father," Sophie said calmly, emphasizing the word she knew could calm him, but had avoided since their time together in his office. "Please, can't we have our first night here with mom? We're just scared, and it'll make it easier if you don't take her away from us so soon," she added. Her influencing powers rivalled Richard's; it was so obvious that they were related.

I saw Richard breathe in deeply, contemplating his daughter's request.

"You can have her for a few hours, my love. But I must have her for the sunset, then we'll all be together for dinner," Richard responded, smiling warmly at Sophie. "Tonight will fly by, and your mother and I will spend every night together from now on, including tonight."

"I can't stand him!" yelled Cale, standing and pulling me from the table. "Let's go, *please* mom," he implored. Sophie glowered at her father, speechless.

I stood, gesturing for Sophie to come with us. "Richard, this is so hard, please …"

"I will come and get you at 4:30, Cadence," he said. "In the meantime, make yourselves at home and enjoy your new rooms." Cale was already half way to the archway leading out of the dining room, and I quickly followed.

Sophie stormed off, but paused under the archway, turning

back towards her masked father. "We're *not* your property to control. What you're doing is making things a hundred times worse than they already are," she said, as Cale and I paused further down the hall to wait for her.

"I know you're angry, Sophie, but know that I love you dearly," Richard responded.

"Treating us like this will make it *impossible* to love you back," she retorted, then sharply turned to follow Cale and me.

Richard stared at the empty archway, his hands tightly bound into fists on his lap. He willed the voice to stay away, but its menacing tone entered his mind, as clear as if its bearer were sitting beside him.

You really screwed that up, you animal. The glass seahorse over there could have done better than you did. That couldn't have gone worse.

"I said what I had to say. I knew this would be difficult and take time," he whispered into the empty dining room. He took a deep breath and sighed loudly as he exhaled.

Yeah, just like twelve years ago, you thought it would take time, yet all time did was make her hate you more. She hated you enough to let you burn in agony. What makes this time any different? Now you have her kids held hostage too, you fucking animal!

"I'm *not* an animal. I'm a father. A husband. Now shut the fuck up!" he said, banging his fist hard on the thick glass surface of the table, causing it to vibrate.

"Boss?" said Leo, staring curiously at Richard from the entrance to the wine cellar, on the other side of the dining room.

Richard was pulled into reality, bothered at having been caught arguing with the voice in his head. He only ever did so in absolute privacy. "Just rehearsing something," he said. "What is it?" he added, impatience clear in his voice.

"Just checking in on you," Leo said, his protective blue eyes not moving from Richard's. "I could hear the girl yelling from the downstairs, and figured I'd better come break things up if I needed to," he said, chuckling to try and ease the tension which was obvious in his boss's rigid posture.

"It's what I expected. This is very hard on them," Richard said, deliberately working to relax his hands and unclench his jaw.

"Maybe. But they also need to realize they're luckier than hell," said Leo. "For God's sake, they've got one of the greatest superyachts in the world as their home! They should be grateful for all you've done for them," he said, shaking his head, agitation mounting in his voice. There it came again, the urge to sprint over to Richard and put his arms around his broad back. To massage the tension out of those muscular shoulders. To show him the affection that nobody here would ever give him. Dammit! The feelings he'd tried so hard to subdue continued to grow stronger. The urge to protect had morphed into an urge to love and be loved back.

Leo always knew deep inside that he was gay. From the time he was in grade school, he could tell that it was the boys, not the girls, to whom he was drawn. But his father was a solid redneck, and the gay jokes were a part of family dinner conversation in their wreck of a house. When his father wasn't drunk, he was mean. And when he was drunk, he was meaner. Leo knew that any inkling of his homosexuality had to be buried so deeply that even he would forget his inclinations.

Through sheer determination and fear, Leo was able to date women, and fuck them while relying on his imagination to come. Eventually he met Cynthia, whom he was able to tolerate, marry, have a child with, and maintain a façade of heterosexuality for a few years. But that façade wasn't sustainable; he could not be what she needed, and just as she began screwing around, so did he, but at long last with men.

Having their daughter, Ella, made the split tricky as resentment had mounted, as Cynthia turned their little girl against him. Bitterness was an understatement, and he poured his angry energy into his career and to one-night stands.

Taking the job with Richard was a no-brainer, from the moment he laid eyes on the man. Although he knew Richard was straight, he couldn't help but wonder if somewhere deep inside there could be a morsel of bi-sexuality that could be released with the help of Leo's sheer passion and determination. Saving Richard's life and sticking by his side for all these years had only solidified his love, and it was a constant struggle to keep his feelings hidden. He'd tried to convince Richard to give up on the idea of abducting Cadence and the kids. He knew at his very core that it was a terrible idea on so many levels. But Richard was a stubborn man who knew what he wanted, and would not be influenced otherwise. Richard was definitely crazy, but the craziness didn't scare Leo away, he was that fucked up too.

Leo had debated whether it was time to quit before Richard had executed this ludicrous plan, but he felt an intense loyalty, combined with a deep love that made it impossible to leave. Yet he felt like a martyr; not only would he never receive the love he yearned for, but he'd have to stand by and watch as a woman who didn't care for Richard received the love that he wanted more that anything. It would be torture every day. But a seemingly unavoidable torture. Leo felt trapped but was not ready to abandon Richard like everyone else had over the years.

Richard interrupted Leo's thoughts. "They will be more grateful in time; I'm sure of it. Thank you, Leo, for making their transition as smooth as possible. They need patience and kindness, even though it will be challenging at times," he explained.

"She's the luckiest lady in the world, that Cadence," said Leo. "If she doesn't realize that, she's crazy," he added.

"We're all a little crazy at times," Richard said quietly, thinking of the voice that thankfully had vanished.

"Very true," said Leo. "I'm going to do the next round of security checks, but so far so good. Nobody on our tail by air or sea."

"Excellent. Thanks, Leo."

"No problem, boss," he said, wishing once more he could give into his urge and feel Richard's flesh against his, but that would never be, thanks to that fucking bitch, Cadence …

The clock on Sophie's wall read 4:20 p.m. I cringed at the thought of Richard's impending arrival. "I think help will come, I really do. We just need to be patient," I said, as the three of us sat on the bed, me in the middle with an arm around each of them.

"Mom, I think you should refuse to go. He can't force you to share his room," Sophie said, for at least the tenth time in the last couple of hours.

"Sophie, he won't give me that choice. But I'll be okay, honey. Nothing bad will happen," I explained, knowing full well that I would not be able to fend off Richard physically for long. But the kids didn't need to know this. This would be my own private cross to bear.

"Okay, mom. I'll take care of Cale and we'll keep praying for help to arrive."

"That's all we can do. And we'll be together at dinner and let's try not to make him mad as I couldn't stand having any of us locked away," I said, reminding them and myself to control our emotions, even though it would be tough.

There was a soft knock at the door a few minutes before 4:30. Sophie walked over and slowly turned the knob. "You're early," she said, as she opened it to see Richard's masked face. He was now wearing a gray turtle neck with black pants, and a gray glove on his right hand.

"I wanted to see if you children wanted to go for a swim or play some video games while Cadence and I enjoy the sunset?" he asked.

Cale and Sophie looked at each other. "Cale, what do you think?" Sophie asked. "Video games are your favorite and it would get us out of here for a while," she whispered.

"Okay," said Cale, refusing to look in Richard's direction.

"Video games would be fine," said Sophie.

"Excellent, we will walk you to the multimedia room," said Richard, as the three of us passed through the door. Richard led us to the set of stairs taking us down one floor to the lounge. Just past the bar, there was a door leading into a dark theater-style room, and Richard turned on the light. There was a large, white leather sectional and a big screen covered one wall. "Up there are the latest versions of PlayStation, Xbox and Nintendo," Richard explained. "We will come back for you by 6:00, and if you need anything you can press the button on the intercom over on the wall here by the door, Sophie," he explained, gesturing towards the familiar looking box we had interacted with in the changeroom earlier today. "But don't leave this room."

"Be nice to mom," Sophie said, arms crossed as she stared up, green eyes looking threateningly into her father's.

"I will be better than nice, Sophie. I have loved your mother for twenty-three years, and I intend to love her even more every day from now on," he said, reaching for my hand with his gloved one, but I instinctively clasped my hands together.

I saw Sophie flinch and Cale tense as he turned away, staring at the blank, white screen. I gave Sophie a look to reassure her that everything would be okay, and gestured for her to join her brother on the large sectional.

Richard motioned for us to leave, and as we exited the multimedia room, I turned back. "I love you, Sophie and Cale. I'll be back soon," I promised, feeling Richard's gloved hand touch my lower back as we walked through the lounge and back up the stairs towards the staterooms.

Chapter Twenty-Three

WE CAME TO A double-doored room at the end of a long hallway, and Richard gently opened one of the doors. "After you, my dear," he said. A massive master suite was laid before us, with a row of windows overlooking the expansive ocean. In the center sat a four-poster, king size bed. To the left there was a sitting area with a white leather loveseat and armchair, beside a glass fireplace encasing soft flames. The air smelled of fresh linen mixed with the sea breeze coming through the large patio doors near the sitting area.

"Can we talk, Richard?" I said, heading towards the armchair, knowing that sitting there would prevent him from getting too close to my personal space.

"We can, Cadence, but let's sit out on the deck, so that we can watch the magnificence of the sunset over the ocean," he explained; just like before, always manipulating every situation, like a general commanding his troops.

"Fine," I said, knowing I'd have to pick my battles, and this one wasn't worth fighting.

"Good, we have a wet bar over here," he explained, walking past the sitting area towards a beautifully appointed bar with a white marbled surface, complete with a wine rack, wine fridge, sink and cupboards. I even noticed an ice machine built in beside the fridge. "I have a beautiful champagne, it's a Dom Perignon from the year of our marriage." He took the bottle, which was laying in a silver ice bucket, and went out to the deck to uncork it, the cork leaving its safe haven to be blown into an unpredictable fate at sea. Much like me and my children.

I walked towards the deck while Richard poured two crystal flutes full of the bubbly vintage. The deck was long, and boasted a hot tub in one corner, as well as a double lounge chair with white cushions and a circular dining table for two. It was clear that Richard had no intention of this being a family area. The sun was on its descent towards the ocean, the sky showing hues of pink and purple as it pressed its way downwards.

"Cadence, would you like to sit at the table or on the lounger?" he asked, reminding me of his constant desire to please me.

"The table is fine," I said, sitting down on the chair that Richard pulled out for me.

He sat in the other chair, at an angle from mine, both of us having an equally spectacular view of the ocean. I closed my eyes, trying to calm my racing heart and the fear and anger that coursed through me. Be calm. Stay in control of your emotions, I reminded myself.

"Cadence, our Sophie is so beautiful. I can hardly believe she is finally here. I would like to toast you and I, together again as we were meant to be," he said, raising his glass to mine.

I did not know how to reply. It took every ounce of my willpower not to slap his masked face. I took a sip of the champagne, feeling the smooth, cool liquid cascade down my throat.

"We're still in shock, Richard," I said, not knowing what else to say that wouldn't include telling him what a monster he was.

"I know, Cadence. And this time will be different. We're going to treasure every moment. Life is short and so precious. I've lost so much of mine, and I intend to savor the life that we have left together," he explained.

I took another sip of champagne.

"Cadence, why won't you look at me?" he asked, as I stared into my glass examining the endless flow of tiny bubbles.

I glanced up at the masked face in front of me. The green eyes peering through their holes. I shuddered involuntarily. "How could you think that this insane scenario could possibly work?" I asked, in a quiet voice.

"Cadence, what's insane is what you did to me. And you are going to see exactly that," he said, leaning further forwards into my personal space. I could smell his minty breath.

"I didn't do that to you, Richard. Maria did and I thought you were dead," I explained, immediately feeling guilty for throwing Maria under the bus. But she would understand. She was safe in Mexico, and I needed to protect myself from him.

"But had you checked my pulse, you'd have known that I *wasn't* dead," he said, his voice calm and his tone certain.

"Richard, she said you were dead and we had to escape the fire," I said. "I'm sorry that ... that you suffered. I didn't mean for you to be ... burned," I said, meeting his eyes. I could see the combination of pain and devotion in their familiar green depths.

"But your actions have shown otherwise, Cadence. We would never have had to enact Plan Z if you hadn't planted that note in your flute. Although, I must admit, I truly admire how clever that was," he said, continuing to stare at me, his lips forming a slight smile. "And now you need to see the results of your actions."

"Richard, there's no point—" I began, but he grabbed my hand, like a snake suddenly snatching its prey.

"There *is* a point! I want you to remove my mask and see what you've done to my body," he persisted, turning his head and forcing my hand towards the leather strap in the back.

"No, Richard, I don't need to see—"

"Yes, you do. Now undo my mask!" he ordered, his voice louder and more intense. He emanated an anger that was more severe than I remembered.

"Fine!" I responded, disturbed by his insistence to show me his face. I fumbled with the strap as my hand shook. It turned out to be a simple clip in the back that unfastened the cover. I carefully pulled off the mask, and gasped at the sight of his face. The whole right side was covered in leathery, dark brown scars, while the left side resembled the man I'd known prior to the fire.

His hand found mine again, pulling it to his face as he leaned towards me. As I tried to pull away he gripped my hand tighter, forcing me to touch his horribly scarred cheek. The surface felt rough, similar to a cantaloupe's coarse texture. I felt pity and anger at the same time towards Richard. He let go of my hand and pulled off his gray turtle neck, revealing a shocking collage of scars, ranging from the same dark brown on his face to a pale-yellow color in places. The flames hadn't missed much of his torso and arms, but the way he was leaning must have somehow prevented the flames from attacking his entire face. Again, he forced my hand to stroke the path of scars on his jagged chest. "Say something," he said, staring at me, trying to read how I was feeling.

"I'm sorry you … you were hurt like this," I whispered.

"You have no idea, Cadence, how painful this was. But losing you again almost killed me, more so than any fire could have."

I felt tears sting my eyes, and turned away. His hand guided mine down towards the rugged terrain of his stomach, feeling a badly scarred surface over his six-pack. "Look at me, Cadence," he demanded, as I swiped away tears with my free hand. I was finally letting myself feel the fear and sadness of this situation. I knew for certain that as long as Richard lived, I would never be free; and now Sophie and Cale were also trapped. My thoughts were interrupted as I felt Richard's hand guide mine onto the hardness under his black pants. I tried to pull away but he forced my hand onto his erection, pressing downwards as he closed his eyes and moaned my name.

Suddenly he lurched forwards and pressed his lips hard against mine. As I tried to move out of my seat, I felt his scars scrape against my skin as he kissed me hungrily. "Richard, please," I said, trying to pull away.

"I can't … it's been too long," he said, his voice hoarse with desire as he pulled me up and scooped me into his arms, rushing to the bed. He placed me down and pulled off my blue sundress in one motion, staring down at my cream-colored bra and panties. "Oh, Cadence, you're so lovely," he said, pulling off my panties as I tried to move away. But to no avail. Within seconds he'd managed to remove my bra and had planted his scarred face between my breasts, the jagged texture of his face scraping my delicate skin as he hungrily kissed and sucked.

"Stop, please!" I pleaded, but he was now in another world, and I knew what I had to do … close my eyes and imagine I was somewhere else. Anywhere else. Count backwards from one hundred … he climaxed at seventy-four. I was finally able to turn on my side and let my tears fall onto the white bedding, as he pulled me into his muscular chest, again pressing his rough scars onto my sore skin.

"Cadence, that was unbelievable. You're so soft, just as I remembered. But I want to please you too," he said, his fingers trailing down, trying to make their way between my legs.

"Not now, Richard … I just want to relax," I said, squeezing my legs tightly together to block his wandering hand.

"Okay, we will have lots of time to get to that. For now, let's just watch the sunset," he said, standing and stretching, catching me off guard with the sight of his badly scarred back and legs. Even his neck was partially covered in dark patches. Under his ravaged skin was the fit, muscular body I remembered. But now, instead of being handsome in his own right, he looked like the monster he was.

He went to the walk-in closet and came out with two white, silk robes. I quickly put mine on as I was unnerved by his staring. He donned his robe and guided me back to the deck, where he insisted I sit in the lounger beside him. He quickly refilled our champagne flutes. The sun was on the last portion of its descent, gently touching the horizon.

"The last time I was this happy was twelve years ago at our

home, before everything turned to hell," he said, stroking my leg. "I never thought when I was undergoing all those surgeries that I'd find happiness again. To be free from the pain, and reunited with my wife. It's surreal."

I didn't respond, instead drinking my champagne to dull the physical and emotional ache, wishing and praying we'd be rescued. Surely a yacht this size couldn't evade the FBI? Yet I knew Richard, and his plan was likely as complex as the patchwork of scars covering his body.

Chapter Twenty-Four

RICHARD CLOSED HIS EYES, deeply breathing in the salty air on the deck as dusk began to fall over the ocean. Cadence had gone inside their room to shower, and despite his wish to wash together, he decided to let her have some time alone. He liked that he could sometimes give her what she wanted, as to please her was his ultimate goal. But he knew it would take hard work, persistence and patience. He wasn't successful twelve years ago, but this time he would be. He had to be. She would grow to love him, even if it took the rest of their lives.

The voice in his head spoke suddenly. Abrupt and firm.

Your own mother didn't love you. You're insane to think Cadence ever will.

"My mother *did* love me," Richard whispered back, just as firmly. An image then filled his mind: he was sitting beside his mother's hospital bed. He used to sit beside her for hours as she slept, and was there for her when she woke up.

"He's dead, mother," was the first thing he said when she came to.

"What?"

"Father is dead, at last. He died of a brain aneurysm. There's nothing they could do."

"Oh my God," she said. Tears welled in her eyes, catching Richard off guard given how horrible his father had treated her.

"But you're going to be okay, mother. *We're* going to be okay," Richard said, gently holding her bandaged arm.

"I want to go back to Montana," she whispered. "To Mountain View, where I grew up. I need to get away from here," she said.

Richard paused before responding. He had no intention of leaving Boston. But he also felt a strong allegiance to protect this weak woman – his only family – even though she had never really been there for him growing up. When he was a child, she should have been his protector, but wasn't. Why should he help her now? His internal battle of what to do ended when he looked at her frail body and he knew that in his heart, he had to do what was right.

"Alright, mother. If that's what you want, we will go together and I can finish high school there," he said, trying to sound mature and confident.

"Richard, it's no life for you in Mountain View. You have the best private school here … there's nothing like that there," she said, her voice weak.

"But I *will* look after you, mother. I … want to," he said, trying to hide his reluctance and fear.

"Okay, then, we will go together," she said, turning away, sorrow etched into the lines on her face.

Richard squeezed her hand gently, but she pulled it away. Affection was not something she had left to give. It was as if her late husband had sucked every last ounce of emotion she had left, and now she existed as a shell of who she once was.

The relentless voice interrupted his image of that life-changing conversation.

You shouldn't have gone to Mountain View. If you had stayed put in Boston, Cadence would be free, as you'd have never have met her and pulled her into your fucked up idea of a life.

"Cadence and I were meant to be. I was a good son and am a good husband. No matter what you or anyone thinks," Richard retorted. "I was there for my mother through her breast cancer treatments. I even postponed college for a year to take care of her. I have no regrets."

She didn't love you, you were just all she had left. She put up with you. But you reminded her of him. Like father, like son. Both crazy in their own right. And now you've passed on those genes to Sophie—

"Shut up!" Richard said, louder than intended.

"I didn't say anything," said Cadence, standing awkwardly at the patio doors in her white robe, her auburn hair pulled up into a towel to dry.

"Sorry, I was just mumbling to myself," he said.

"It sounded like you were talking about your mother."

"Yes, Cadence … I had some memories come back … of my mother." He closed his eyes and images raced through his mind. Memories of when the cancer spread and after more chemo and an unsuccessful surgery to remove the tumor, he made the decision midway through the school year to go back and be with her. The doctors spoke of how the tumor could not be fully removed, as it would completely damage her brain to do so. As it stood, she had already lost some of her memory. Richard pictured entering that big house the day he arrived back to nurse her through her final weeks.

"Mother, I'm back," he called out.

No response.

"Mother, are you here?" The house smelled musty as the tightly closed windows had not let the house breathe. He climbed the stairs, heading towards his mother's bedroom. As he turned the corner, he felt something slam hard against the side of his head. He fell to the ground, his head throbbing.

"Get out of my house!" his mother screamed. She held a baseball bat in both hands, ready to strike at him again. Her eyes were wide with rage, as she looked angrily down at her son, sprawled in pain on the floor. Gray patches of hair grew on her otherwise shaven head, a testament to her recent surgeries.

"Mother, it's me, Richard, your son!"

"You look like my husband, you monster," she scowled.

"He's dead, mother. It's me, Richard," he pleaded, her eyes looking distant and confused, evidence that the brain tumor had eroded more of her rationality since he last visited prior to the surgery.

"Stop lying, and get the hell out of here!" she screamed.

Richard forced his eyes open to pause the scene, looking at Cadence staring at him nervously in the patio door.

"Richard, are you okay?"

"Yes, I just get these memories … flashbacks. Sometimes they throw me off, but no need to worry. It's nothing new," he explained.

"I'm worried about the kids, I'd like to see them." I changed the subject, despite being perplexed at what I'd just witnessed. Richard was never vulnerable like this, and blurting out angry words to himself made him look even more disturbed.

"There's a black dress hanging in the closet for you. We can get them for dinner shortly," he said, standing to walk towards his wife. She abruptly turned back into their room. He ached for the day she would walk willingly into his embrace. Be patient, he thought. That day will come.

Chapter Twenty-Five

I WAS ABLE TO close the walk-in closet door, as I pulled on the black cocktail dress that awaited me. The all too familiar feeling of my every day, every meal, every activity planned out felt suffocating. But now I had a different focus: helping my kids to get their lives back. While at the same time ensuring their safety around these unpredictable men.

The closet door opened behind me, but I was facing the other way, putting on the black high heeled sandals sitting below where the dress had hung. I knew the drill. I stiffened as arms encircled me from behind. "God, I've missed you, Cadence," he said, his rough skin scraping my neck as he planted a soft kiss. "I have a gift for you," he said, gently placing a necklace around my neck, and carefully doing up the clasp. "It is a very rare, five carat Alexandrite. It changes color in different lights; emerald by day, and dark ruby at night. Rare and complex, just like you, my love," he said.

I stared down at the greenish-blue, oval shaped stone hanging on my chest from a platinum chain. "It's very … unique, Richard. Thank you," I said, feeling more possessed by the minute. I didn't want to turn around and face him.

"The blue-green that it is now reminds me of you and me, and how we came together to create Sophie. She's so beautiful, Cadence. And intelligent. And talented. I couldn't ask for more in our daughter," he said, grasping my shoulders and turning me around to face him. His face was once again masked, and he wore a white, long-sleeved shirt.

"If you love her so much, you will set her free to live her life," I said, not able to help myself.

I gasped as he forcefully grasped my shoulders. "I love her enough to give her the experience of a lifetime on the Great White, where she will be able to grow up seeing exotic parts of the world, expanding her horizons and getting one hundred times the education that she would at a traditional school. So not another word about setting her free, Cadence! She is finally free to see the world and be with her true father as well as her mother."

"Let go of me," I said, glaring up into his eyes.

"I didn't mean to be rough, I just need to get through to you."

"I want to see the children."

"Fine, but I meant what I said earlier, Cadence. If any of you insult me, there is always the isolation room. I will not take the same treatment I took from you twelve years ago. My rules are firm," he said, as if I were a child.

"Don't threaten me," I said, my arms tightly crossed, and the anger inside me at the boiling point.

"It's not merely a threat, Cadence. I love you and trust me

that I do not want to act on it, but I will if you disobey me," he added.

I stormed ahead, needing to get away from him before I lashed out and ended up in the isolation room myself. Richard followed closely behind, motioning me towards the stairs that led to the lounge where Sophie and Cale were. We could hear yelling coming from the lounge when we were half-way down the stairs, and instinctively I sprinted towards it, Richard on my tail. When we entered the lounge, the door to the multimedia room was open and when we got there Sophie was in a screaming match with Leo, while Cale cowered in a corner, tears streaming down his cheeks.

"What is going on?" shouted Richard.

"He's scaring us!" shouted Sophie.

"She was trying to use your satellite phone, boss," said Leo, his face nearing the same red shade as his hair, while he shook his head and glared at Sophie.

"Yes, I was trying to call home to tell dad that we're alive!" retorted Sophie. "And he grabbed me, and bruised me, and pushed Cale!" she exclaimed.

I cringed, knowing this discussion was quickly going downhill. Even I had trouble controlling myself, but Sophie was her father's child: persistent, stubborn and confident.

Richard's next move surprised me. He walked up to Leo, arms crossed and green eyes blazing, changing color almost like the stone in my new necklace. "Leo, is this true? You hurt my Sophie?"

Leo looked taken aback, his steel blue eyes looking anxious, avoiding Richard's glare. "I didn't hurt her, I was just pulling her away from your phone and out of your office, boss. She broke all the rules, and I swear I wasn't rough."

"You were so rough," retorted Sophie, now having moved beside me, along with Cale, who was now crying in my arms. "Look at the mark on my arm," she said, showing her right arm that was already beginning to bruise.

Richard lurched forwards and grabbed Leo's shoulders. Although Leo was muscular, Richard was taller and much more intimidating as his rage permeated the room. "Never lay a hand on my daughter again," he commanded. "Is that clear, Leo?"

"Yes, boss. But I won't let her get away with risking everything we've worked for," he added.

"But you will do so in a non-physical manner," said Richard. "I do not want her scared; she means the world to me and will not be harmed by anyone on this yacht."

Leo turned to look at me, his gaze filled with a myriad of emotions; anger of course, but also a mix of fear and hatred. "I would like to go check your office, where I found them, and make sure she didn't take anything else," he said, trying to rebuild Richard's confidence in him.

"Did you take anything else?" Richard asked Sophie.

"No, I didn't," she said, looking up into the eyes that matched her own.

"You know the rules, Sophie. You were to stay in the multimedia room and use the intercom if you needed anything. You broke the rules," he said, matter-of-factly.

"You broke the law," she replied, equally confident in her tone.

"Are you calling me a criminal?" he asked, anger mounting on his masked face.

"You're a criminal and a monster!" screamed Cale, catching

us all off guard.

"Leo, take the boy to the isolation room. Now!" ordered Richard.

"No!" shouted Sophie, grabbing her brother, at the same time as I tightened my arms around Cale.

"You know the rules, and you broke them by calling me that," Richard said, hurt intermixing with his rage.

"Take me instead," begged Sophie. "Cale is too young."

"Nope, it's the boy who broke the biggest rule: of treating me with respect. And may this be a lesson to you as well, Sophie, that there are consequences to your actions here. Now the boy must leave, or I will allow Leo to use force," said Richard.

"Noooo!" I said, tightening my grip further. "You are truly a monster if you do this, Richard," I said, tears falling from my bloodshot eyes as I stared at him, irate.

"Now!" said Richard. Everything happened quickly then. The feeling of Richard holding me tightly back, while Leo grabbed Cale from Sophie and me, and hauled him out of the room, as he kicked and screamed.

"Help, mom! Help, Sophie! Help, help, help!" he shouted.

Sophie was pulling on Leo's arm, but his strength allowed him to move quickly towards the door, and when he got there, he maneuvered in such a way that he pushed Cale out, blocked the doorway, and then closed the door. Sophie tried to follow, but it was locked. She banged and screamed repeatedly, tears now pouring down her pink cheeks. "Cale! We'll get you out of there soon!" she screamed.

I was flailing as well, tugging and pushing and yanking my way out of Richard's arms, but he stood steadfastly. Once Sophie realized she could not leave the room, she ran back to us, and tried to pull her father's hands away from me. "Let mom go!" she yelled.

Richard seemed to hear his daughter through his anger, and released me.

"You can't lock up Cale. He's too young. Please let me go instead," she begged, her young tears still flowing. "Please, father," she added, emphasizing the word she knew could get through to him.

"No, let me go, Richard. Neither of the kids should be locked away. It's cruel!" I exclaimed.

"He will stay in there for the evening. His dinner will be brought to him and he will be able to come out in time for bed. It's the only way you will all learn the rules," he explained.

"You're so cruel," I said "He's nine years old, Richard. Just a child."

"He's old enough to understand the rules. Hopefully this will be the last time he, or either of you, will need to be punished," he added "Now, Sophie, would you like to freshen up, and then we can all head to dinner?"

"I can't stomach eating with you," she said. "I've lost my appetite."

"Fine. Your dinner will be brought to your room for when you are hungry," he said.

"I will walk Sophie back to her room, Richard," I said, telling and not asking.

"Join me in fifteen minutes in the dining room, then, Cadence, and don't be late," he replied, equally as assertive.

"Fine," I said, choosing not to argue this time. I quickly followed Sophie, but true to her style, she could not help but turn around, hands on hips, tears streaming down her face, and glare at Richard as she declared, "You're the worst father ever." Then we left.

Richard paced back and forth in the multimedia room, his mind a flurry of thoughts and emotions. Should he have been so forceful? Yes, he *had* to be. It was all to be expected. It would get better. Yet the despair he felt was mounting. He sensed the initial connection he'd had with Sophie in his office ebbing away, being replaced by loathing. *Of course,* the voice came back into his head, its deep tone reverberating against the walls of his brain.

Now look what you've done. As if stealing Sophie wasn't bad enough, you're forcing her to hate you more each minute. You've made things so bad that they will never forgive you.

"I did what I had to. Rules must be enforced. This is the only way that they will learn."

The only way they will learn to hate you, you mean? You've done a stellar job of that. Your mother hated you. And now your wife and daughter hate you too.

"My mother loved me, she was just sick and I reminded her of him."

And with that he was back at the house in Mountain View, Montana.

"Mother, the nurse will be here shortly, but do you need anything in the meantime?" asked Richard, cautiously standing in the doorway of her large bedroom. The air smelled of medicine and antiseptic. The shutters were drawn, giving the room a dark and sad atmosphere. Yet his mother refused to open them for fear of germs entering the house: one of her many newly developed phobias as the rationality depleted from her brain.

"Get out, Alexander. Get the fuck out of here," she snapped.

"Mother, it's Richard. Your son. Alexander is dead. He died back in Boston from a brain aneurysm," he explained for what seemed like the one hundredth time that week.

"Stop screwing with my brain as you always do, Alexander. Now leave me in peace. Go screw your next whore instead of screwing with my head."

"I'm not him. I'm *Richard*."

"Richard's our son. But I'm afraid that he's turned out like you, Alexander."

"Mother, I am nothing like him. I am kind and loving. I detest whores. And I am going to find a wonderful woman to marry one day, whom you will love."

"I hope Richard never marries; he'll abuse his wife just like you've abused me all these years, Alexander," she said. "Now leave me alone."

As the scene faded, Richard realized that tears were trailing down his cheeks.

You do have a lot to cry about. You've made your own wife and daughter cry so much today, now it's your turn to feel the pain. The voice in his head was getting nastier by the minute.

"I've suffered enough and I know things will get better. It's just the early days that will be tough."

Let's see about that. If you couldn't even get your own mother to love you, how on earth will you ever be loved by Cadence or Sophie?

"Watch me," he said. He took a few deep breaths, trying to force the voice out of his head. He focused on when he first met Cadence, hoping that happy memory would make the voice disappear.

He was back at his mother's house, in her bedroom doorway, twenty-one years old and crying.

"I told you to leave my room," she said, her eyes now closed as her weak and thin body lay in the bed, being ravaged by relentless cancer.

"Sleep well, mother." Richard ran through the hall and down the staircase, pausing briefly to lock the big front door behind him. He ran out into the forest. He ran and ran and ran for what felt like miles. He didn't slow down even as he ran up hills. Tears and sweat poured down his face. He finally slowed down and stopped cold when he heard a melody echoing over the hills. He stood, taking in the beautiful notes that flowed through the picturesque Montana countryside. A few more steps forwards and she was in sight. Standing in the distance, playing a flute. Her long, auburn hair blowing ever so gently in the mild breeze. He stood frozen there for several minutes, then carefully sat down on the slope to watch and take in every note. She was meant to be his. At that moment, he knew he had found his soul mate. His savior. The woman who would love him and allow him to unleash all the love that he had bottled up inside since he was a child.

Chapter Twenty-Six

CHRISTIAN SAT ACROSS FROM Agent Kent, both men exhausted and on the edge of their seats since the call came in that morning. The call they had both dreaded for twelve years, and hoped would never come. The day had been spent in interviews, capturing every detail of Christian's communications with his family, and all of the information leading up to the trip.

"I can't believe this is happening," said Christian, running his hands through his dark brown, curly hair. His brown eyes raw from tears. Grief. Loss. His family gone. Not only Cadence and Sophie, but Cale as well. That monster had no right whatsoever to Cale. His son. He wished he could tear Richard White to shreds. Or better yet, put a couple of bullets through his psychopathic brain.

"I know, it's beyond shocking. The team we've assembled is only the best of the best. We have not only our best FBI agents, but the Navy and even the Coast Guard are on high alert and searching. Our assumption is that Richard White would quickly reach international waters and would have radar deflectors and jamming devices making him more challenging, but not impossible, to find."

"We have satellite technology trying to zero in on the yacht's location. We have the yacht builder giving us all the information we need to estimate its speed capacity and thereby pinpoint the radius in which it's likely in at any moment. We also have the best hackers trying to track down any possible electronic communications that might be coming from White and his group." Jack Kent sighed deeply. "I'm really hopeful this nightmare will end soon, Christian. I truly feel for you all," he added. As usual, he was calm, and his dedication to their case over the past twelve years, even when it no longer was an FBI priority, gave Christian hope that they did indeed have the very best searching for his wife and children.

"Thanks, Jack. I appreciate it. I'd like to be on one of the search vessels, as soon as possible, so that when they're found I can get there quickly," Christian said.

"I think that's workable. I'd have to pull some strings as it's against protocol, but given the nature of what you've been through, I think it is the least we can do. Maybe one of the Navy vessels has a chopper and we could fly you to them or vice versa when they're found. And they *will* be found. You have my word that I'm doing all I possibly can to make that *when* happen very soon. I'm glad I've put off retirement and I won't be going anywhere until Richard White is behind bars or executed."

"Thanks, Jack. This is more horrible than I ever imagined. And trust me, I've worried about it a lot over the years. I just hope he doesn't … harm them," he said, his voice choking up.

"There was never an indication of wanting to harm in the past, so we're going on the fact that he truly is trying to build a family. He's deluded himself into thinking he can buy a family, and unfortunately, he had the means to fool us despite all the precautions we took. I'm sorry we couldn't foresee or stop this. And I feel terrible that Adam and Drew were killed in the line of duty, two of our most talented security guards."

Christian swallowed, fearing for his own life. He remembered how vulnerable he felt after being attacked twelve years ago. The feeling of always looking over his shoulder, and wondering if each night when he went to sleep (or tried to sleep) would be his last. He had been assigned twenty-four-hour protection as soon as the call came in, and the day had flown by like a fast-paced nightmare.

"We are going to hold a news conference right away. The more eyes out there looking for them the better," said Jack. "And they're going to want to hear from you, Christian. A plea to bring back your family."

"Okay. Whatever I can do …" Christian replied.

We're live this evening from Manhattan, with breaking news in connection with the deaths of two security guards in San Diego, who have been identified as Adam Brown and Drew Walters. They were hired by the FBI to protect Cadence Davidson and her twelve-year-old daughter, Sophie, and nine-year-old son, Cale. This woman and her two children are believed to have been abducted on a superyacht owned by Richard White.

As some of you may remember, Richard White is the elusive billionaire who kidnapped Cadence from her San Francisco apartment twelve years ago, and held her captive for over three months. Cadence's husband, and the children's father, Christian Davidson, would like to make a statement.

Christian took a deep breath, looking into the camera as he began to speak. "A father's worst nightmare has come true for me today. The family I love, my wife and children, have been taken against their will. I hope and pray that they are not harmed, and that Richard White has some semblance of humanity in his soul and sees the right and only course of action is to set them free. I thank the FBI for all they are doing to find my family, and I ask that anyone at sea or who spots them anywhere in the world to please call for help as Richard White is dangerous and unpredictable. Cadence, Sophie and Cale, if you can hear me, I … love you so much," his voice cracked, as he brushed tears off his cheeks and turned away from the camera.

Chapter Twenty-Seven

Leo was livid as he led Cale to the isolation room, which was on the bottom, engine level of the yacht. It had no windows, and was very simple with a single bed, a small white desk with a chair, and a door that led to a tiny bathroom, with only a toilet and a sink. The walls were a blank canvas with a crisp white color without any artwork. No TV. No music. No electronics. There was a small bookshelf lined with a combination of children's and adult books.

Cale looked around through his tears, his brown eyes wide and terrified. "Don't leave me here, please, mister. I want my mom!" he begged.

"Not gonna happen, kid. You're in here for a few hours. Next time I'd suggest taking Mr. White's rules more seriously and treating him with the respect he's due," Leo explained. But inside he felt anything but respect for his boss. He was angry at Richard's reaction and at how he'd been manipulated by Sophie. Leo was loyal and wanted to be at Richard's side, whereas the rest of his "family" wanted to leave him. He didn't care for Sophie and detested her mother, but he did feel sorry for the boy. Richard should never have included Cale in his plan. It was clear that Richard wouldn't be able to bond with the kid, and it just added to the tension that was already rocket high here on the Great White.

"I'm scared," cried Cale, looking pleadingly up at Leo.

"Just relax, do some reading. Your supper will be brought down soon and that will be a distraction. The time will go by quickly," he reassured Cale, and being reminded of the fact that he'd missed out on his own daughter, Ella, at this age. A wave of bitterness filled him at the thought of his lost fatherhood due to that bitch, Cynthia. Sometimes he felt like killing his ex-wife and taking Ella away on this yacht too. But he wasn't as confident as Richard, to think that Ella would ever love him after being forced to be here.

"Please don't leave!" begged Cale.

"Gotta go, kid." Leo closed and locked the door, quickly walking past the engine room and back up the stairs to the lounge level. Even if Cale was banging on the walls and screaming at the top of his lungs, it would be difficult to hear from the floors above, for which Leo was grateful.

He decided to head to his room, which was on the same floor as the lounge and multimedia room, but on the other side with the staff quarters. Decent sized, comfortable rooms with porthole windows. Each had its own bathroom, entertainment system, and working area. He flicked on the news to see what was going on with their scenario back in America. He landed on Christian Davidson pleading for the safe return of his family.

Yep, he looked a lot like the boy. The same hair and eyes. The man looked utterly devastated. "Yeah, I wish I could ship 'em all back to you, man, as it would be a whole lot better here without 'em," he said to himself, feeling bitter to the core.

Leo paused, allowing his imagination to wander. What if he could ship them back? What if they could go back to their lives before, without all this drama? What if, by some slight possibility, he could seduce Richard? Bring out his bisexuality, like fanning a tiny flame into a fire? Was there a chance that Richard could be bisexual, and decide that women were a dead-end after all this drama? Could the two of them build an amazing life together cruising around the world on this yacht?

Cadence was the biggest barrier. So long as Cadence was in the picture, there was no way to seduce Richard. But what if Cadence could be sent away for good? Leo smiled, thinking of getting that bitch off the Great White. Away forever. And if he had the choice, he'd send the boy with her. If Sophie stayed, though, wouldn't Richard be happy enough to have his daughter? Wouldn't his daughter bring him some of the joy he was missing all these years? Did he really need Cadence around to feel loved and happy? Leo could bring him love and devotion, both physically and emotionally, like he'd never felt before. Richard was starved for affection, and Leo had so much to give him. So what that he wasn't a woman, did that matter? And he wasn't, Cadence, the bitch … damnit, that *did* matter. Richard had built her up on some sort of pedestal that she didn't deserve. But perhaps it wasn't insurmountable. He'd continue to brainstorm, as it made him feel a glimmer of hope.

He turned off the television, disinterested in the reporter commenting on the world-wide search for Cadence, Sophie, and Cale. He flipped open his laptop and opened the video app that focused on Richard in the shower. His erection grew in response to just flicking on the video. He hadn't had a chance to watch the footage for the last few days. He'd installed the same type of miniature camera in Richard's shower that the team had installed years ago in the Davidsons' apartment in New York City. The way the master bath was laid out, with a molding around the ceiling, allowed for perfect camera placement that would be nearly impossible for Richard to find, even if he was looking for it; but he would never suspect someone on his own team would install this in his private quarters.

The image of Richard in the shower was one that Leo yearned for, studying it in detail as often as he could. Sometimes he'd masturbate to the footage, imagining his hands all over Richard. Other times he'd just watch and smile, forcing himself to stay put and not go find Richard and admit his love. The best times were when Richard had an erection in the shower and masturbated himself. He sighed, then grimaced realizing that was when Richard was likely thinking about Cadence.

He fast forwarded to today, and saw Cadence's naked form in the shower. He saw her stricken face as she turned on the shower. Her body had red marks in various places, likely from Richard's scars. Leo longed to feel those scars on his body, and had often fantasized about kissing and touching them. He fast forwarded until a while later, when Richard entered the shower on his own. No erection. He looked somewhat content, a look Leo wasn't used to seeing on his scarred face. Fuck this, thought Leo, as he slammed the laptop shut.

Chapter Twenty-Eight

SOPHIE AND I SAT in her music studio, on the floor whispering so we wouldn't be detected by any potential recording devices. "Sophie, Cale will be okay. I will convince Richard to let him out early. I'll do whatever I can so he doesn't have to stay in that room for too long," I promised, feeling sick to my stomach that my little boy was locked away like a prisoner in solitary confinement.

"I'm so mad that he's in there. I wish I could do something to get him out right now!" cried Sophie. "He must be so scared."

"He's strong, Sophie. He knows we will get him out as soon as we can," I said, trying to calm both of us. But it was time to put our fears and tears aside, and strategize on a plan to get through this. "I know help is coming. I feel it."

"Oh, mom, what if it doesn't?"

"Don't think that way. We just need to be sure to follow the rules as much as we can so that he doesn't punish anyone. I know, from last time, that his threats are real. He can go from kind and sweet to angry and threatening in seconds when provoked."

"But I think I can get through to him, mom. I think I can influence him," Sophie said, looking hopefully at me to agree.

"He does love you, I know that for sure, Sophie. In his own way, of course."

"If I pretend I love him, maybe I can get him to promise not to lock any of us away again," Sophie contemplated.

Suddenly there was a knock at the door. "Cadence?" I heard Richard's voice, as he went ahead and opened the door, walking through Sophie's room towards the music studio.

"We're in here," I said.

Richard stared down at the two of us through his mask. He looked noticeably calmer since our last encounter. "Ah, my lovely ladies," he smiled at us adoringly.

"Hi, father," said Sophie, working to sound sweet and calm herself.

"Darling, it's so good to see you relaxed. Are you hungry after all?"

"Yes, can I join you and mom for dinner?"

"Certainly. I'm the luckiest man alive to have my two beauties with me as my dinner dates. Can I help you up?" he asked, as we both began to stand. He used his gloved right hand to help each of us, then proceeded to kiss each of our hands ever so gently, so we wouldn't feel the roughness of his face.

He led the way to the dining room, and seated us at either side of him. Candles lined the table, as dusk set over the Pacific Ocean. Jazz played in the background. "Miles Davis, one of my favorites," explained Richard. "I hope you enjoy him, too," he added, as Pierre came in to take our drink orders.

"Father?" asked Sophie. "I was hoping to spend some time with you tomorrow. To get to know you better," she said. Clearly playing her card of tugging at his heartstrings.

"Of course, my love," Richard said. "There's nothing I would enjoy more. What would you like to do?"

"Learn more about you. Maybe hang out in your office. See some photos of when you were younger," she said. "Hear about your family."

I could see Richard tense. "My family wasn't the best. But I can tell you one thing: our family *will* be. I do have a few photos to share and will tell you about me, and I'd like to hear all about *you* too. I'd also love to hear you sing."

"Okay," said Sophie. "But I have a favor that would mean a lot to me, father," she said, looking pleadingly at him, as he leaned in towards her. I could tell he was basking in the potential of pleasing her.

"It would actually make me feel a lot better to eat with Cale tonight, instead of you and mom. Even if I have to eat in the isolation room, I'd rather be with him, and that would give you and mom more time together," she said, awkwardly.

Richard was silent. I could tell he was contemplating. Would he choose not to upset Sophie yet again? Or would he maintain his firm position of power and follow through on the punishment he was so clear about? "Okay, I will let you go and eat with him. He cannot get out early as that sends the wrong message, but it will give you a chance to see the room too, and to understand why respect in this family is so key," he explained. "I trust you to explain that to him."

"Thanks so much, father," she said, standing and surprising Richard as she wrapped her arms around him, and he returned the hug, locking eyes with me, smiling as widely as he could with his scars. Yes, Sophie was right. She was the only one who could get through to him. Like putty in her hands, it seemed.

When Sophie let go, Richard pulled his walkie talkie out and radioed Peter to come and take her to the isolation room, just as Pierre walked in with our drinks. "Pierre, can you please send Sophie whatever she would like with Cale's meal, as she will be dining below deck tonight with her ... brother," Richard said, stumbling on the word brother, as if it were a word he'd rather not say. He had wished countless times that Cadence would not have any children with that man, but then along came the boy, he recalled resentfully.

When Peter came, Sophie kissed Richard on the cheek and followed Peter to the kitchen to get her meal and meet the chef. Richard reached for my hand, and despite the urge to pull away I let him take it. The calmer and happier we could keep him, the better our temporary lives would be here. Together, Sophie and I could ensure Cale was not mistreated again. Perhaps keeping Cale apart from Richard was the best plan.

"I'm still thinking of our lovemaking," Richard said, as we both sipped the red wine he'd selected.

I didn't respond, instead taking another deep sip of the smooth vintage to try and dull my senses from this madness.

"So, Cadence, what do you think, overall, about the Great White?" asked Richard, reminding me of the twenty-one-year-old guy I had dated so long ago.

"It's ... huge," I said. "And beautiful and impressive," I added, knowing he was basking in pleasing me.

"I knew you would like it. And there's so much of it you haven't even seen yet. I know you'll be comfortable and spoiled here, just the way you deserve to be," he added.

"I'm really nervous about Leo, Richard." I changed the subject, using this as a chance to voice my uneasy feeling since the moment I had met that creepy man.

"Leo? He's a good guy, Cadence. He's just protective of me. What happened twelve years ago stuck with him, and it will take some time for him to warm up to you and the children," he said, unexpectedly including Cale.

"I think he hates me," I said, "and I worry about Sophie's safety given how rough he was with her today."

"It won't happen again, Cadence. Trust me." He leaned in, looking steadily at me through his white mask. He was close enough that I could smell his spicy cologne, which I knew all too well.

His mask looked creepy in the candlelight. I had a hard time looking back at him wearing it. "You don't have to wear that," I said. "It really doesn't matter to me." He looked surprised.

"It matters to me, Cadence. I do not want you to have to look at my grotesque face every day. I want you to remember and see me as I was," he explained.

"But it must be uncomfortable and hot. I really don't mind and I'll get used to it, as will the kids," I replied.

"When we're alone together in our suite I will take it off, but not out here, my love," he said. "Speaking of that, I want you *now*, Cadence. I'll have Pierre bring dinner to our suite."

"Richard, I'd rather eat out here—" but before I could say another word, he had pulled me from my chair and was leading me briskly through the archway and down the stairs to the master suite. As we entered the room and he slammed and locked the door, I regretted my comments about his mask and willed myself to be back in New York, at least in my mind.

"Cadence, be here in the moment with me. Let me please you, too," he said, as he kissed

me hungrily.

"I'm … not in the mood, Richard," I said, my mind having moved from New York to picturing myself and the kids on a lifeboat being intercepted by the Coast Guard.

"Oh, Cadence, what does he do that I don't," he whispered, as he nibbled my left ear. I felt his right, gloved hand grazing my nipple. It was an odd sensation.

"He gives me a choice," I responded.

Richard pulled back, obviously hurt. "If I stop and wait for when you are ready, how long would I have to wait?" he asked, his eyes filled with lust, and his mind fighting to restrain his body.

"Richard, this is all so overwhelming. I'm still in shock and—"

"You don't need to say any more. That's my answer. I will need to just take charge or it will never happen. But one day, I swear that you will like it. One day you will want me as much as I want you. Even if that takes years, it will be worth the wait." And with that Richard swiftly removed our clothes, threw me onto the bed, and rolled on top of me, ravenous as a starving lion.

Chapter Twenty-Nine

Sophie sat on the bed with Cale, both cross-legged as they ate their dinners. "At least the food is good here," Sophie commented. It had taken about twenty minutes when she got here to calm down her brother, who was hysterical.

"I miss our own food," said Cale. "I miss dad so much," he added with a sniffle.

"We will see him again soon, Cale," Sophie whispered, sure there was a recording device somewhere in here, perhaps even associated with the intercom that was mounted by the door. "We just need to make sure we keep our mouths shut about how we feel about Mr. White, as we don't want any of us, especially you, to end up in this room again."

"I hate his guts," said Cale.

"I know, Cale. You can say whatever you want to mom and me, but don't say anything bad around him, okay?"

"Okay," he said, taking another bite of his drumstick. Their dinners were the same tonight, roast chicken complete with mashed potatoes, carrots and broccoli.

"I'm going to find a way to communicate with dad, Cale," Sophie whispered directly in his ear. "I'm learning my way around here and I know I can get online and reach out. The FBI can then track where we are. I've seen it on crime shows."

Cale smiled at his sister, hugging her tightly. She read to him to calm him further, and the next two hours passed quickly, with Peter arriving to bring them back to their rooms.

Richard lay on the bed naked, his scarred body fully exposed. I had put on my robe as soon as it was over. I begged to go get the kids, but he insisted on two more hours, as he wanted to be sure that Cale had learned his lesson.

Our dinner, which was spinach and feta stuffed chicken, on a bed of wild rice with sautéed vegetables, was served to us on the deck. Now that the sun had set there was a cool breeze, but as usual Richard had planned for every scenario, and turned on a large overhead heater that warmed up the entire deck. Candles lit up the table, and soft deck lighting was built in around us. I was engaged, trying to hold back my thoughts so as not to rile him. I knew that if I started, I would say something that was bound to get me thrown into the isolation room for my first night here, which I wanted to avoid at all costs.

Later his walkie talkie buzzed, and he reached for it on the nightstand. "Peter confirmed that they are back in Sophie's room."

I stood immediately, heading for the door. "I need to see them, to tuck them in."

"I will come as well, to tuck in Sophie," Richard said, donning his robe and glove, and picking up his mask from the nightstand.

Sophie's room was just down the hall, and when we entered, they were both sitting on her bed. Cale ran to hug me, crying in my arms. "Sweetheart, I love you," I comforted.

"He wants to sleep with me in here," said Sophie.

"He has his own room, next door," said Richard, "and besides, I want some time to say good night to you in private," he added. I noticed how he still had not said Cale's name, and rarely looked in his direction. It made me hold Cale even tighter.

"Richard, they should be together. This has been a very traumatic day for them both," I said, firmly. "Why don't I help Cale get ready for bed in his room, and when you're done saying good night to Sophie, he can join her?"

Richard looked at me, contemplating his answer. He could choose to dictate things, like where the kids slept, but he also wanted to make Sophie and me happy. "Fine, Cadence, if that pleases you and Sophie, we will do it that way."

"Come, Cale," I said, leading him to the door. "Let's brush your teeth and get your jammies on." With that I led my son to his room.

"Sophie, I've dreamed about tucking you into bed ever since you were born. I watched you fall asleep in your crib, and wished you could have done so in my arms," Richard said.

"You watched me fall asleep?" asked Sophie, staring curiously at the masked man who was sitting on the edge of her bed.

"Yes, I had a small camera hidden in your nursery so that I could be part of your life. It kept me alive through the surgeries and pain, knowing I could zoom in on you and see how beautiful my baby was," he explained with a smile.

"But that's illegal," Sophie commented, her inquisitive eyes meeting his.

"That's one way of looking at it, Sophie. But I had the legal right to be your father and that was taken away from me. I felt I at least had a right to watch you grow up from a distance."

"It feels weird that you did that, but I guess you are my father, not some stranger, which would've made it creepier," Sophie said.

"Nothing about it was creepy, Sophie. I loved and admired and cherished you every day. My dream was to read you *Goodnight Moon*, as I saw that was your favorite book as a young child. Actually, I have a copy of it here. Would you oblige me in reading it to you this one time?" he asked, hopefully.

Sophie paused, debating whether his request was cute or creepy. But again, she knew she had to build trust so that she could keep her mother and brother safe. "Sure, why not."

Richard knew exactly where to find the book on Sophie's shelf. He was back in an instant, sat beside her on the bed, and began, "In the great green room there was a ..." This moment made Sophie long for Christian, her true dad. He had read this book too many nights when she was little. He had also played soft melodies on his cello while she fell asleep. She couldn't help but silently cry as Richard read the story.

"Oh, sweetie, you're crying," he said, taking her hand in his gloved one.

"I'm just sad ... sad about how everything has gone. I'm

sad you were burned," Sophie said quickly, avoiding the real reason for her tears.

"Sweetheart, it doesn't hurt like it used to. It looks much worse that it feels. And I could not be happier right now about having you with me again." He squeezed her hand.

"I'm glad it doesn't hurt," Sophie said. Richard finished the book, and kissed his daughter on her forehead, being as gentle as he could. The timing was perfect, as Cadence and the boy were entering the room just at that moment. "Good night, the moon and sun of my life … my world … my Sophie," he said.

"Good night, father."

Chapter Thirty

AFTER TUCKING MY CHILDREN into bed, I quietly cried myself to sleep beside Richard. When I woke up in the middle of the night, reality came flooding back about where I was and whom I was with. How could this be happening again? I thought this was a nightmare? Richard was oddly still wearing his glove, but slept naked otherwise, spooning and touching me as often as he could.

I counted down the hours until morning, when I could see the kids again. I prayed help would come, and that the FBI would find a way to locate us. I tried to send positive thoughts to Christian that we were all okay. I went to shower while Richard was still sleeping. The hot water was soothing, and I rubbed my favorite bath gel over my sore body, wiping away the smell of Richard; the spicy smell that I remembered so well. Although much about Richard was like the way he used to be, he had also changed. He had hardened and softened at the same time.

He seemed more tormented in his mind, yet also slightly softer, especially when it came to Sophie. I found myself wavering at times between hating him and feeling sorry for the way his life had turned out. But I also felt sorry for Sophie and me, that we were entwined in his life. And I felt even sorrier for Cale, pulled into this drama at such a young age, and it was clear that Richard was struggling to even acknowledge his presence, let alone try to make him comfortable or even welcome.

When I got out of the shower, I quickly dried off and put on a pale-yellow sundress from the closet. Richard was no longer in bed. I found him out on the deck, in his robe on the double lounger, with two coffees on the end table. "Cadence, good morning, my love. Join me for our morning coffee?" I still flinched when I saw him without his mask, saddened by the extent of damage to a once handsome face.

"I'd like to see how the kids are, Richard," I replied, but eyeing the coffee as I was exhausted from my restless night.

"I'm sure they're fine, honey. Just stay for a few minutes, while your latte's hot. It's done exactly as you like it, with a shot of hazelnut," he explained.

He had closely followed me while we were apart, as he knew the tastes I'd developed. Like before, in some ways it was a comfort to have the things I liked around me, but also a violation that made me shudder with each new discovery. Richard never missed a detail.

I sat at the bistro table, despite Richard wanting me to relax beside him, and drank the delicious latte. I looked out into the ocean, wishing to see a ship on the horizon coming to save us. Maybe a warship or a battleship. One that could take out this yacht with ease.

"We have so much to explore together," Richard said. "Once we get through the transition period, things will be so much easier. We will eventually start to feel like a family."

I didn't know what to say. I couldn't lie. But I also didn't want to provoke him. "Yes, the transition is difficult," I agreed. "I would like to see the kids now," I said, as I stood, taking my latte with me.

"As you wish," he said. "Breakfast will be a nice one today, so let me know if they are awake and I can instruct the chef to get started."

"Okay," I said, leaving the master suite and heading to Sophie's room.

When I got there and opened the door, only Cale was in the bed. I rushed over and gave him a hug, planting a kiss on his soft, brown curls.

"Is Sophie in the bathroom, honey?"

Cale moved to whisper in my ear. "She's exploring the yacht. She's looking for a way to go online and contact dad," his little voice explained.

I trembled. "Oh, no!" I whispered back. "That's too dangerous, I need to go find her," I said, not adding my biggest fear, of Leo finding her before I could. I also didn't want Richard to find out, as it would damage the trust she was building. Sophie was stubborn and resourceful, just like Richard, so I shouldn't have been surprised at what she was doing. But I was absolutely terrified at the same time. "Stay put here, Cale. I'm going to find your sister and bring her back here," I whispered. "Don't tell anyone what you told me, okay?"

"Sophie already told me that. I can keep secrets, mom," he replied.

"Good," I said, planting another kiss on his curls, and running out of the room, closing the door quietly behind me. I didn't know where to start looking and wondered if she'd be upstairs, in Richard's office. I tried to put myself in her shoes. Would she go to Richard's office where she'd already been caught yesterday, or try to find another computer or device on the yacht? The latter, I guessed. But where? Should I go up or down? Most of the staff would be up by now in the kitchen area, wouldn't they? So, I headed downstairs.

I quickly entered the familiar lounge room, passing by the white sofas and chairs with their light-blue accent cushions, and the marble bar with its perfectly placed white, leather bar stools. Not a soul was in sight, so I kept walking to the end of a room, which had a set of doors I had not yet been through. I opened one of the doors to find a hallway with several more doors. What were in these rooms? I quietly walked down the hallway, my bare feet enabling me to move quietly on the wooden floor. At each door I paused to listen, placing my ear gently against the wood. Not a sound. Everything smelled new. My heart raced. Just then one of the doors near the end of the hall on the right slowly opened and Sophie appeared. She jumped, shocked to see me staring at her.

"Mom!" she whispered. "You won't believe what I just found."

"What?" I whispered back, my heart pounding even harder as I stepped closer to her.

"It's bad," she said. "The Internet doesn't work, but there's a video of you in the shower on the laptop I found in there!"

"Oh my God," I whispered, the feeling of violation bubbling in my gut like volcanic vomit. Richard knew no end to his spying. "Show me," I reacted.

Sophie quietly opened the door, moving like a mouse across the room to a desk with a laptop sitting open on it. "Mom, I saw Leo and Peter leave through the lounge; I hid behind a sofa when they passed so I knew they came from here. I'm not one hundred percent sure whose room this is, but the laptop was open and not password protected. I think they were just on it," she rambled nervously, clicking open a screen that showed the shower I'd just used. Sophie pressed the rewind button, and in seconds I was on the screen. I was livid, as this meant somebody besides Richard, which was bad enough in itself, was violating my privacy.

Just then the door swung open and there stood Leo, his blue eyes bulging and pale skin reddening. "What the fuck are you doing in my room?" he roared.

"What are *you* doing with a naked video of my mom?" Sophie retorted, hands on her hips.

"Yes, answer that, you pervert!" I added.

Leo looked shocked, his eyes focusing on the screen in horror. This couldn't be happening, he thought. It took every ounce of his self control not to strangle Cadence. But if he did, he knew he'd be dead too. He could blame the video on Richard, but he knew it would get back to him and there was no telling what Richard would do to Leo, but he knew it would not be good.

Suddenly a lightbulb went on in his brain. An idea ignited based on his ongoing debate about how to get Cadence out of his life for good. "Here's the deal," he began, locking eyes with Cadence. "If you don't mention this to Richard, I will get you and the boy off this yacht tonight. You can get help and reunite with the girl later," he explained.

"I'm *not* leaving Sophie," I said.

"It'd kill Richard to lose both of you. Only one of you can go. And I don't recommend sending two kids off on the lifeboat."

"Then it's mom and Cale," declared Sophie.

"I can't leave her," I pleaded. But my intuition told me that Cale was in danger here. Richard was capable of violence and he was acting strange around Cale. The isolation room was one thing, but what if he hurt my son? Getting Cale off the yacht as soon as possible needed to be my priority. Sophie was not in danger, although leaving Sophie felt wrong.

"Mom, it's only temporary, and it's the best chance we have. Help hasn't come and may not even find us out here."

"She's right, lady. The chances of anyone finding us have diminished now to almost nil. I'm only going to offer this deal once, as I'm risking everything," Leo said, sweat trickling from his red forehead. He swiped it away, agitated yet determined to maintain the upper hand.

"How do we know we won't die in the lifeboat?" I asked, trying to understand the risks associated with this plan.

"Cause it's not your typical lifeboat. It's large and safe, with an excellent motor. You will have a radio to contact help that will work once we're far enough away so that we can't be tracked. Trust me, you'll get away safely if you do what I ask; just don't mention the video to Richard."

I considered his steel blue eyes, which held so much rage. I knew he hated me, just as much as I hated him. But why would he risk his life for us? If Richard found out, I was certain he'd have Leo killed or even do it himself.

"Don't get me wrong, it's going to be set up to look like you took the boat. I had *nothing* to do with it. If you mention that to the FBI or to anyone, there'll be hell to pay. You'll never see

Sophie again, that I can promise," seethed Leo.

"Don't threaten me, you bastard," I retorted.

"It ain't a threat, it's a fact. I never thought Richard should've included the boy in this plan anyway. The boy deserves to be with his dad. And frankly, I think you're ungrateful and don't appreciate what Richard has built for you. You're treated like a fucking queen here, yet all you wanna do is leave. You don't deserve him," he added.

"Just let us all go," I begged.

"Nope. No way. This is my final offer, take it or leave it."

It was clear that Sophie could not leave with us. And it was obvious that Leo was loyal to Richard, so why would he orchestrate our escape behind Richard's back? I was perplexed, but the way Leo spoke of Richard showed true respect. But he showed himself to be a pervert with those videos. Would he be a danger to Sophie? I cringed, not knowing what to do.

"If you ever lay a hand on Sophie, or spy on her like you spied on me, our agreement is void, and I will tell Richard what you've been recording," I said.

"I won't touch her. Kids aren't my thing, and I'm not that type of guy," he added. "So, I suggest we do this at night. I'm thinking a couple of ground up sleeping pills slipped into Richard's food should do the trick," he said, bringing back the memory of when Richard was drugged on White Island. "I have some pills that I can get to you before the evening. It's your job to get them into him."

"Okay, I can do that. Where do we meet you?"

"You and the boy will meet me at the bottom of the stairs off the lounge floor at 2:00 a.m. sharp. At the same landing where Peter originally brought you up."

"What if anyone else sees us?" I asked.

"I know all the schedules, and I will make sure the guy on night watch is sleeping, if you catch my drift."

"I could help distract people too, if I need to," suggested Sophie.

"No, best if you stay in your room. Your job will be to calm down your father when he finds out in the morning, as he will go absolutely nuts," said Leo.

I swallowed, my heart pounding in my ears. I couldn't believe that I was contemplating leaving Sophie and planning an escape in collaboration with one of Richard's henchmen. Why on earth was Leo so willing to risk this? I was missing a key piece of the puzzle.

"You'd best get out of here. The boss will be suspicious by now," he said, slamming his laptop shut and glowering at me. "And let's not risk talking about this today, as he has eyes and ears everywhere," said Leo. "Oh, and I'll make sure that there will be plenty of water and food on the lifeboat. But bring a change of clothes, just in case, as you may need it depending on how quickly help finds you tomorrow." I quivered, thinking of the movies I'd seen where people were lost at sea for days or even weeks.

Chapter Thirty-One

CHRISTIAN STOOD ON THE deck of a ship that was assisting in the mission to find Richard's yacht. He had gotten a special exception to be onboard, given what happened twelve years ago and given what was now unfolding; plus, he hoped to be there when his family was found.

Agent Larissa Brody, an expert in hostage negotiation, was one of a few FBI agents who were onboard, and walked over to stand beside Christian as he stared out at the ocean. She reported to Agent Kent, who was overseeing the case from the FBI's field office in San Diego.

"Hanging in there okay, Mr. Davidson?" she asked. She had short red hair and bright blue eyes. Her voice was deep for a woman and radiated confidence.

"Trying. I wish there was more I could do," he said, clasping the metal railing as if it were a lifeline. It felt cool against his jittery fingers.

"It won't be long, I'm sure, before you will be reunited with your family," Agent Brody said. "This ship moves at quite a clip compared to a yacht, and we know where they *aren't*, which is helping us zero in on where they *are*."

"I just want them off the yacht safely, and then nothing would give me more pleasure than to see it blown to smithereens," said Christian, uncharacteristic of his gentle nature.

"I'm sure it would. Or maybe it should be donated to your family for all the hell you've been through," said Agent Brody, trying to lighten the mood.

"As much as it would be amazing to have a yacht, I'd never want to set foot on that lunatic's vessel," said Christian. It was still hard to believe that his family was somewhere out there on the expansive Pacific Ocean. Held captive by that monster. This would be the last time, vowed Christian. He would never let this happen again, even if they had to go into hiding. Nobody should have to go through this pain twice.

Sophie and I hurried back upstairs, and found Cale in Sophie's room playing a handheld game. I would wait until bedtime to tell Cale about the plan, so that we wouldn't risk him bringing it up during the day. There was a knock at the door and Richard came in without waiting for an answer, which was his way. "Good morning," he said. "Ready for some breakfast?" Richard was now wearing a white turtleneck with beige khakis. He smelled of his fresh, spicy cologne.

"Yes, I'm hungry, father, and so is Cale," said Sophie.

"Alright, a delicious breakfast will be ready for us shortly," he smiled. "And then you and I can spend some time together, Sophie, like you wanted to."

"Yes, for sure. And Cale was hoping to see where the captain sits," Sophie said.

"That's fine; Peter or Leo can take him."

"I can go as well," I said, not wanting to leave Cale's side.

"Sounds like a plan, Cadence."

Shortly after we headed up to the dining room, where Pierre served up plates of blueberry pancakes, bacon, sausages, and fresh fruit.

"It's a sunny one out there today. You kids should go for a swim this afternoon, and your mother and I can sit by the pool and catch some sunshine," said Richard. I wondered if he would wear something other than his customary turtleneck and pants.

"That'd be fun," said Sophie enthusiastically, good at putting on an act. I knew she was nervous underneath her cheery facade, and I was still debating the merits of our decision to leave her behind. My mind was spinning with the pros and cons, the what ifs …

"And I know that you and your mother enjoy yoga, Sophie, so I had a small yoga studio built that I look forward to showing you. It's on the same floor as the pool, near the sauna," he explained. I looked at Richard, hoping that by this time tomorrow he may never see me again. But I detested the fact that Sophie would be stuck here until we could rescue her. It was all so unfair. So unfortunate. So insane.

Sophie was in her music room, waiting for her father, who

would be there any minute now to spend some time together. She was singing *Castle on a Cloud* from *Les Misérables*, facing the panel of windows that overlooked the ocean. The acoustics were perfect, and she enjoyed filling up the space with the notes of this song she loved. It helped distract her from the drama that would unfold over the next day. She remembered when her parents took her to the musical for her eleventh birthday, and how much she dreamed of being on Broadway one day. She turned around to see Richard standing in the doorway, holding a bouquet of pink roses.

She kept singing, her father smiling at her, his lips stretching against his scars. When she finished, she took a small bow and Richard clapped. "Bravo, darling. You're amazing! These flowers are from your biggest fan," he added, walking over to her, taking her hand in his gloved one and planting a soft kiss on top. Then he placed the pink roses in her arms. "I'm so proud of you, Sophie. I want to give you roses all the time, but out at sea the florists are limited," he chuckled. "But I stocked up in San Diego so at least I can give them to you and your mother for a few days."

"Thank you, father."

"I will have our housekeeper, Anna, come and put these in a vase in your room when she tidies up," he said, motioning for her to put them on the side table by the sofa. "And I have a request: *Somewhere over the Rainbow.* I heard you sing it before, but I was one of many watching. I'd like to have a private viewing of my daughter's talent."

"Okay, sure," said Sophie. She took a deep breath and then began: "Somewhere, over the rainbow, way up high. There's a land that I heard of once in a lullaby ..."

Richard sat on the armchair, watching his daughter with love and admiration. A small tear threatened to escape as he felt emotion overwhelm him. She was his own flesh and blood, the perfect combination of him and Cadence. Lovely, talented, beautiful, sweet. He couldn't ask for more. She sang directly to him, smiling at certain points, and looking serious at others. He wished this would never end. When she came to the final note she held it for a few extra beats, then took a bow. He couldn't help but give a standing ovation, then moved forwards and hugged his daughter, lifting her off the ground and twirling her around, smelling the sweet berry aroma of her long, strawberry blonde hair. He couldn't help planting several kisses onto her soft hair. "I am the luckiest father in the world, Sophie," he said. "You're amazing and very talented. It's an honor to listen to you sing."

"Thank you, father," Sophie replied once she was planted on the ground.

"Let's go to my office and see some photos and get to know each other better," he said.

"For sure," Sophie replied. The subtle, sweet aroma of the roses had begun to fill the room, and Richard breathed deeply, associating the sweetness with his daughter.

They headed up to his office, where they sat across from each other at his desk. "So, what questions do you have for me, Sophie?" he asked, staring intently across at his inquisitive child.

"How did you make all of your money?" Sophie asked, looking around the office and out the window that overlooked the pool below.

"Well, I learned a lot about business at Harvard, but it wasn't until I got out there and bought my first business with the money I'd inherited from my parents, that I really learned how to build wealth. That first company was in telecommunications, and I grew it into a billion-dollar enterprise from five hundred million. I worked long hours, as I was single and driven like nobody else. I was able to exceed the success my father had by the time I was twenty-six. But that wasn't enough, I knew I could be much more successful than that. So, I sold that business and chose to buy and invest in a series of other businesses that interested me. High tech and energy were two other industries I got to know very well. I brought on the right people to run the companies and my role was very strategic. I could call the shots on the direction we were headed, and had the intuition of when to sell and reap the greatest rewards. Time after time, I built upon my wealth as I wanted to be able to build a life that very few people get to experience. I learned from every mistake and became wealthier than I could have predicted. I wanted Cadence and my family to live in absolute luxury, to be served and have the very best adventures and opportunities possible. It feels great to have achieved that goal, and I don't have to work so hard now. I don't run companies anymore and instead just ensure that my investments are moving forwards, so that I continue to make money in my sleep. Plus, I can spend a lot of my time with family, enjoying all that life has to offer."

"That's amazing. I've never met anyone as rich as you. You must be so smart. I can't imagine what it's like to be able to buy anything I want or go anywhere I want," Sophie said.

"Now you don't have to try to imagine, Sophie. All of this is *yours.* What's mine is yours. You can do anything you want and become anything you wish."

"I want to have friends and go to school and be in musicals,"

Sophie said. "Those things may not cost millions, but they make me happy," she stated. Sophie knew when to weave in the points she wanted to make. She was wise beyond her twelve years.

Richard paused, not knowing exactly what to say, as those wishes would not be in her immediate future. "One day you will have those things again, Sophie, just somewhere different than New York."

"And I want to see my dad again," she said, ignoring his last comment. "You're my father, I get that, but my dad is also important to me and has been really good to me and mom." Sophie had a calm way about her, stating the facts matter-of-factly and with confidence.

"Sophie, one day you will see him again, I'm sure, but not for some time. It's your time with *me* now. He had twelve years of your life, and now it's *my* turn for a while. It's only fair," he said, rationalizing this crazy, illegal scenario as if it should be common sense to anyone.

"I wouldn't exactly call it *fair*, but I do like that you say 'a while,' and not forever. I want to live a normal life again one day. I want to make my own decisions and not be forced into anything."

"Nothing is ever really *normal* in life, Sophie," Richard replied, fixated on her point about living a normal life again. He had pondered at length about normality. "It's just that things are *different* from what they used to be. Our life on the Great White won't be what you're used to, but there will be some parts that you will find are even better. I know that it will take some time to enjoy those things though."

"Tell me more about your life growing up," she asked, changing the subject. "And about your parents."

"It was a childhood I'd rather forget, Sophie. My father, your grandfather, Alexander White, was a smart businessman. He was very successful but also very nasty to me and my mother. He was cold and distant and didn't show us any love. To be honest, I feared him until I finally stood up to him when I turned sixteen. I'd had enough. He had hurt my mother one too many times, and I had no choice but to confront him. He died shortly after that of a brain aneurysm, so I never did have the chance for a proper goodbye, which would have involved telling him more of what I truly thought."

"That's sad," Sophie said, feeling genuinely sorry for her father.

Richard smiled at her. "And my mother, your grandmother, was named Constance White. She had the same green eyes that you and I do. But her hair was darker than ours, a chestnut brown color. She was very beautiful when she was younger, and wore her hair long, just like yours. She was very intelligent, but my father did not want her to work again after she had me. She was a lawyer, and worked hard to get an education as her family had much less money than my father's family. Over the years, as she was mistreated by my father, she became depressed and isolated herself, which was very hard for me to see. After my father died, we moved to her hometown of Mountain View, Montana, where I finished high school. Then when I was going to Harvard, she was diagnosed with cancer, so I returned to Mountain View to be with her, and that is where I met your mother."

"I've never seen a picture of you two when you met. Do you have one?" Sophie asked.

"I sure do," said Richard, standing and walking to a bookcase beside his desk. All the albums were the same brown leather, their spines neatly labeled by year. He pulled one out, and placed it on the desk between them. He opened it to display photos of what looked like a high school prom.

"That's you and mom!" Sophie exclaimed, pointing to a photo of her mom in a light blue gown, beside a handsome looking Richard in his tuxedo, smiling broadly down at her. "You two look so young," said Sophie.

"I was very much in love with your mother, pretty much from the moment we met. I was planning to propose to her, but she was young and not quite ready. But I know she cared for me. We had a lot of great times together. I know she was, and still is, my soul mate," he explained.

Sophie ignored the comment, not sure what to say, but images of Christian and her mom kept flashing in her mind. Wasn't Christian her mom's true soul mate? "And this is Danielle, mom's friend, right? I recognize her as she came to New York a few times to visit us. She looks so young in these photos!"

"Yes, I do remember Danielle well. She made your mother very happy."

Richard grabbed another album from the bookcase when Sophie was done looking through the prom photos. "This is our wedding on White Island off the coast of Jamaica," he explained, smiling as he opened to a picture of him and mom standing amongst lush tropical flowers and bushes. She was wearing a white, strapless gown and beautiful diamond jewelry. She was only half-smiling in the picture, her auburn hair pulled back into a beautiful updo. Beside her, Richard was smiling widely, looking very handsome in a light gray suit.

"You two looked beautiful," Sophie commented. "But mom looked sad."

"She was tired, that's all. But we had a beautiful ceremony

and the most amazing starlit dinner on the beach. I will never forget it, Sophie. It was the best day of my life, next to hearing about your healthy birth, of course," he smiled across the desk.

"This island looks beautiful. So many flowers and palm trees. And the sand looks so soft and white," said Sophie. "Do you still own it?"

"I wish I did, but I got rid of it for my own security purposes. Plus, it would have reminded me too much of my time there with your mother, and what I was missing all these years. One of my trusted staff members, Alvin, drugged me and some of my staff, and stole your mother in the night, holding her for ransom. It was one of the scariest times of my life, thinking that I had lost her. Thank God, I found her, but she had been in a serious car accident and was badly hurt. I will never forget the fear I felt seeing her on that stretcher ..." he looked out the windows.

"I never knew any of this happened. How scary," Sophie said.

"That's why I am so thankful that we had you; *you* bond Cadence and I together forever, Sophie," he explained. "Now I want to know more about you. I feel like I know a lot from observing your life, but there are some things I don't know. Tell me what truly makes you happy," he asked, leaning in and staring intently at her through the white mask.

"Singing. Being with my family and friends. Central Park on a warm spring day. Soft serve vanilla ice cream dipped in chocolate ... and lots more," she explained.

"Ah, well some of those things will definitely be available to you here, my darling. And so much more. Now tell me, Sophie, what are you thinking you want to be when you grow up?"

"A singer on Broadway, that would be my dream. But I also

want to go to college. I can't decide between business or education … or maybe even psychology. I find people interesting," she said, locking eyes with her father.

"Yes, indeed they are. I have found that there is a fair bit of psychology in navigating the business world. And business opens a world of possibilities. Education is a bit more limiting, in my opinion, but in the end, I want you to pursue whatever dreams you have."

"That's exactly what mom says too," she said, deliberately leaving out Christian so as not to irritate Richard. She was intuitive and noticed how he flinched each time she said "parents" or "dad." But she couldn't help but think of how supportive and encouraging Christian had been all along.

"Your mother is wise. I'm glad we see things the same way. She may not feel it quite yet, but I stand by what I said earlier … we are soul mates."

Sophie chose not to respond. She looked out the window instead, at the vast blue ocean surrounding them. She imagined her mom and Cale escaping in the dark of night, under the stars, while her father was knocked out in a deep, drug-induced sleep. In some way, she couldn't help but feel sad for him. It was so clear how much he loved her mom, yet her mom's heart would always belong to Christian. It was a sad, one-sided love story that would never work out the way her father wanted. But she could see the hope in his eyes, and it tugged at her heartstrings. At the same time, she was angry – livid – that he thought it was okay to steal them away from their lives. She was also disgusted that he felt the need to lock her nine-year-old brother in an isolation room. Sophie needed to continue reminding herself of these things when her empathy for Richard surfaced.

"What are you thinking, Sophie?" Richard asked.

"Just taking in the view. It would be fun to go for a swim, I think."

"Excellent plan. Let's go find your mother," he said, as he stood and put a hand on her shoulder and they walked out of his office together.

Peter had finally come to get Cale and me, and led the way up several flights of stairs to the bridge. A tall, lean man with white hair and a British accent greeted us. Peter made the introductions: "Captain Jeffries, meet Mrs. White and her son, Cale."

"Pleased to meet you. Welcome to the brains behind the Great White, where we control her every move," said the pleasant man, shaking my hand. "And you, young lad, I imagine you'd like to see how this vessel works?"

"Yes, I'd like to, please," said Cale, staring curiously between this stranger and the fascinating control room. There were a series of computer screens on the black console that surrounded two sleek, black leather seats. The view from this height was panoramic, with the ocean a gorgeous blue, and not a cloud in the sky.

Just then a second man, slightly shorter and perhaps ten years younger than the captain, walked into the room. "This is George, the first mate, who watches over things. We also have a second mate, Mitchell, who is sleeping right now so that he can take over for the night shift, later," Captain Jeffries explained. "George, meet Cale and his mother, Mrs. Cadence White."

"Pleased to meet you both," said George, gently shaking

our hands, while looking at me with curiosity.

"Nice to meet you," Cale and I said in succession.

"Cale, would you like to sit in my seat and take a closer look at the controls?" invited Captain Jeffries.

Cale slid into the black leather seat, which dwarfed his small form. "This is so cool," he said. "There are so many controls."

"Yes, indeed. Even in rough seas, the Great White is smooth and she maneuvers like no other vessel I've ever captained. We also have a mechanic, who works down in the machinery control room to help monitor all our systems. His name is Don, and he's a wizard with these types of yachts. Of course, with the latest technology, we're able to monitor most of the systems from here on the bridge."

"What happens if it ever sinks?" Cale asked, his brown eyes wide and curious.

"Good question, lad. We have a total of six additional boats on the Great White, three lifeboats and three work boats. In an emergency, it wouldn't take long to lower the boats into the water, as the hydraulic lowering equipment is very efficient. Our lifeboats are motorized and very sturdy and stocked with water and dried food, allowing people to survive for weeks if needed. Because they are enclosed, survivors are protected from the elements."

"How many people are on board?" asked Cale. I was glad he asked, as I'd been wondering the same thing.

"Fourteen in total, including our three newcomers, as in yourselves," answered Captain Jeffries. "And if there were ever an emergency, we have the chopper and our pilot, Owen, on board to get us to land in a hurry if needed. He's also trained as a paramedic."

Captain Jeffries and George went on to discuss the various controls, the terms and acronyms clearly over my head. Instead, I took the opportunity to walk around the bridge, staring out the windows and wondering if we would be able to pull off our plan tonight, as well as the repercussions if we failed. I continued to contemplate leaving Sophie. I knew Richard wouldn't hurt her, and would protect her fiercely from any source of harm. I also knew that she was resourceful and persistent, yet patient; qualities that would help her find a way to contact us, while at the same time we worked to zero in on the yacht's location.

My other choice of us all staying on board seemed risky in terms of help finding us. The fact that no one had saved us yet was not a good sign. At least if I left with Cale, I could have more control over our fates, and have a fighting chance of getting both my children back to their former lives.

Suddenly I felt arms encircle my waist from behind. "Hello, my love," said Richard, kissing the top of my head. I stiffened, and at the same time Sophie came around in front of me and gave me a tight hug.

"You're doing okay, Sophie?" I asked, hugging her back while Richard released me.

"Yes, father and I had a good chat, and I was thinking a swim would be fun as it's so nice out. But this room is amazing and I'd like to see some of how this yacht works, too," said Sophie, walking over to Cale and Captain Jeffries. Richard couldn't help but join in, ignoring Cale and focusing solely on Sophie. The whole dynamic was awkward, and soon the children had seen enough and asked to go swimming. We left the bridge as a "family," hoping that this unfortunate reality would soon end.

Chapter Thirty-Two

RICHARD HAD STOCKED A drawer of swimwear for me. "Would you consider wearing this bikini?" he asked, holding up an indigo colored, sexy-looking number.

"No, Richard! Not around the kids. That would barely cover me, and after having two kids I wouldn't want to even try it."

"You look hot, Cadence. You have not lost your body, from what I can see. But fair enough, we will save it for our own hot tub," he replied, passing me a red, one-piece swimsuit.

"My skin does not do so well in the sun anymore. I think it got a lifetime's worth of heat. I'm going to most likely wear my robe," he explained, pulling off his khakis, turtleneck and glove, followed by his underwear. He walked naked to his dresser and pulled out a pair of gray swim trunks. "I will wear these underneath as I may need to cool off at some point."

I opted to change in the closet, away from Richard's gawking stare. I momentarily thought of the bathroom, but remembered the camera mounted in there and cringed at the memory of seeing myself fully exposed in the shower.

"There's sunscreen at the pool, Cadence. Ready to head up there?"

"Sure. Let's see if the kids are ready."

They found Cale and Sophie in Cale's room, each wearing swimsuits that had been perfectly selected for their sizes and tastes. Sophie's was a purple one-piece, and Cale wore blue and green striped swim trunks.

We walked up a flight of stairs, which led to the floor that the pool was on. There were a few doors down the hallway leading to the pool. "Check this out," said Richard, opening a door and gesturing for us to go inside. "This is the yoga studio, complete with a big screen to project the best yoga videos available. So, you have a built-in instructor whenever you want," he beamed at us. The room smelled new and fresh with pale wood walls and floor, and a bank of windows overlooking the ocean.

"This is really nice, father," said Sophie.

"Yes, it is," I added.

"Good stuff," he said, as he motioned us back out the door and noted the door to the sauna, as well as the changeroom. I winced at the memory of being locked in there the day before, and marveled at how so much could have happened in one day.

The pool looked clear and beckoning, and the kids quickly jumped in. Richard motioned for me to sit with him on one of the double lounge chairs, like the one on our private deck. He sat on my right side and tried to hold my hand with his non-scarred left one. I let him but not for long, as my instincts were too strong to pull away.

"Cadence, there is no place on this earth that I would rather be than right here with you," he said. Anyone looking at us would see a perfect scenario: a family enjoying an incredible day together.

I didn't reply, instead picturing the blue sky above us black and full of stars as Cale and I pulled out into the dark night towards our freedom and Sophie's eventual rescue.

—

After an hour in the sun, Richard suggested we cool off in the pool. He removed his white robe and stood to jump in the pool.

"Eww!" exclaimed Cale, who was sitting on the opposite edge of the pool with Sophie, staring at Richard's scarred body.

"Cale!" I exclaimed. "That's very rude!"

"What happened to his skin? It's so—"

"Cale, shhh!" scolded Sophie.

"I don't wanna be in the pool with him," said Cale, pulling his legs out of the water, and walking to a lounger, glaring across the pool at Richard.

"The boy seems to have the same manners as his father," Richard stated coldly.

"Richard, that's not true, and don't insult their dad," I responded coldly back.

Richard ignored my comment, and dived into the pool, swimming underwater and not surfacing until the far end. He emerged for a deep breath, then went under again all the way to the opposite end. He emerged and held onto the edge of the pool, kicking his legs and trying to calm down the resentment he felt mounting towards the boy. He couldn't help but be reminded of Christian every time he glanced at the kid. Prior to meeting him, he had hoped that he could form some sort of stepfather/stepson bond, but he was simply too repelled by his presence. He had visions of throwing the boy overboard. A growing hatred that he wasn't sure he could control. The voice in his head suddenly spoke:

You're treating the boy just like your father treated you. Cruel. Heartless. Cold. You are wired like him and there's no getting away from that.

Richard whispered as he treaded water at the deep end of the pool, making sure his lips barely moved. "That was different. He was my real father and this kid is not mine. It's going to take time, that's all," he said, trying to convince himself.

A leopard cannot change its spots. You will never be able to love the boy, and therefore you will never have the loving family you hoped for. This plan is a miserable failure.

"It's not a failure at all. Sophie has warmed up to me. Cadence is in the process of warming up. It's going in the direction I need it to," Richard whispered. "But I regret taking the boy. It was a mistake. A stupid mistake to please Cadence."

But now you're stuck with him. There's no turning back from your idiotic mistake.

"There may be … there just may." Richard pulled himself out of the pool and dried himself off with a towel from the shelves against the far wall. He then walked back to the lounger and pulled on his robe to hide his expansive scars. "Cadence, I have to go make a call. You stay and relax here. Lunch will be served in about an hour in the dining room, so if I am not back shortly, head down and change and I will see you in the dining room."

"Okay," I said, turning my head when his lips tried to

meet mine, resulting in them landing on my cheek, the coarse scarred texture like sandpaper on my skin. Richard left, and Cale walked around the pool to give me a hug.

"I hate him, mom. He scares me. And he looks scary too," said Cale.

"Oh, Cale. Don't be afraid, I'm here. Just don't say anything to him; I can't have you locked away in that room again. We will get away, I promise, sweetheart," I whispered, running my fingers through his damp, dark locks. I was confident with tonight's plan that I could fulfill my promise.

"Okay, mom," he said, and jumped back into the pool to join his sister.

Richard sat at his desk, across from Peter and Leo, whom he'd radioed for an immediate meeting.

"I need a plan to get the boy off here. I cannot stand his presence and I do not want to risk hurting him, as Cadence would never forgive me. But it cannot look like I had anything to do with it. We need to be creative. I want him removed safely by one of you. I know Cadence would never forgive me if she knew I set this up."

Leo stared at his boss. How he wished that Richard had listened to his warnings about bringing the boy along. He hated seeing the pain in Richard's eyes. It was evident that Richard was struggling with this decision. Leo wished he could tell him that the boy was leaving tonight, and that Richard would never have to set eyes on him again. But the accompanying fact of Cadence also leaving would devastate Richard. He wondered, suddenly, if he could make it look like a botched job, where the plan went wrong and Cadence snuck aboard the lifeboat at the last minute? Could this actually work in Leo's favor?

"How about we blame it on me, that I knew you'd harm the boy if he stayed, so I took it upon myself to get him away and back to his father?" Leo quickly explained. "I could take him in the middle of the night by lifeboat. That way it wouldn't be seen as your decision, boss," said Leo, proud at how his plan was coming together. "You could get really pissed at me when I get back, so that it would all be very believable. You could even punch me so that she'd be convinced that you weren't involved."

Richard tapped the fingers of his gloved hand on the gleaming, wooden desk in front of him. Calculating green eyes stared through the white mask at Leo. "I need to think it through, but I like your strategy, Leo. She already dislikes you, so it does not matter if she hates you more. You could ensure the boy was safe somewhere so that help could get to him and bring him back to his father, then head back here. I would need you to keep your distance from Sophie and Cadence after, as they will both be livid. Maybe I could have you locked in the isolation room for a while to build further credibility. What do you think, Peter?" Richard asked the man who was silently observing the conversation.

"I think it could work, if this is what you really want, boss. I mean, it's only been twenty-four hours, and these relationships take time to build. I know you wanted to try and make it work for the lady, but there is no going back after this. The boy's a nice kid, but I know it irks you that he's not your own," said Peter.

"Irk is an understatement. I detest him. He reminds me of all the years I lost with Cadence and Sophie. Of the fact that another man screwed my wife while I could only watch her from a distance. He also reminds me of the man who stole Cadence's heart from me; he's the spitting image of him. I fear that I might not be able to restrain myself when it comes to the boy. I think Leo's idea of disappearing with him and taking the full blame could be believable. I know Cadence will miss the boy, as will Sophie, but time will make it easier. And it's safer this way. I know they would rather see him alive and well with his father, than hurt by me here," Richard concluded.

"Why don't we do it tonight? I think it's a good decision and there's no point in delaying it," explained Leo. "Peter and I can flesh out the details and let the captain and his crew know that I'm leaving via a lifeboat tonight. We can chart a course to get the boy to land, and a plan for me to intercept the Great White again."

"Okay, keep planning you two. I need to join my family for lunch." Richard left, a confident bounce in his step as Leo's gaze trailed after him.

Leo smiled, scrolling through details of the plan in his mind. It must be a tremendous relief to Richard that the boy would be leaving tonight; but unbeknownst to Richard, Cadence would be in Leo's place. It would be difficult to prove that Cadence did so on her own without support. It would just take some careful planning on his part. He shuddered at the thought of what would happen if Richard ever found out the truth.

Lunch was uneventful. Richard once again ignored Cale, while Cale glowered in his direction. The tension between them was palpable.

"I am going to hit the gym this afternoon. Would you two like to try out the yoga studio?" Richard asked Sophie and me.

"Sure, that sounds good," I answered, knowing that I needed a chance to be on my own to hopefully get the sleeping pills from Leo.

"Do we have yoga clothes?" Sophie asked.

"Of course, my darling. The brands that you like. I did my homework," he smiled across at Sophie.

"But what will I do, mom?" asked Cale.

"You could hang out in your room for a bit, honey. Or bring a book or sketchpad and come with us," I offered. Cale loved to draw, mainly planes and rockets.

"I'll come with you," he said, finishing the last bite of his fish taco, and washing it down with a glass of milk.

—

Richard bench pressed with all his strength, using the exercise to calm his agitated state of mind. The plan to get rid of Cale both excited him and made him nervous. Was it indeed the best option? Would the pros outweigh the cons? He lifted and groaned through the motion, and when he finished and sat up, Leo was standing in the doorway of the gym staring at him.

"Nice to see you back working out, boss. What are the ladies and boy doing?" Leo asked, the sleeping pills stowed in his pocket ready to pass onto Cadence.

"They're in the yoga studio," he answered.

"I chatted with the captain," Leo said, changing the subject. "If we leave at around 2:00 a.m., I should be able to get the boy back to San Diego by late morning. Extra gas tanks will be put on the lifeboat so that I can cover the distance. The ocean looked fairly calm so it's a good time to do it," he explained. "I'll drop him off at a safe location and by the time he spills his story, I'll be on my way back. I'll likely intercept the Great White late tomorrow evening."

"Sounds like it's falling into place. It's much safer for the boy this way. And I trust you, Leo, completely. You have always been there for me and I know you will carry this out flawlessly," said Richard, not typically one to give praise.

Leo felt warm inside, his heart pounding as he observed Richard's taut muscles through the thin t-shirt he wore to work out. He ached to have Richard, and could barely stop himself from touching him. Once Cadence was out of the picture, that intimacy might come in the future. There was always the glimmer of hope. If Richard knew he could never have Cadence again, would he live out the rest of his life celibate? Or, like straight men who are in jail, might he be willing to release himself in Leo's expert hands as his lover? Leo swallowed, realizing his growing erection might become obvious, so quickly excused himself.

Sophie and I followed the yoga sequences on the screen from the lithe and skilled Daisy, our on-screen instructor. We both wore designer yoga tanks and tights, hers colorful and mine black and gray. Cale lay on his stomach on a yoga mat, sketching images of fighter jets. The door opened and Leo stood at the entrance. "Can I have a quick word with you, Cadence?" he asked.

"Yes, sure. Keep going, Sophie, I'll be back in a minute. I

walked over to the door, but rather than go into the hall, Leo motioned that we stay in the confines of the yoga studio.

"Here you go," he said, discretely passing me a small baggie containing two pills. "You'll need to get them into his food or drink at dinner. Best is if you can dine together in your room again. There are no cameras in the room or on the private deck. Be sure to grind them up. They're powerful and will work through the night. But be very careful, because Richard doesn't miss any detail. If something seems off, he'll figure out what it is," he whispered. "There are also no recording devices in here, by the way," he added.

"Got it. I know the way he works. When will you come and get us tonight?"

"Once Richard is asleep I want you to get Cale and come up to the lounge. I will share more details with you then about the next steps. Say your goodbyes to Sophie before she goes to sleep. There's no point waking her up after."

"Okay," I said.

"Remember, you only get one shot at drugging him. If he finds out, there's gonna be hell to pay."

"Got it. Thank you," I added, and with that he left.

Chapter Thirty-Three

AFTER OUR WORKOUTS, RICHARD and I went back in the master suite. "I want to have you in the shower, Cadence," he breathed into my ear. I immediately thought of the camera. I doubted that Leo had the chance to uninstall it, and cringed at the thought of his watchful eye. "How about the hot tub, instead?" I asked, surprised at the sound of my request. It was only the promise of leaving tonight that made one more time tolerable.

Richard was as surprised as I was with my suggestion, stripping us both naked in seconds, scooping me into his arms, and stalking towards the hot tub. We practically fell in as he ravaged me with kisses, sucking my earlobes and nipples, as the warm water helped calm me. I tried to imagine he was Christian. After Richard climaxed, he hugged me tightly, whispering how much he loved me.

"Can we have dinner here tonight, on the deck?" I asked.

"Yes, Cadence. Of course, anything you want," he said, loving the opportunity to grant me my request.

"The seafood is so good here. Maybe scallops?" I asked.

"Oh, yes, Chef Marcus makes amazing garlic butter scallops on a beautiful risotto. I cannot wait for you to try them, my love." He leaned in and nibbled my earlobe again, planting a prolonged kiss on my lips. My mind was focused on how to plant the crushed pills in his risotto. That could work very well, I thought, filled with optimism around tonight's escape plan.

"The kids would probably enjoy eating in the multimedia room, maybe watching a movie?" I asked.

"Sure thing, my darling, their movie choices in there are endless. Plus, it will give us more time to ourselves," Richard whispered into my ear. I looked at him, without his mask, getting used to seeing his half-scorched face. I felt a pang of pity for him, knowing that this would be his last night of feeling his own version of happiness. I knew that he would never move on, and I felt sad for this man who was so hungry for love.

"I wouldn't mind a nap; I didn't sleep very well last night," I said.

"Absolutely. You must be exhausted from all of our love-making. I'll take care of putting our dinner and wine requests into the chef. And I'll make sure the children are taken care of for their dinner as well." He climbed out of the hot tub, and before wrapping himself in a towel, held a fluffy, white one out for me. I climbed out and into his arms.

"God, I love you," he said, bending down to meet my lips again. This time I didn't turn or flinch. Surely, I could kiss him back, knowing that this was one of the last times I'd ever have to.

—

I lay in the bed attempting to nap, imagining what the night would be like at sea. The sleeping pills were now stashed in my underwear drawer. I'd need my energy for the night ahead, and for staying strong for my son as we escaped into the black ocean. Somehow, I drifted into a fitful sleep, awakening when Richard entered the room.

"Sunset is coming in the next hour. I have some appetizers and champagne being brought up. And I have a gift for you, my sleeping beauty," Richard said, sitting on the edge of our king size bed. He handed me a small, white box. I yawned, and took the box.

"You don't need to—"

"Yes, Cadence, I do," he said.

I opened the small white box. Inside was a ruby ring, in the shape of a flame and set in platinum. Richard laid across the bed and took the ring, slipping it onto the ring finger of my right hand. "This symbolizes the fire that threatened to separate us forever, but didn't succeed," he said. "It's a very rare ruby that I was able to obtain and have custom designed for you, my love."

"It's … it's so unique," I said, glancing down at the large, sparkling stone on my finger.

"And I think it's time we take off your other wedding ring and replace it with ours," he said, fishing another small box from his pocket.

"I don't know, Richard," I stammered, shocked that he'd have a replacement for the one I wore out of the Oregon woods the day I escaped. I had donated it towards a charity for young musicians' scholarships, and never looked back. And now, out of this box emerged an exact replica of the ring that he proposed to me with so long ago.

"I insist. I married you first, so my ring belongs on that lovely finger," Richard said, gently removing the ring that Christian had given me, placing it in the box, and carefully slipping on his. "When you donated it, I bought it back from the scholarship group, at double the price they wanted, so it was a win/win," he smiled proudly. Of course, I thought foolishly, for imagining the ring (and Richard) would be gone forever.

I glanced at my hands, weighed down with a ring from Richard on each ring finger. I took the box with Christian's ring and placed it on my bedside table, making a mental note to slide it on my finger later once Richard was asleep. "I know that you love him, so I am not going to take that ring away. But I do hope that you will find it in your heart to return even a small percentage of the strong love I have for you, Cadence." He squeezed my hand with his gloved one, and the air smelled subtly of his cologne.

If only I could love this man back. He was starved for love, acceptance and appreciation, none of which I could willingly give. In return, he took my freedom. My choice. His actions gave me no alternative but to do everything in my power to leave again.

After a quick shower, in which I made sure to face away from the potential eye on the wall, I dried off and changed into a simple, red sleeveless dress. I'd made sure to grab the sleeping pills discretely, along with my underwear. In the privacy of the locked bathroom, I put on my makeup, styled my hair, and carefully ground the sleeping pills on the marble counter, using the handle of my round brush much like a rolling pin. I then scooped them into a makeup powder container that I'd emptied, and placed it back in my makeup bag for later.

When I came back into the bedroom, Richard was facing away, buttoning up a long sleeved, white cotton shirt. He seemed in good spirits, whistling as he buttoned up his beige khakis. "I'm going to check on the kids," I said.

He turned around, looking at me appreciatively. "Sure thing. You look fantastic in red, by the way. I'm glad you chose that dress, as it matches your new ring, which is dazzling on you, my love."

I gave a weak smile, then left the room to check on the kids. I walked down the hall and found them in Sophie's room. "Hi, darlings. I hope you're okay eating in the multimedia room together while I eat with Richard tonight?" I asked. "I'll come by and say good night in a couple of hours," I added, knowing by then that Richard would be drugged and asleep.

"He told me that earlier," said Sophie, eyeing me knowingly. "We're fine eating there together."

"But I don't want you to go!" added Cale, his wide eyes looking scared.

"Honey, you'll be fine with your sister, and I'll spend some time here with you later. I promise." There was no point in alerting Cale to the plan until I was sure Richard was drugged and our escape was underway. I gave him and Sophie a hug and a kiss, and then headed back to the master suite.

When I got back to the suite, I used the bathroom, and put my lipstick and the powder container into a black clutch. When I came out onto the deck, Richard had soft jazz music playing in the background for the sunset, and a lovely looking bubbly rosé on ice. He poured two glasses and insisted on us sharing the double lounger, with me sitting between his legs. I placed the clutch on the side table. "What a perfect night. Not a cloud in the sky. The sunset will be magnificent," he said, kissing my neck. He wore his mask, and despite me reminding him that I was fine with it off, he insisted on keeping his scars hidden.

Pierre brought us a shrimp cocktail as our first course. We sat at the bistro table and ate the large, succulent shrimp. I was anxious, so quickly finished my glass of the rosé to calm my nerves, which seemed to work. Our salads came as the sun did its final dip out of sight. I wanted to make sure Richard was relaxed, so encouraged him to enjoy some more wine with our main course. He chose a New Zealand sauvignon blanc to pair with the scallop and risotto dish, which had just arrived under covered dishes.

"Richard, I know I shouldn't worry, but I'd really like to know how the kids are doing, and I have to use the bathroom anyway. Would you mind checking on them before we eat?"

"I can radio Peter or Leo right away, Cadence," he said, reaching into his pocket.

"They still scare Sophie, so I'd rather have you, her father, go and check," I said, nearly stumbling over the word "father."

Richard looked down at me. I could see that he was debating the merits of leaving while we were enjoying his perceived romantic dinner. "Okay, but only for you. I will go quickly so that this beautiful meal doesn't get cold. You really shouldn't worry, Cadence. They are just fine. Remember, no news is good news," he added, bordering on sounding like a parent and not a spouse.

"Thank you," I said. My heart pounded.

Richard left and I stepped into the bedroom as the door closed, making sure he'd truly gone. I rushed back to the deck, grabbing my clutch and standing at the table. Looking over my shoulder every few seconds, I took out the loose powder container, carefully twisting off the lid. I then removed the silver cover from Richard's plate and pulled my fork from my cloth napkin, using it to stir the powder into his risotto, making sure the fine powder disappeared into the creamy sauce. I replaced the silver lid, and wiped my fork on my napkin. I then put the empty powder container back in my clutch, and clicked it shut.

Surveying the table, everything looked exactly as it did when Richard had left. I took a sip of my wine, and then headed to the bathroom, holding the clutch tightly. I locked the door behind me, then took out the empty powder container, and replaced some of the powder which had found a temporary home in the corner of my makeup case. I applied a fresh coat of lipstick, hastily peed, then headed nonchalantly back out.

I nearly bumped into Richard, who was standing outside the bathroom door. "What took you so long?" he asked, eyeing me skeptically.

"Slightly upset stomach, and I needed to touch up my makeup. But all good now. How are the kids?"

"Perfect, just as I thought. No worries, darling. Now let's go eat."

We sat at the candlelit table. The fresh sea breeze smelled of salt water. Richard lifted the lids off our plates. "I would like to feed you, Cadence," he said, taking his fork and scooping a piece of the warm risotto, and moving it towards my mouth.

I froze momentarily in disbelief. Really, could this be

happening? It seemed that he knew something was up. "I'd prefer to feed myself," I said, observing the disappointment in his intense, green eyes.

"Just one bite, please, Cadence," he said, moving the fork to my mouth, as if I were an infant who didn't have a choice in the matter. Just one small bite shouldn't affect me much. And it could look suspicious if I refused.

"Just one," I obliged, opening my mouth. As I chewed the rich risotto, I made sure to keep some in my cheek to spit in my napkin if I could do so discretely.

"Your turn," I said, scooping a forkful from his plate. His eyes were closed as I gently slipped the delicious bite into his mouth. "Good?"

"Yes, mmm," he said, chewing slowly. "One more," I said, taking advantage of Richard's closed eyes to use my left hand and napkin to carefully spit the contents stored in my cheek, like a chipmunk dumping its winter store. With my right hand, I gently fed him another scoop. He opened his eyes as he swallowed. "Let's toast to the fact that, despite the circumstances, this is an amazing meal and a beautiful evening," he said.

"I agree, Richard. It is a gorgeous evening and meal." I stared at this strange man across from me, his eyes burning into mine.

He suddenly leaned forwards, clasping my hand in his gloved one. "What's going on, Cadence? You are not acting how I would expect you to on our second night together," he said, staring quizzically at me. I felt my heart begin to race, but willed myself to remain calm.

"I'm just making the best of it, Richard. It's not like I have a choice," I added for good measure, taking a bite of my delicious dinner.

"Fair enough. I'm just not used to it. Nothing seems normal right now. Yet … I don't know what normal even feels like," he said, gazing out at the dark ocean, and taking another drink of his wine.

"I think that Sophie is becoming fond of you," I said simply. "You are so much alike. I'm glad you got to spend some time together," I said, speaking honestly.

"And me of her, Cadence. *Thank you* for bringing her into this world. The day I heard about your impending abortion, I was terrified. I felt helpless as I was recovering from yet another surgery. My head was full of nightmares about our baby dying. I could not imagine going on if he or she died. And for that I owe you *everything*," he declared, staring at me. His eyes peering out from the mask revealed the intensity of his adoration for Sophie and me. I almost felt guilty as I hoped the sleeping medication would begin to take effect soon.

"You're welcome," I said. "I can't imagine not having Sophie, either." I took another bite of risotto. "Richard, I think this is the best risotto I've ever had," I said.

"I know, Chef Marcus is a master. And the scallops are fantastic, too," he added, taking a bite of both scallop and risotto.

As we ate, I watched every bite of risotto enter his mouth. All of a sudden, my head felt funny, like I was in a daze. What was happening to me?

"Are you okay, my love?" Richard asked.

I yawned as I felt myself losing touch with reality. "I'm just … tired," I said, fading faster than I could control. "Let's skip dessert and head to bed. I need to … rest," I said.

"Your pupils are dilated. What exactly did you put in my meal, Cadence?" he demanded.

"What?" I asked, fear igniting somewhere deep in the recesses of my brain.

"I swapped our meals, as I sensed that you were up to something. I need to know that you are not going to be hurt by whatever was planted in there," he stated.

"Nothing. I dunno ... what you ... mean ..." I murmured, as my head bobbed, and sleep overpowered the fear and failure that flickered like distant flames in my head. I felt Richard take me into his arms, and place me on the bed. Then sleep engulfed me.

The door to the multimedia room swung open. "I need to speak with you *now*, Sophie," ordered Richard. "Just you," he added.

Sophie leaped off the sectional and ran to her father. "What's wrong?" she asked, fear apparent in her eyes.

Richard closed the door to the multimedia room so they were alone together in the lounge. "I need to know the truth. What did your mother try to drug me with tonight?"

"She wouldn't try to drug you," Sophie said. Like Richard, she was quick on her feet. "It must've been someone else," she added, wanting to implicate Leo, but needing time to think through the best approach given that he seemed to be her mom and Cale's only hope of escape.

"Well, my meal was drugged, Sophie. And your mother was acting odd prior to eating our main course. I swapped our meals. Her pupils were dilated and she passed out quickly. I want to make sure I don't need Owen, our paramedic, to pump her stomach," he said.

"Oh God, I don't want anything to happen to her!" Sophie looked terrified. Should she tell the truth about the sleeping pills? Her instincts said no. Sleeping pills weren't lethal, her mom would be okay. The risk of Richard's wrath felt much more of a danger now than the sleeping pills in her mom's system.

"I want you to wait in our room and keep a close eye on her. I'm going to speak to Leo and Peter ASAP. The boy can wait in here for now."

"I want Cale with me," said Sophie. "He'll be scared!"

"No! He stays here until further notice."

Sophie knew that her father's tone meant no further discussion. She hadn't yet experienced Richard in this state, and was too scared to argue. She opened the door to the multimedia room and ran over to Cale, letting him know that she'd be back as soon as she could.

"Don't be long, *please*, Sophie," he pleaded.

"I promise, I'll be back as quickly as I can, Cale," she said, and gave him a quick hug.

Sophie sat on the bed beside her sleeping mom. Cadence was breathing deeply, appearing to sleep peacefully. "Any changes or signs that she is sick, press the red emergency button on the intercom, and I will be here with Owen right away. I'm going to send him here shortly, anyway," Richard said.

"Okay. How long will you be?"

"I don't know, but I am going to get to the bottom of this." He shot her a serious look before he left, and she shuddered imagining how this would play out if the truth was unveiled.

She squeezed her mom's hand, vowing to do everything she could to protect her mom and Cale, and to reunite them all with Christian as soon as possible.

"I love you, mom. I'm sorry this is happening. I won't let him hurt anyone, I promise," Sophie whispered, planting a soft kiss on her mom's cheek.

Chapter Thirty-Four

RICHARD'S PRIORITY WAS MAKING sure that Cadence wasn't at risk from whatever she'd ingested. He had radioed Owen, the helicopter pilot and paramedic, to meet with Peter, Leo and himself in five minutes in his office. He ran all the way up there, his anger mounting. Once in his office, he paced back and forth, anxious for the men to get there.

The voice came alive with a vengeance: *If she had her way, you'd be the one passed out and maybe she would have killed you. She hates you. They all hate you. It will never be any different. You should end everyone's misery and shoot yourself with that gun in your desk. A quick, painless death.*

"Shut up!" Richard growled. "Cadence doesn't hate me. I know she doesn't. And I have fought this hard for what I want. I am *not* going to disappear. But I *am* going to find out who gave her whatever knocked her out. And when I do, they will pay."

You can't trust anyone on here. You think they are loyal, but all they see you for is a paycheck and the monster you are.

"I am not a monster!" Richard roared, as a knock came at his office door. "Come in!" he barked, the anger in his office thick in the air.

"You okay, boss?" asked Leo, eyeing him with a combination of fear and curiosity at the statement they'd just heard loudly through the door.

"No, Leo, I'm *not* fucking okay." He motioned for the three of them to take a seat. Peter and Owen looked concerned, glancing at each other then back to Richard, who stood at the other side of his desk, staring at them through his mask. "Cadence has been drugged. Something was slipped into my meal, but I sensed something was up and swapped meals to be sure. And unfortunately, I was correct. She passed out quickly, and I need you to go and check on her, Owen. I need you on high alert until she wakes up and we make sure she's okay. I need you to keep an eye on her vitals just in case we need you to pump her stomach."

"Yes, sir," said Owen. "I can check her out right now. What were her symptoms before she passed out?" Owen was originally from South America, but had lived in the United States for the last twenty years. He wore his dark hair in a military-style buzz cut, and his dark eyes reflected both intelligence and honesty. Richard had grown to like and trust him over the last decade. Owen had previously worked with Leo, so came with a glowing reference. He would not be a risk, as he disliked law enforcement and the FBI as much as the others.

"The only thing I could see was her pupils dilating. And then she looked exhausted. Her head started bobbing. I had to carry her to the bed, as she was about to pass out on the deck.

Can you intercept Pierre so that he does not throw the rest of her meal out? I would like it stored in the fridge for potential testing," he ordered.

"Roger that. I'm on it," said Owen, standing to leave.

"Before you go, I'm going to ask this once and I demand the truth. Did you have *anything* to do with drugging my meal, or do you know who did?" Richard asked, staring fiercely through his mask.

"No, sir. Absolutely not," said Owen, staring confidently back at Richard.

"If anyone avoids the truth, there will major consequences. You know that I am serious, right, Owen?"

"Yes. I don't know what's going on. I swear," he answered, beads of perspiration forming on his dark forehead. "But I should check on her as soon as possible," he added.

"Go! Sophie is with her right now."

"Okay," Owen said, walking rapidly out of the office, and closing the door behind him.

"Now I want the fucking truth! How the *hell* did a drug get into my meal?" he roared, looking from Peter to Leo.

"Haven't a clue, boss," said Peter. "I swear I don't know. But *I will* help solve this mess," he promised.

"You two are my right-hand men. I trust you. You wouldn't dare to screw me over, would you?" He was now focused on Leo.

"Never, boss. Maybe she stole some meds from Owen's supply? Who knows. Between Cadence and the girl, they could've gotten their hands on something. Or maybe from one of the staff's bedrooms?" he added.

"Owen's supply is under lock and key, and all the staff know to always lock their doors. I will get to the bottom of this, and

I swear the punishment will be severe," he warned.

Leo swallowed, thinking about leaving his door open this morning, and the repercussions that were resulting from his stupid error. He tried desperately to think up a way to incriminate Cadence or Sophie, but their threat around the video hung heavily in his mind. He could remove the camera from the master en suite and delete all evidence on his laptop; then it would be his word against theirs. But the fact that they both saw it was too much of a risk. The girl, especially, could sway Richard, and he felt it was too much of a risk to take. He'd best play dumb. He'd have to trust all parties would do the same.

He needed to get Richard's attention back onto tonight's plan of getting the boy off the Great White. That way, Leo could get away too, until things calmed down. Maybe he wouldn't come back. But the thought of leaving Richard for good was one he couldn't fathom. Even in his angry state, Richard was every bit as appealing as he'd always been. His rage made him even sexier, so masculine and powerful. Leo felt the familiar pull to protect Richard, and vowed never to collaborate with Cadence again. If she wanted to hurt Richard, she'd have to do so on her own accord. Fucking bitch, he thought. "I'll help you figure this out, boss," said Leo. "Do you still want to get the boy off as planned tonight?"

"I need to think about that. My priority is Cadence's health. I need to understand what happened before I can focus on the boy. There are too many variables at play." Richard closed his eyes, grasping the sides of his head as if he had a headache. He then opened them, staring firmly at Leo and Peter. "No, the boy stays for now. And I command you two to get to the bottom of this. Within twenty-four hours, I want an answer to what happened. Is that clear?"

"Yes, sir," said Peter.

"We'll do everything we can, boss," said Leo.

"I want everyone on this yacht questioned, and their rooms searched. I want the remainder of that meal tested, so Owen will need to fly it to a lab, I'm guessing. Something like this can *never* happen again," he seethed, punching his fist on his desk with a loud bang.

"We'll make a plan and get started immediately," said Leo, standing beside Peter.

"I won't take *any* excuses. I want answers first thing tomorrow," Richard declared, glaring through his mask.

They nodded and left, closing the door behind them. Richard was sweating under the mask, his rage boiling throughout his body. He undid the mask, placing it on his desk and wiping his sweaty forehead. "Fuck," he said, again slamming his fist on the desk so hard that it throbbed.

Owen entered the master suite to check on Cadence. "Hello, Sophie. I'm Owen, and I'm a trained paramedic here to check on your mother."

"She'll be okay, right?" asked Sophie.

"I'm sure she'll be fine," he answered, taking her vitals. "All seems okay. I'm going to take some blood as well, so it can be tested." He removed a needle from his medical bag. He swiftly found a vein, and Cadence barely flinched as he smoothly inserted the needle and drew a couple of vials of her blood.

"I suspect it was a heavy-duty sleep medication. She will

likely wake up some time tomorrow morning, a little bit dazed and confused, but all will be fine as the day progresses."

"Thank you, Owen," said Sophie.

"No problem. I'll come check on her again in the next two hours, but the emergency button on the intercom will reach me if you need me at any time."

"Okay," said Sophie, eyeing the intercom on the wall near the doorway. As soon as Owen left, Sophie burst into tears. She sobbed for her mom, trapped here with an obsessive, controlling, stalker who happened to be Sophie's biological father. She cried for Cale, who must be so scared. She cried for her dad, who must be worried sick. And she cried for herself, caught up in this crazy situation in the middle of nowhere.

"Honey, don't cry," said Richard, who had been standing in the doorway quietly watching his daughter. "It's going to be fine, Sophie," he said, walking to the bed and sitting beside her, folding her into his arms.

Sophie continued to sob, gasping for air as she cried harder than ever before. It was as if all the stress from the last two days was pouring out of her. "I'm scared," she sobbed.

"Sophie, you're safe here. There's nothing to be scared about," he soothed.

"There's you. Your temper. Your possessiveness of mom," she said through her tears, not making eye contact.

"Sophie, I love your mother so very much. There is nothing to fear. As long as she's with me, and she doesn't try to escape, she'll be safe" he added.

"If you love someone, you shouldn't trap them," Sophie said, finally starting to calm down.

"Love takes on many forms, Sophie. In time neither of you

will feel trapped."

"What about Cale? Why did you trap him? He doesn't deserve this," she said, now making eye contact with her masked father.

"I knew that you and your mother would miss him too much; that if you'd had a choice, you would have wanted him with you," Richard said. "Maybe ... maybe I was wrong though," Richard admitted.

"But there's still time to do the right thing, father. Let mom and Cale go. Keep *me,* but don't punish them," said Sophie, her reddened eyes begging Richard to agree.

"Sophie, at most I would consider letting the boy go, but *never* you or Cadence. Never!" his voice rose unexpectedly, startling Sophie.

"You don't have to yell. Do you want to be scary and mean?" she asked. "We'll never want to be around you if you're so nasty all the time," she said, storming towards the door.

"Sophie! I'm sorry," he yelled after her, but she was gone.

The voice answered in her place: *What a father you are. Terrifying monster. Abuser. Control freak. You swore you'd never be like your own father, and now you are every bit as mean as him, but even crazier.*

"Shut up! Shut the fuck up!" Richard answered.

You can tell me to shut up all you want, but I will never go away. I'm with you. I'm trapped in your fucked up head and I'm going to keep telling it like it is. You should let them go and then jump into the ocean. Let the sharks take care of the rest.

"Aaargh!" Richard yelled, then sobbed through his mask, tearing it off so that he could use the tissues tucked in his bedside table. He sobbed and sobbed. He was six years old again. Trapped in his closet. Scared. Alone.

"Get the fuck out of there, you little coward," shouted his father. The door swung open and his father was glaring down him.

"Please, don't hurt me," sobbed Richard. "I love you, father."

Richard's sobs gradually subsided, and he felt weak from the emotions, past and present, playing through his tortured mind. He put his arms around his wife and whispered, "I love you, Cadence. I love you so much. Please don't ever try to hurt me again," ending his request with a kiss planted on her sleeping lips. Then he fell into a deep sleep at her side.

Chapter Thirty-Five

SOPHIE RESCUED CALE FROM the multimedia room, and they were now back in his room, sitting on his bed. She comforted her little brother and whispered in his ear. “Cale, trust me, mom and I are working on a way to get off here. Don’t worry, it’ll all be okay.”

“I want mom,” he whimpered. “And dad.” As the tears flowed down Cale’s cheeks, Sophie’s resentment and determination to get him and her mom off this yacht grew.

“Mom’s asleep. She wasn’t feeling well, but she’ll be fine tomorrow. I promise you’ll see her then, Cale.”

“Can you sleep with me here? I’m scared.”

“Yes, for sure. I just need to do a couple of things, and then I’ll be back. You can relax and read for now.”

“Okay, but don’t be long, Sophie.”

“I won’t.” She kissed his cheek, and gently closed the door behind her. She needed to find Leo. She needed another plan for getting her mom and brother off here. And she was scared for her mom, and for what Richard might do if he found out she had indeed drugged his meal in order to try and escape. Leo was scary and intimidating, but her only option for freeing her family. One day she would get back her own freedom, but for now her focus was on their safety.

She headed through the lounge, past the lonely sofas and chairs, and towards the staff quarters. She nearly bumped into Peter, who was quickly walking down the hall. "You aren't allowed here, Sophie," he said, looking anxious and preoccupied.

"I'm looking for Leo. I have to talk to him," she demanded.

"About what?"

"That's my business."

"It's actually my business to ensure the security of everyone on this yacht, Sophie," he replied, his angry red face contrasting with his white hair.

"Oh, sorry, I thought you were only in the business of illegally abducting families," she retorted.

"You're a lippy little one," he replied, as he turned around abruptly, walked a few doors down the hall and knocked on Leo's door. "Leo, the girl wants to talk," he said, glaring back at Sophie.

Leo emerged, surprised to see Sophie standing a few feet away. "What do you want?" he asked.

"I need to talk with you, in private," she said.

"Fine, kid, but I don't have much time. Peter and I are both busy trying to get to the bottom of the drugging incident." He gave her a firm glare, as if she was to blame.

"Which is also my goal," she lied, knowing Peter's inquisitive eyes were watching her every reaction.

"Peter, I'll join you in the security room in about twenty," Leo said.

"Okay," Peter replied, rushing away.

"Let's sit over in the lounge," said Sophie, leading the way.

"The far corner over there is private," said Leo, heading to a corner with two large, white armchairs. They sat down, looking angrily at each other.

"We need a new plan to get my mom and brother off here, as soon as possible," Sophie said.

"That's the least of my worries, kid," scowled Leo. "If the boss finds out about the pills, I'm dead."

"He won't find out from us. I promise that. But this can't go on much longer. We need a plan."

"I'm *done.* I ain't plannin' nothin' with you two. I work for your father."

"Don't forget that we know about your sick videos," Sophie retorted.

Leo lurched forwards, wanting to grab the girl by the neck, but stopped within inches, controlling himself with every ounce of his willpower. How dare she blackmail him! A twelve-fucking-year-old brat!

Sophie jumped back, turned and ran. Leo tried to grab her, but was blocked by one of the armchairs, profanities flowing as he bashed his shin into a coffee table. Sophie sprinted through the lounge, ignoring Leo's shouts from behind her. She ran up the staircase and towards her parents' room. Leo was close behind. "Stop right now, kid! Stop or you'll be sorry!" But Sophie was quick, strong-willed like her father, and had the benefit of a slight head start, which landed her through their door, where she found her parents sleeping.

"Father, help!" Sophie shouted, startling Richard awake.

"What's wrong?" he mobilized quickly, leaping from the bed.

"Leo tried to hurt me!" she screamed, as Leo appeared at the door.

"Boss, that's not true," he yelled. "She's trying to get me to help them escape, and I won't betray you," Leo snapped, glaring at Sophie, hands in tight fists against his muscular legs as he shook with rage.

Richard was in front of him instantly. "I told you to never scare my daughter!" Richard sneered. "Look, you've terrified her." He pointed to Sophie sitting beside her sleeping mother, shaking and crying. "But Sophie," he asked, "is it true that you were trying to orchestrate an escape?"

"That's *not* true. I was trying to help figure out what happened to mom," she declared. "But I don't want to stay if *he* stays, he's crazy and will hurt us! He hates us, father," she added, not taking her eyes away from Leo.

"Sophie, I'm the boss. I will decide who stays and goes. Is that clear?" Richard tried to glare at Sophie, but it was apparent that he had trouble doing so.

"You're a controlling stalker. That's what's clear!" she snapped, immediately regretting her words.

"Isolation room. Now!" Richard replied calmly, walking over to the intercom, and entering a code. "Peter, please come to the master suite and escort Sophie to the isolation room immediately."

"I can take her, boss," said Leo.

"I'm not finished with you. The way you have terrified my daughter is unacceptable, and I will be addressing it shortly," Richard scowled. "My office, fifteen minutes."

"Yes, sir," muttered Leo, turning around so that Richard couldn't see the combination of pain and rage on his face. He left abruptly, and walked down a floor to calm down in his room. Fucking little lying bitch, he thought. Like mother, like daughter. He was running out of patience for this bullshit. Their manipulation of Richard was so tough to see. The man he respected and admired was like a moldable piece of plasticine when it came to those two.

Leo's mind spun with ways to deal with this situation. Every cell in his body wanted to hurt the girl, but that would be a deadly impulse. He was already in deep shit. He hated being berated by the man he loved. He'd do anything for Richard, but being demeaned was almost too hard to take. He took a glass from his bedside table and hurled it across the room, pieces shattering everywhere like his broken heart.

—

"Please don't make me go in there. I'm sorry, please, father," cried Sophie, as Peter appeared in the doorway.

"You know the rules, Sophie. Your words were cruel and there is a price to pay for treating me that way. It will only be for a couple of hours, so that you can think about the repercussions of calling me those painful names," he said, looking away from Sophie as he talked. He knew that making eye contact with his crying daughter would put him at risk of softening her punishment further.

"I promised Cale that I'd be back soon. He's scared. If I go, he goes. It's our pact," she demanded.

"No, the boy stays where he is. You need to learn this lesson on your own, Sophie. And that's final. Take her *now,* Peter," he added, while turning away.

"Yes, sir." Sophie screamed as Peter took her arm and pulled her out of the room.

"Cale! Cale!" she yelled, her screams fading as they made their way down the hall and down towards the isolation room.

Richard lay down again at his wife's side. She had not moved or responded to all the commotion. "Cadence," he whispered, stroking her hair. "I'm sorry this isn't going as smoothly as I had hoped. But one thing is for sure, it *will* get better. I will find out what happened, and I will ensure it never happens again. It breaks my heart to see you this way," he said, feeling an overwhelming sadness replace his anger.

The voice in his head responded. *Sending your daughter to a dungeon; how could you? She'll never love you now. All you are is a replica of your father. No better than a terrible, abusive prison warden.*

Richard felt torrents of tears come, for once speechless to the voice. He was a kid again, crying so hard that he thought he would choke. All he could say was, "Why, why, why, why, why," as his tears soaked the back of Cadence's red dress

Chapter Thirty-Six

Leo waited outside Richard's office. He barely felt the cuts on his hands from roughly picking up the shards of glass. He didn't care about the cuts and the pain, as they were a welcome distraction from how horrible he felt inside. He wanted them off this yacht, all three of them. He wanted the life he had before they arrived, with the chance of his relationship with Richard morphing into more.

Yet now he felt trapped and coerced by the fact that these ungrateful bitches had seen his video footage. His anger had reached a fever pitch inside his tormented brain, impacting his whole body. He felt as though he'd explode. Breaking the glass was only a momentary reprieve from what he really wanted to do.

Suddenly Richard stalked past Leo and opened his office door, grunting at Leo to follow and gesturing for the door to be closed behind him.

"Have a seat, Leo," Richard said, motioning to the chair

across from his desk. Instead of walking behind his desk, he uncharacteristically sat in the chair beside Leo and faced him. Richard looked stricken. His eyes, peering through the mask, were red and bloodshot. He'd obviously been crying. He ran his hands through his thick, blond head of hair, a mannerism Leo knew well when Richard was thinking. "I need the truth, Leo," Richard demanded. "The *whole* story, not bits and pieces of reality and lies. If I can't trust you, who the hell can I trust?"

Leo's time was up.

"The truth is, they all want off. Cadence and Sophie blackmailed me into getting your wife and the boy off here on one of the lifeboats tonight, and I felt backed into a fucking corner," Leo said, the truth coming out, despite his better judgment.

"What would they have to blackmail you about?"

"Boss, I can't say …" Leo said quietly, turning away from Richard.

In a second, Richard lurched forwards, grabbing Leo by the shoulders, turning him around, and pinning him against the office wall. Richard was bigger, but Leo was also strong and muscular. Leo reached out to hold Richard at bay, but Richard was intent on a physical fight. "I am your boss, you do not keep *anything* from me, Leo! I'M YOUR FUCKING BOSS!" Richard yelled, shaking Leo.

The closeness. The physical contact. The testosterone. It was all too much. Leo hugged Richard tightly, pressing against him. He looked up into the mask of the man he loved. "Fine. No more secrets," Leo said hoarsely. "I *love* you, Richard. Let me show you what we could have together," he added, feeling himself growing hard against Richard's tense body.

The momentary pause, during which everything stood still, except for Leo's growing erection, ended with Richard hurling Leo onto the floor. "Don't ever touch me again!" roared Richard, stomping around to the back of his desk, while Leo slowly got up. "I saved your life … I'd do *anything* for you," promised Leo, feeling the hurt of rejection mixed with longing. "She'll leave you again, hurt you again. I *know* it. I'd stick by you and protect you no matter what."

"I'm not gay and I never will be. Cadence is the love of my life. How dare you try to predict my wife's actions. You are leaving this yacht by morning. I *never* want to see you again," declared Richard, glaring through his mask at Leo, who was now leaning on one of the chairs, in pain from hitting the hardwood. Richard turned around to face the panel of windows that looked onto the pool deck, the aqua colored water now glowing in the dark of nightfall. "Get out, pack up your things, and await further orders," said Richard.

The shot fired before Richard could comprehend what was happening. He crumpled to his office floor.

Peter stared in disbelief at Leo's laptop. At the image of Richard showering. When Peter was locking her in the isolation room, Sophie had told him about the video recordings, about how Leo was an electronic Peeping Tom on her father, and more recently her mother. She had described how Leo had caught her and her mother watching the footage. About how Leo didn't want Richard to find out. About how her father had a right to know, but she didn't tell him as she feared Leo and his volatility.

She also described how Leo had come very close to hurting her earlier in the lounge. "It's true!" she declared to Peter. "He's a risk to our safety, and if you don't check into this, I'll tell my father *everything* tomorrow."

Peter was hesitant. He'd worked with Leo for many years. Although he didn't particularly enjoy Leo's company, he didn't have a reason to distrust him. Leo was fiercely loyal and protective of Richard and all the staff; the hallmark of a prized security hand. If he was watching over anything on this yacht, it was for a damn good reason. But Peter felt the urge to go see for himself. If anything, he could discover the truth and prove Leo was in fact trustworthy. It had to be a misunderstanding. There must be another security reason for Leo to have installed a camera in the master en suite.

Yet somewhere deep inside, Peter had a flicker of doubt about Leo. Something about the way Leo protected Richard. Admired him. Something about the way Leo's demeanor had changed, subtly but noticeably, when Cadence and her children came aboard the Great White. It wasn't just about nerves or the tension in the air. Was it jealousy? Was it resentment?

And here it was, the video footage Sophie had promised, indeed existed. Richard showering. But not from today, or yesterday, or the day before that. It was from over a month ago. Why on earth were there months of video footage of the master en suite on Leo's laptop? And why was the video currently paused on this full frontal scene of Richard, from one month ago, instead of the present? Would there be a safety reason for videoing this bathroom?

When Peter had opened Leo's laptop, it was password protected. Peter, however, knew the password from when all the devices were set up on the yacht. It only took three guesses to determine that *White$$$* was it. Similar to the other passwords in their arsenal aboard this high-tech yacht. But now what? Should he confront Leo first, or go directly to the boss?

Peter's thoughts were interrupted by the sound of a shot firing from above. He mobilized without pause, racing out of the room, and pressing the emergency button on the intercom system in the staff hallway, which would alert everyone to follow the emergency protocol that they'd practiced so many times. The familiar alarm started blaring all over the Great White.

Peter's heart was racing as he ran down the hall, through the lounge, and up three flights of stairs, calling out to ask if anyone was hurt, and heading towards the security room, which was beside Richard's office. He noticed Richard's office door was open as he ran through the upper living room. "Boss?" he yelled, entering the office, where he spotted Richard crumpled and bleeding on the wooden floor.

"What's going on?" asked Owen, who had just entered the office as Peter knelt beside Richard.

"Come quick, he's been shot!" yelled Peter.

Owen was down on the floor examining Richard in an instant. His paramedic training went into autopilot. Richard was shot through his right shoulder, not low enough to puncture his heart or lungs. He was also bleeding from a contusion on his head, perhaps from cutting himself on the corner of his desk during his fall, Owen surmised. "Peter, bring my medical bag from the shelf in the security room," he said, in the meantime having pulled off his own shirt to press down on Richard's bleeding shoulder wound.

Peter entered the security room, where several staff members were beginning to gather, panic stricken on their faces. "Mr. White has been shot," said Peter, "Owen is treating him in his office. George, bring him his medical bag!" he said to the first mate, who ran the bag next door. "I need to secure the yacht and find out who did this," he said, reaching for the intercom. "Leo, where are you?" he asked into it. No response. His suspicions were quickly being confirmed. "If anyone sees Leo, radio me immediately!" said Peter, knowing the rules: his number one priority was to keep Richard's family safe and onboard.

Chapter Thirty-Seven

LEO DUCKED BEHIND THE bar in the lounge, his mind a mix of rage and regret. He'd shot the man he loved, the man he'd sworn to protect at all costs. He had to get away, and *fast.* He could take a boat, but it could be risky.

An idea suddenly came to him: the chopper. Both Owen and he were trained to fly it. He could go into hiding quicker with the chopper than with a lifeboat. He could start a new life, and teach Richard a lesson, as he knew how key the chopper was to safety and medical emergencies on the yacht. So, to take it would be the ultimate "fuck you" to the Great White and Richard.

Yet, despite the adrenaline rush of this plan, Leo was devastated by Richard's rejection and dismissal. He'd dedicated himself to this man for over a decade: as a physical protector, a confidant, a strategist and an admirer. And now that he had revealed his true feelings, he was forced to leave. Like none of those years mattered. To never see Richard again. No, if he was going to lose what he loved, so was Richard White. Leo would take away the love of Richard's life, that bitch Cadence. He could taste the sweetness of revenge, imagining Richard's heartbreak when he found out she was gone for good.

But, Leo pondered, Cadence *also* needed to be punished. She was ungrateful and had caused immeasurable pain to Richard and now Leo too. What would hurt her the most? Leaving without both of her kids, thought Leo, a sinister smile forming on his face. Leaving the boy on the yacht would be a double blow; payback to both Richard and Cadence. Richard would have to deal with a kid he didn't want, both of them pining after Cadence; and Cadence would be more desperate than ever to get her kids back. Yep, that was what needed to happen. The answer was clear. So, after he saw Peter running through the lounge, he quietly darted out in the other direction to head down to the master suite and get Cadence.

Cale was reading on his bed when he heard the shot from above. What was it? A loud bang, like a gun. He was terrified. Where was Sophie? She'd promised to come back quickly but hadn't. He needed to go to his mom. In his blue and white striped pajamas, he quietly opened his door, looking right and then left down the hall. All was quiet. He tiptoed quickly down the hall towards the master suite. As he passed Sophie's door, he paused and turned the knob. It opened, and he called out, "Sophie, are you here?"

No response.

He walked further down the hall to his mom's room, and knocked gently, calling out to her. No response. Sophie had said their mom wasn't feeling well; she was probably sleeping. But he needed her. Cale slowly turned the knob and the door opened. His mom was asleep on the king size bed. He ran over to her. "Mom?" he asked, touching her arm. "Mom, are you okay?"

No response. She was sleeping deeply. The masked man was nowhere in sight, which was a huge relief. Suddenly he heard loud footsteps running down the hall. He instinctively ducked and slipped under his mom's side of the bed. He curled up, feeling safely hidden as the footsteps drew nearer.

"Your wish has come true, *Mrs. White.* You're leaving this boat," said Leo, ripping the blanket off Cadence. He lifted her over his shoulder, making sure he still held tight to the gun in his right hand. He may need it before their departure. He could smell the familiar scent of her perfume, which made him gag. What was so attractive about *her* anyway, when he had so much more to offer Richard as both a lover and protector?

He took the back way to the helipad to avoid encounters with the other staff. There was a small, metal staircase on the opposite end of the hall meant for maintenance and emergency purposes. He opened the door to the staircase with his left hand, a challenge as he held tight to the bitch's sleeping mass and to the gun. He hiked up the stairs, pausing at each landing as he was out of breath from the exertion. "Almost there, bitch!" he said.

Cale resisted the impulse to scream. To yell for help. To punch this man who was stealing his mom. Although Sophie and his mom had assured him that they had a plan to escape, he sensed that something was wrong. And for his mom to be taken away sleeping like this by Leo, and for her not to wake up, was odd. Especially upsetting was hearing Leo call her a bitch.

He needed to follow. To protect his mom. His small form moved quietly, silently following them to the doorway at the end of the hall and then up the metal stairs. Leo was mumbling profanities from a flight above him as they made their way to the upper decks. Where was he taking her? One thing was for sure, Cale was *not* going to let his mom get hurt.

—

Richard groaned as Owen treated his shoulder and head wounds. Owen administered morphine before successfully removing the bullet lodged in Richard's shoulder. Thank God, for his training in the military where he'd dealt with similar wounds in Iraq and Afghanistan. Who would've thought this would happen here in the middle of the ocean, on a luxury yacht, and in spite of the extensive security protocol.

With the help of George and the second mate, Mitchell, they lifted Richard's large form onto a stretcher, and moved him from the office floor to one of the sofas in the upper living room, where the housekeeper, Anna, had laid out fresh, white bedding. Owen sat in a chair beside Richard to continue to monitor his vitals, which were all stable.

—

Peter stared at the rows of screens on the back wall of the security room, scanning for where Leo could be on this giant yacht. A few members of the staff were standing around nervously behind Peter. Suddenly his eye caught an image from the camera that overlooked the helipad. It was an image of Leo, maneuvering towards the chopper with a body over his shoulder. "Shit!" yelled Peter. "Leo's taking Mrs. White onto the chopper! We've gotta stop him!"

Peter sprinted out of the security room, grabbing two guns from the wall, while calling others to follow as backup. Captain Jeffries followed closely behind, with Don chasing directly after them. Peter took the fastest way he could to the helipad, which was the metal staircase just off the security room. The helipad was on the same floor as the bridge, on the back deck of the yacht. He took the stairs two at a time, swearing under his breath at that son of a bitch, Leo. "Fuck, Leo, you bastard," he said, picturing Leo starting up the chopper. The nerve of him, to steal what wasn't his. The chopper was one thing: a replaceable, material possession. The lady was on another level; the boss would hunt him down and kill him for taking her. Leo's life would be very short once Richard found out what was going on.

When Peter reached the top of the staircase and entered onto the helipad deck, he saw Leo hoisting Mrs. White into the back of the chopper, through the open sliding door on the side. Unexpectedly, the boy was crouched behind the chopper, craning his neck up to see what was happening. Cale looked like a small cougar ready to pounce. Peter silently handed one of the guns back to the captain, and whispered, "Back me up."

Peter then drew his gun and pointed it directly at Leo, taking a few steps closer as Leo finished placing Mrs. White inside the chopper. "You're not going anywhere, Leo," he growled.

Startled, Leo turned around, while simultaneously aiming his gun straight at Peter. "I'll shoot!" shouted Leo.

"You're a dead man if you do," Peter replied. Captain Jeffries held his gun up as well, a few steps behind Peter.

Leo's thoughts swarmed in his mind. If he died, he would not be punishing Richard or Cadence, only himself. He couldn't get shot. But he had to leave *now.* He'd take his chances. While keeping the gun pointed, he slid the fuselage door closed, not bothering to check if it was secure. He then inched beside the open pilot door, and with one swift motion, learned from many escapes during his CIA days, he climbed inside. He then slammed the door shut, while still holding the gun towards the window. Leo quickly started the chopper in a few swift motions, the sequence of steps automatic as his adrenaline surged. He saw Peter run forwards in his peripheral vision.

Peter yelled into the window. "I'll shoot you if you don't stay put!"

It was impossible to hear over the roar and wind caused by the large chopper blades beginning to turn. Peter needed to act. He had no choice but to fire. He pulled the trigger, the bullet breaking through the glass of the pilot's window, narrowly missing Leo. Backed against the pilot's seat, Leo's heart pounded as he aimed his gun right back at Peter. His shot narrowly missed Peter and hit Captain Jeffries in the leg. Peter fired again, but his aim was off due to the gusts of wind blowing in his face, and the shot flew in front of the chopper. The rotor was now in full motion, the large chopper lifting off the Great White's helipad. Peter aimed and fired again, this time hitting the pilot's door, the bullet being deflected so again not reaching its target.

Leo focused on lifting off as quickly as he possibly could. He narrowly avoided yet another bullet that came through the broken hole in the window, whizzing past his face and crashing through the opposite window. "Come on, come on, boy, come on," he said, breathing heavily as he guided the chopper higher up. "Yes, yes, yes," he said, "fucking yes!" He heard crying behind him. Was she waking up already?

"Don't crash!" sobbed a small voice. He craned his neck around and saw the boy clinging to his mother.

"How the *fuck* did you get in here, kid?!"

"I'm not letting you hurt mom," he replied through his sobs. "Please take us home," he begged. Leo quickly weighed the option of tossing the boy out the window, but the chopper was high enough above the helipad that it could kill the boy to be dropped from this height. Plus, it would just slow Leo down. Every second counted. He knew Peter would be mobilizing additional off-site security forces to try and intercept the chopper, so the quicker he could fly them back to San Diego, the better. He knew Richard and Peter well enough to know what the plan would be, and he would outsmart them by being one step ahead. Yep, he was going directly back to San Diego, back to where this all started. And a hell of a lot quicker that this monstrous yacht had taken to get to this point.

The boy continued bawling. "Shut up, kid. I don't wanna hear another sound. You and your mom will live, but only if you shut the fuck up," he threatened.

Cale reacted with whimpers, doing his utmost to remain silent, yet shaking from the fear of sneaking on board just as the sliding door was about to close. Leo didn't catch him as he was focused on shooting Peter and fleeing. Cale's legs were barely in when the door shut. What was even scarier, was being shot at, and the sound of glass smashing only a few feet away from where he was curled beside his mom. Cale thought for sure that this was it. They were all dead. It was so noisy and Leo was crazy. But he'd rather be here than held captive by Richard White, who was even crazier. Cale closed his eyes and clung to his mom as they flew up into the black night sky.

Chapter Thirty-Eight

"FUCK YOU, LEO!" PETER screamed, his head looking up towards the belly of the chopper as its lit form grew dimmer and disappeared into the darkness. He radioed the paramedic. "Owen, Captain Jeffries' been shot in the leg, please come up to the helipad as soon as you can," he ordered. Captain Jeffries was sitting and pressing on his upper thigh, blood soaking through his white pants. Don, who'd followed them and witnessed the whole scene, sat beside the captain, asking if he could pull off his belt to tie the wound and stop the bleeding. Captain Jeffries nodded, a weak but grateful smile on his sweating face.

"Listen, guys, I gotta run and get security in place to intercept that son of a bitch to ensure Mrs. White and the boy's safety. Standing orders are that the family and their safety is top priority. Don will take care of you, Captain Jeffries, and Owen will be up shortly, so hang tight."

"I'll be fine," muttered Captain Jeffries, clearly in pain but trying to put on a tough act.

Peter raced downstairs, stopping by where Richard was sleeping, temporarily knocked out by the morphine. "Boss, I got this covered. I know what calls you'd want me to make," he said, as he strode past Richard towards the security room.

—

Sophie was beyond mad about being locked up in the isolation room for the second time in less than twenty-four hours. Like her father, she felt emotions very strongly, and her anger had a physical edge to it. She literally hurt inside as she threw herself across the bed and sobbed. She was glad, though, that she'd seemed to get through to Peter about checking out Leo's video footage. What a creep! He deserved to be thrown off her father's yacht and eaten by the sharks. But her thoughts were cut short by a distant bang. It sounded like a gunshot coming from the floors above. Normally, very little could be heard from down here, but the sound was unmistakable.

She leapt from the bed towards the intercom on the wall, and pressed the alarm button, knowing that it would grab someone's attention. She needed to get out of here. She felt so alone and trapped. No response. She tried again, pressing the button hard and more than once. Nothing. She then tried paging security directly. Peter's voice came over the intercom. He sounded rushed and out of breath. "Can't help you now, Sophie, we're dealing with an issue. I'll be by later," he said, cutting out abruptly.

The time passed by slowly. Sophie's mind went to places of worry: anxious about how her mom was doing; worrying about Cale alone in his room, no doubt wondering where she was. She couldn't believe it when the door finally opened, but it wasn't Peter this time, it was Anna, the housekeeper. She was a short, energetic Filipino woman who had a kind smile, and dark, bright eyes. Her black hair was tied back in a French braid. She smelled like roses. "Thank you for coming," said Sophie, holding back her tears. "What was that loud sound I heard earlier?"

"Your father was shot, but he's doing well," said Anna, looking anxiously, yet kindly, at Sophie.

"What? I want to see him. Now!" Sophie mobilized, feeling a rush of fear for the man she'd just spent time wishing she'd never have to see again.

"Okay, dear, follow me," said Anna, leading them back through the engine floor, and up several floors to the upper living room, where Richard was asleep on one of the long white sofas. On a nearby sofa, Captain Jeffries lay down while Owen treated a wound on his leg. She noticed Captain Jeffries wincing in pain, and felt sorry for him. The air had a faint smell of antiseptic mixed with ocean air.

"How's my father?" Sophie asked the man sitting next to Richard. She didn't recognize him. He looked Asian, maybe Japanese, and was slim and dressed in a white captain-looking uniform.

"He's going to be fine," he replied. "He had enough morphine that he fell deeply asleep and the worst of the pain is over. He is lucky that the shot wasn't a few inches lower. By the way, I'm Mitchell, the second mate, and you must be Sophie?" He was polite and made her feel at ease.

"Yes, nice to meet you, Mitchell. And thanks for helping

him," she replied.

"All I did was help get him in here on the stretcher. It was all Owen's work removing the bullet," he replied, glancing over at Owen, who was focusing intently on his task of fixing up the captain. "He's good, really good. He used to fix up badly hurt soldiers in the Middle East."

"Thank you for helping him, Owen," she said, raising her voice only enough for him to catch her words, but not wanting to disrupt his focus.

He looked up briefly, said, "No problem," and went back to work.

"I'm glad my father got help from someone so good," she said, glancing again at Mitchell. She then looked down at her father. He was bandaged from his chest up to his shoulder, as well as around the side of his head. The bandages, in combination with his many scars, made it look like he was in rougher shape than he probably was. "Did Leo do this?" she asked Mitchell. The question had been burning in her mind since she learned that her father had been shot.

"Yep, he shot Mr. White from behind, in his office," he said, confirming her suspicion. "Coward," he added.

"I thought so. Leo's a monster. Where's he now?" she asked, looking around anxiously.

"He's taken the chopper and—"

"Escaped with your mother and brother," answered Peter, who'd suddenly appeared behind them. "Sophie, I'm very sorry. We're doing everything we can to get them back, dear."

Sophie's world froze. Fear coursed through her body, and she started shaking uncontrollably. She turned to face Peter. "Noooo!" she cried. She had never felt more alone. Her only family here was a knocked out father whom she barely new and deeply resented.

"We're tracking the chopper, and our guys will intercept Leo wherever he lands. Don't you worry, Sophie, we'll get your mother back."

"What about Cale?" she blurted. "He can't be hurt by that madman!"

"Don't worry, Sophie, we'll make sure that doesn't happen. It may be that he gets brought back safely to his father. Leo was against having the boy on here from the beginning, so he may be planning to hand him back to his father," Peter added, tipping Sophie off for the most likely outcome, given Richard's wish from earlier in the day.

"What? Who does he think he is? He can't pull me and my brother apart! That's heartless," she said, swiping tears away with her delicate hand. She turned and pulled her long hair forwards to hide her face. Her mind was a mix of thoughts. On the one hand, her dad would love to see Cale, and Cale was miserable on this yacht. But if her mom was separated from Cale, she'd be even more distraught than she already was.

"Well, we don't know anything yet, but I promise that we are doing our best to catch Leo, and to make sure your mother and brother are safe. You can discuss the details with your father when he wakes up, my dear. And if I know Richard White, he'll make sure that your mother returns to you both here again. I'd bet my life on it."

"But mom can't be separated from Cale. She'd never be happy," Sophie replied, still swiping at her tears.

"Like I said, it's too early to know. The chopper will be in the air for at least four or five more hours as it seems he's heading to San Diego, but we'll know more as time goes on. I gotta go back to the security room. Try to get some rest, as it's gonna be a long night, honey," Peter said, softening his voice to soothe Sophie, whose tears were now morphing into sobs. She went to a comfy white armchair beside Richard's makeshift bed. Curling up in a ball she cried for a long time before falling into a nightmare-filled sleep.

Chapter Thirty-Nine

I FELT MYSELF WAKING, disoriented and hearing a loud noise surrounding me. My eyes fluttered open, and shock filled my system as the realization set in that I was on … on a … helicopter!

"Mom, are you awake?" asked Cale, who was beside me, his small arms encircling me as best he could on the row of leather seats.

"Where, what ... what's happening?" I asked, awareness creeping in, my mind trying to latch onto reality. I'd been drugged with the sleep medication meant for Richard.

Cale leaned in so he could speak directly into my ear. "Mom, Leo stole you and took the helicopter from the yacht. I followed you, and snuck on just before it took off." I glanced ahead but couldn't recognize Leo from behind the back of the pilot's seat. The helicopter was loud enough that he likely couldn't hear us, plus he wore a headset.

"Oh, Cale, I'm so glad you're safe," I said, as I hugged him tightly back. "Where's he taking us?"

"Dunno. He told me that I had to shut the eff up or we may not … live," Cale's voice broke and he began crying into my shoulder. I stroked his soft curls, comforting him as best I could in my groggy state.

"How long have we been flying, honey?"

"Not sure, but it feels like a long time. I don't have a watch and can't see the time from back here."

"Sophie … she couldn't get on here with you?" I asked, my anxieties now laser focusing on my daughter. I felt an overwhelming fear at the thought of her being left behind.

"No. I think she was in the isolation room. I heard her yelling from the hall when she was being taken there. You were asleep, mom. I was hiding under your bed when Leo came and stole you," he explained, my brain flashing to the images of what this must've been like for my sweet, little boy. How terrified he must've been.

"Oh, Cale, you're so brave to have followed us. You must've been so terrified, honey," I said, as I continued to stroke his hair, planting a kiss on its soft top.

"Mom, I'd *never* let you go alone," he asserted, his innocent young voice like music to my ears.

"Oh, Cale, I love you *so much.* Everything will work out. We'll find a way to get Sophie back once we're safely on land," I said, now beginning to wonder why Leo had taken me in my drugged state. The pieces of the story didn't make sense. He'd made a deal to take Cale and me that night by lifeboat, while Richard was drugged. Now with the scenario flipped, and me drugged, I was surprised that he'd risked stealing me.

"Oh, mom, it was so scary with Leo and Peter shooting at

each other," he continued.

"What?" I shuddered in shock to hear that Richard's top two security guys, who I thought were close, would try to kill each other.

"Yeah, it was so loud. Peter almost shot Leo, breaking the windows and everything. He fired a few shots that felt like they'd break the helicopter. Leo was shooting back at Peter too. It seemed like someone got shot, but I couldn't see for sure as I was hiding here with you. I was really scared we might get shot. Oh, mom, it was so bad," Cale said, his voice cracking again as he relayed this nightmarish story.

"Oh, sweetheart, I'm so very sorry. I'm *so* glad you're okay. But I wish … I wish Sophie was with us," I added. Then curiosity overcame me. "Cale, where was Richard?" I asked, realizing his name had not yet been mentioned. His persona was always in the back of my mind. But he wasn't part of this story, which was unlike him. He was always in control, front and center in the drama that he forced to unfold in his dream world.

"I dunno. He wasn't in your room, and I didn't see him on the stairs or on the helipad. I'm not sure where he was," Cale said. "But I hope I *never* have to see him again," he added.

"Oh, Cale, I'll do *everything* I can to make sure we don't have to go back and that we get Sophie back as well," I promised, my voice confident, trying to avoid the trickle of doubt I felt when I thought about our safety being in Leo's hands. He'd given me an uneasy feeling ever since I met him, with the shower video solidifying my distrust. And now here we were at his mercy on a chopper high in the dark night sky. I was tempted to move to the front and take a seat beside him, but it seemed even noisier up there with the air blowing in from the broken windows. I wanted to demand answers, but thought better, as I didn't want to distract him from safely flying us to wherever he planned to land.

"They're an hour-and-a-half away from San Diego, Pete," answered the deep voice through one of the radios in the security room. "We've mobilized two teams on the ground, as well as two choppers to track them, so Leo can't get far. We'll have a team wherever he lands to intercept them."

"Good, Mike. And to be clear, Leo must be shot on sight, but not at the risk of harming the lady. Getting the lady safely back to Mr. White is our top priority. The boy needs to be brought to a safe location where he can call the authorities to connect him back with his father. The boy is not to be brought back to the yacht. Is the team clear on that?"

"Yes, all clear. Roger that," answered Mike.

"Good. Keep me posted, and I'll check in for another update at the one-hour mark," said Peter.

"For sure. Signing off," said Mike. It was good to have Mike as the lead of their US security team. He'd been in Richard's employ for the last two years, during which time the final planning for the abduction onto the Great White had taken place. Like Owen, Mike was ex-military, and was bright, confident, and disgruntled enough with society that he was happy to work on an illegal operation in return for loads of cash under the cover of the White Operation, or White Op as they called it in code.

Peter was tired. It was almost two o'clock in the morning.

The adrenaline helped keep him sharp, but his old body felt exhausted from the evening's events. Plus, the shoot-out had sucked a lot of his energy. In the meantime, he decided to go over and check on Richard. He saw that Richard was stirring, so it was good timing. Owen had dozed off on an armchair close by to both of his patients. A storm had blown in unexpectedly, so the yacht moved more than usual, and the sounds of thunder and lightning brought an eerie feeling to the dimly lit upper living room.

"What … how?" Richard mumbled. He reached to touch his face, as if it were a habit he did upon waking. Was he feeling for his scars? Feeling for his mask? Who knew, Peter thought. Richard's eyes flickered, then suddenly opened, as if he willed himself to become alert, his sheer determination overpowering the morphine. His eyes locked with Peter's. "What's going on, Peter?" he asked in a ragged voice.

"You were shot, boss. By Leo," Peter explained plainly, knowing all too well Richard's impatience with people not getting straight to the point.

"That fucking …" Richard began, then his gaze fell on his daughter, curled up in a ball on the armchair across from where he lay. "Is Sophie okay? Where's Cadence?" His next two questions came in quick succession.

Peter took a deep breath, bracing for what he had to relay. Please don't shoot the messenger, he thought. "Sophie's fine, just rattled. I'm sorry to report that Leo stole the chopper, and flew off with both your wife and the boy," he said, trying to be calm.

"What? How could you let this happen?" Richard growled, trying to sit up, but wincing from the sharp pain in his shoulder.

"Boss, I got to him just before he took off. I fired a few

times. I tried to kill the bastard. Captain Jeffries is my witness. He was shot in the crossfire. It was a battle. I never … um … expected Leo would do something like *this.* Shoot you and then—"

"Aaargh!" Richard roared, now sitting up despite the pain. "You let him get away!"

"Boss, it's under control. Mike's on top of things back in San Diego. We've got two teams on the ground, as well as two choppers tracking Leo. He won't be able to escape from us, as we'll know exactly when and where he plans on landing. He'll be killed on sight, and your wife will be brought back here. The boy will be sent back to his father, as per your wishes, boss," Peter explained. He tried to sound confident and on top of things, but inside he felt a mounting anxiety over having failed to kill Leo here on the Great White.

"You sound so sure, Peter. Just like I was sure that I would never lose Cadence again," Richard seethed. He shook his head, his green eyes dark with rage.

"Boss, rest assured that this plan will be executed exactly as I've said. I swear, you can count on getting your woman back."

"Would you bet your life on it, Peter?"

Peter swallowed. He knew there was only one answer that would satisfy Richard White. He knew with certainty that giving a nebulous answer was akin to risking his life. "Yes, I would, boss," he replied without hesitation.

"Okay, then, Peter. I truly hope you're right. For all of our sakes."

Sophie had been awakened by Richard's roar. She was emotionally torn, glad that her father was awake as she'd been worried for him. Yet at the same time, she was angry over what he was saying. She couldn't help but interject into the conversation. "Don't threaten Peter, father. Leo's the bad guy here," she said, uncurling herself from her sleeping position in the armchair across from them.

"Sophie, please don't interfere. I'm glad you're safe, honey. I'm so relieved to have one of my ladies still with me. We'll get your mother back soon, I *promise* you, Sophie," he said.

"She won't want to leave Cale," Sophie said, matter-of-factly.

"I know," said Richard, "but that won't be her choice. The boy will be in better hands with his … father," he said, barely choking out the word. "He will be safer there than with me," he said, his eyes looking into the distance. Sophie caught a look of extreme sadness in his eyes. What had made Richard this way, Sophie wondered. He alternated from super confident and in control, to like a monster and even very sad. Yet it was hard to feel sorry for this man who was calling all the shots on her life, as well as her mother's and brother's, without considering *any* of their wishes.

"We're all like pawns on your chess board, aren't we? How can you think it's okay to dictate our lives and pull our family apart like this?" she asked.

"I am trying to bring us *together*, not pull us apart. I tried giving it a chance with your brother, but I am not his father and never can be. It's better if he's with a father who can … can love him. My focus will be on you and your mother, the two most cherished and loved women in the world."

"If you love someone, you let them *choose* where they want to be. Love isn't about controlling, it's about setting free."

"Sophie, don't get philosophical on me. You are twelve years old. You will understand when you are older. Sometimes the people you love don't know what they need. It's the people who love them most who know what is best."

Sophie closed her eyes and took a long, deep breath, trying to ease her tension. Her heart pounded. Her father could rile her up like nobody else. How she missed her dad, Christian, and his calm nature. Her tears came involuntarily. "I miss them," she whimpered, avoiding Richard's eyes. Those intense green eyes she knew so well, that bore into her, trying desperately to read her, but failing to understand what she truly needed.

Richard tried to stand, groaning from the pain. Owen was also awake, and had been checking on Captain Jeffries, but turned abruptly at the pained sound Richard made. "I recommend staying seated, or better yet lying down, Mr. White," said Owen. "You're quite weak and lost some blood. It's best if you can rest as much as possible," he clarified. "Ideally, we'd be flying you to a hospital, if the chopper wasn't gone." Owen's voice gave away his disgust at what had taken place. "And given the circumstances, we can't risk your stitches breaking and an infection."

"I just wanted to go and hug my daughter," said Richard, his voiced edged with defeat.

Sophie felt sad for her father. She was so confused; one minute she hated his guts, and the next she wanted to tell him that she loved him. But she needed to contain her feelings, and figure out how to get her way if she was ever going to get back to her family. Arguing with him non-stop wasn't going to work. He wasn't reasonable nor logical, and reasoning with him would get her nowhere. Instead, she listened to her instincts. She stood and walked across to his sofa, sat beside him and hugged him gently, careful not to press against his bandaged shoulder. The feeling of his arms around her, and the comfort his warmth brought, made her tears flow more. She cried for what felt like a long time.

Richard relished having Sophie in his arms. He loved being able to comfort her. To be needed. He stroked her soft, long hair and gently kissed her head. He felt intense sadness over his daughter's suffering, and for having lost her mother to the man he'd wrongly trusted. How could Leo have done this? This breach of trust was too hard to bear. And he shuddered at the thought of Leo making a pass at him. How could he not have seen the signs all these years? He was angry at himself, which brought on that damned voice in his head, yet again.

You think you're brilliant, and on top of every little detail? Yet you miss a glaringly obvious one right in front of your face! Shame on you. And this fuck up led you to lose Cadence again after only two days here. Two days! So much for brilliance, more like a stupidity.

Richard bit his tongue, holding tight to his daughter and willing the voice to leave his exhausted brain alone. Yes, he had fucked up, but no, he would *not* give up. He would bring Cadence back and make a life for the three of them. No matter what, the three of them would be the White family, and live without this constant drama and fear. "I'll make sure things get better, Sophie. Much better. I love you and promise you that."

Sophie eventually cried herself to sleep in her father's arms, despite feeling scared for her mother and brother … and herself.

Chapter Forty

Leo's mind had been circling through multiple scenarios. He knew how Richard worked, and fully anticipated being intercepted by a team wherever he landed. Orders would be to shoot him on scene, and his only chance was to land somewhere that would be possible to escape from. Like somewhere crowded where they wouldn't be able to open fire as easily and he could disappear into a crowd. He was quick and crafty when it came to escape, and stood a good chance in the right area.

Another tempting option was to ensure that Richard never got the bitch back. The way to increase those odds was to land where the cops or military would be plentiful so that she could get immediate help. That scenario would also decrease the odds of Richard's guys killing him, but dramatically increase his chance of arrest. It would feel damned good though, to know that Richard would be without the love of his life, suffering alone for the rest of his days, just like Leo. But how good would it feel to be in a foul jail cell, while Richard lived in some opulent place? Maybe, he strategized, he could cop a plea and help the FBI find Richard once and for all. He could negotiate being set free with a changed identity, while Richard rotted in jail, or better yet, was executed. It tugged at Leo's heart to think of Richard dead, despite the massive rejection he'd suffered. And what if he couldn't plea bargain his way out of a sentence? Or what if . . . what if Richard paid off the right people and ended up killing him anyway? That was entirely possible. Richard's wallet seemed as deep as the ocean, and there was no telling what he'd do when provoked. The odds were already heavily stacked against Leo. There seemed to be no ideal solution to his dilemma.

"I need to know where he's taking us," I said to Cale. The grogginess was starting to wear off, and as much as I didn't want to startle or provoke Leo, I also wanted to know the plan so I could protect Cale and increase my odds of getting our lives, and Sophie's, back. "I'm going to speak with Leo, Cale. Stay here, I'll be right back," I said, kissing his cheek.

"Mom, I'm scared," said Cale, his voice barely audible over the sound of the rotor, but his eyes wide with fear.

"Don't be, Cale. We'll be home soon. We'll be safe," I assured him. "I just need to make a plan with Leo for when we land." I squeezed his small hand, then maneuvered my way from the back row of seats, past the two seats in the middle, and up to the passenger seat beside Leo. I sat down, startling him slightly as evidenced by his flinch. It seemed even noisier up front.

He glared at me with his steel blue eyes, his face tight and angry, and his red hair sweaty and disheveled. He reached down and grabbed a headset, motioning for me to put it on. His nasty, gruff voice was now clear in my ears. "We're less than an hour away," he stated. "And then I *never* have to see you again. Hallelujah." He scowled as he glared over at me.

I hadn't realized just how much he detested me. What had I done to him to deserve this level of disdain? Who cares, I thought, so long as I could keep things civil and safe. "Where are you taking us, Leo?" I asked, eyeing him skeptically.

"I'm taking us back to San Diego, and I'm gonna land at the naval base. So that they don't think we're a threat, I'm gonna radio ahead and tell them that I ran out of fuel and need to do an emergency landing there. I know that area well and can disappear quickly cause Richard's guys will be on us like flies on shit. They're less likely to get into a shoot out there with all those Navy Officers and security guards around. And the authorities will be able to protect you and the boy, so that Richard never gets you back," he explained.

"Leo, why don't you stay with us? Or land by a police station? I can explain that you saved us," I said, knowing exactly what types of men Richard hired, and the speed with which they would snatch us. Being that it was the middle of the night, Leo could provide some degree of protection for us, as I wouldn't stand a chance on my own if help didn't come quickly.

"I would get fucking arrested. The cops may be good for you, but not so good for me," he said, his voice increasingly sarcastic and irritated.

"I'd make sure you didn't get arrested, Leo. You saved Cale and me. I owe you, and I give you my word that I'd vouch for you," I explained.

"I only took you to pay that fucker back. Let me be clear, I hate everything about you, Mrs. *White*," he said, stretching out the last name with disdain. "And I didn't intend to save the boy, he snuck on. My only intent is to make Richard White suffer like he deserves."

I didn't know what to say. Hatred emanated so strongly from this man. Our lives were in his hands, and I needed to think quickly. The only thing we had in common was needing to escape from Richard's men. Couldn't we figure out a better plan together than apart? "You'd make Richard suffer more if you help us catch him, once and for all," I said, trying my best to reason with this cold-hearted man.

"I dunno, those guys are quick and if they see me as a threat, I'm dead. I'd rather land and get the hell away. I'm faster on my own, and you're a liability to be around."

"I still think you'd have a better chance if the police were involved. Together we could help them catch Richard," I repeated.

"Yeah, it would be good to see him rotting in jail. But not at the cost of my ass in a jail cell. No way, not gonna happen. We're landing at the naval base and that's that. I'm not gonna rot in jail while Richard drinks champagne and eats caviar, while watching the sunset," he sneered.

"Why did you do this, Leo? Why did you leave Richard? And why didn't he stop you?" I asked, curiosity getting the better of me.

"Long story. But in the end, I shot the bastard," he said, gazing ahead.

"What? Where?" I asked, shocked at this revelation.

"In the shoulder."

"But … but you were loyal to him all these years," I said. "What made you turn?"

"He fired me," said Leo, plain and simple.

"Did he see the videos?" I asked.

"Nope, but let's be clear on those, woman. I had zero interest in watching *you.* God knows why he's obsessed with you," he said, shaking his head.

"I didn't ask for his obsession. I didn't want his money or lifestyle. I just wanted to be left alone," I said, trying not to take offense at his hurtful words.

"Funny, I would've done anything for that man. *Anything.* And all he does is pine after *you.* An ungrateful, stuck up bitch," he said. He gazed ahead, a clear look of loss and hurt beneath his intense rage.

It finally sank in. He *loved* Richard. He was recording Richard naked, for no other reason but to watch him. Despite his nasty words, I felt a moment of pity for this man who was rejected after so many years of loyalty and unrequited love. I didn't respond, and sensed that Leo wanted to be alone. I slipped off the headset and moved back to Cale, sitting beside him and holding his warm body in my arms. We would get away. We would not be taken back to the Great White, I vowed, as we flew through the starry night sky.

Chapter Forty-One

"Boss, it's a half-hour till they land. Our choppers will be following them shortly, and the two ground teams are in strategic locations where they can intercept quickly."

Richard stared up at Peter, while holding his sleeping daughter protectively in his arms. He loved the warmth of her. The fact that she was his. An extension of him and Cadence, and their love that seemed so elusive. "I'd like to speak directly to Mike, to confirm the details," he said, not able to trust anyone but himself. Leo's betrayal felt raw. Traitorous. It made him doubt whether he could trust Peter to execute such a critical plan.

"Sure, but you can trust me that it's under control, boss," Peter said, looking nervous yet trying to sound confident. His anxiety had been mounting ever since Richard's earlier threat. He hung onto the fact that Richard needed him, even more so now that Leo was gone. But he couldn't help but contemplate how he'd escape if he had to do so in a hurry.

"Get me the satellite phone, now," ordered Richard, trying to speak quieter than he normally would, while Sophie continued to sleep deeply. Her deep, rhythmic breathing helped calm Richard's nerves.

"Okay," said Peter, rushing back to the security room.

"Sophie, I love you so much," Richard whispered, gazing down at her. "I'm sorry this has been difficult. I promise you that things will get better. You can trust me, darling, I will always protect you." Peter came back moments later, handing him the satellite phone, having already pressed redial to reach Mike.

"Hi Pete," answered Mike.

"It's Richard."

"Boss, you okay?" he asked.

"I've been better. I need to make it very clear, Mike, that Cadence *cannot* get hurt. I need her back. Absolutely nothing can go wrong," Richard asserted.

"You can count on me, boss. Between the two choppers and our two ground crews, they won't be able to get far. I'll make sure we get Mrs. White back," he said.

"You know I will not accept failure, right Mike?" asked Richard. Mike didn't appreciate the threatening undertone. He was not one to be intimidated, yet he felt uneasy about the ever so slight chance that something could go wrong. Unless they could take over the helicopter in the air, which was too risky, there wasn't a way to predict exactly how this would go down. It all depended on where Leo decided to land. The more public a place it was, or if it was near a cop shop, the greater the risk of them not being able to seize the lady.

"Yes, boss, I know. You hired me because I'm the best. I'll make sure we get your lady back." Mike swallowed, glad that

Richard couldn't see the hint of doubt he felt.

"Good. And I don't want to see that boy ever again. There's no way he can come back with her. Is that clear?"

"One hundred percent clear, boss."

"Good. And I want Leo dead. I want him shot more than once so there is no doubt of him surviving. Clear?"

"Yep, one hundred percent clear," replied Mike, put off by Richard's condescending tone, but the money made it well worth it. But what if something went wrong?

"Good. Now go get the job done, and there will be an extra bonus if you execute it quickly and with no problems," said Richard.

"Alright. Signing off, boss."

Richard hung up, feeling Sophie stir. He had tried to speak quietly, but the conversation had awakened her. She stretched and her eyes gradually opened, looking into his. She flinched slightly, as the realization of where she was set in.

"What's happening?" she asked.

"I was just speaking with the head of my security team back in San Diego. Your mother is landing shortly, and we should get word of her being on her way back to us in about half an hour."

Sophie looked away, nervous for her mom and Cale. "I hope they land safely," she said. "Leo's crazy and I'm scared for them," she added.

"My team will make sure they are safe. You can count on that."

"I hope so, father," she said, pulling herself off his lap.

"I know so, honey," Richard replied. "I'm going to use my bathroom and change my clothes," said Sophie. "I'll be back soon."

"Okay, honey," he said. He missed her warmth already, and shuddered at the fact that the events of the next half hour were so critical and out of his direct control.

I could see the lights in the distance, and felt the beginning of our descent. "Cale, when we land we'll need to run quickly to the nearest building. We both need to scream for help as Richard's men will be trying to capture us. Hold tightly to my hand. I won't let you go," I said.

"I'm scared, mom."

"Oh, Cale. It'll be okay. The naval base is a safe place. There will be lots of help around us there. I'll lead us to safety and we'll be okay, my love." I kissed his curls, and gave him a long hug. I felt terrible for the trauma he'd endured over the past two days, which felt more like two hundred.

"About ten minutes till we land," Leo shouted from the front.

"Okay," I yelled back. I saw another chopper in the distance, heading our way. Richard's men?

We continued to descend, and the lights below became brighter. The other helicopter was now flying parallel to us, so there was no doubt it was going to land wherever we did. I caught sight of another one behind us, through the opposite window. Richard never settled for basic. I felt waves of anger and fear coursing through me.

I could now make out the shapes of buildings below. Of a few cars driving in the middle of the night. The blackness of the ocean below us felt ominous. I thought about Sophie, praying that she was okay. I forced myself to take deep breaths to combat my mounting anxiety. My heart raced and my palms felt cold and clammy as I held onto Cale, bracing for the landing. I could see the battleships at the naval base. The lights of the buildings. Please, *please* let there be help. I said a silent prayer in the moments before we touched down.

Everything happened quickly from the moment we landed on the pavement. Leo was out and running, while simultaneously another chopper was landing, and a van was heading right for us. We were in some sort of open space, with buildings all around us. I opened the door, hopping quickly off and lifting Cale into my arms, as I feared holding hands would risk him being pulled away from me. I ran in the opposite direction from where Leo had gone. "Help us!" I screamed. "HELP! HELP!"

Cale joined in, his little voice yelling as loud as he could. "HELP! PLEASE HELP!"

A gun fired somewhere behind us, but not at us. I was running as fast as I could, Cale clinging to me so tightly that I could barely breathe. We were being chased. "HELP US!"

Two officers dressed in navy uniforms came out of one of the buildings ahead. "Who's there?" one of them yelled.

"HELP!" I screamed, and then felt arms grab me from behind. I did what I'd been planning to do during the helicopter ride; what I knew I must do if it came to this. I released my son. "Run Cale! Run and get help!"

"No, I'm not leaving you mom!" He tried to reach for me but I felt myself being dragged backwards.

"Run to those men before it's too late, Cale!" I screamed at him.

Cale stood for a moment, looking frozen with fear, then bolted towards the men who were now running in our direction.

I struggled to escape the tight grasp with every ounce of my strength. More shots were fired behind me. A flurry of bullets. Screams. Chaos.

A deafening blast numbed my senses, as the man who was holding me from behind was shot and crumpled to the ground. Those arms were replaced by someone else's, who held me around my neck this time. "Put your guns down or she dies!" shouted Leo.

"Please, no!" I felt his gun touching the side of my head. Terror engulfed me.

One of the Navy Officers was in the distance with Cale, and the other was approaching us with his gun pointed at us. "Let the woman go!" he ordered.

"It's those guys you want, they're trying to abduct her!" shouted Leo.

"Get more help!" I yelled, knowing that two Navy Officers were no match for Richard's crew.

Before he could even react, a bullet hit the officer, throwing him to the ground.

"Let her go, Leo, or you're dead," said a man I didn't recognize.

"No chance, Mike," said Leo, backing us up in the direction of the building where Cale and the other officer had disappeared. Leo was rough, dragging me away with him. I could smell his sweat, and feel its dampness on my neck.

"I mean it, Leo," said Mike, now flanked by two men. I noticed another helicopter landing near the first. "I've got a big team, you're gonna die if you don't let her go *now,*" threatened Mike.

My body shook from the recoil as Leo fired a series of shots at Mike and his men. The man on the right fell, while the others were now running towards us. Leo fired more shots, hitting the one on Mike's left.

I could now hear an alarm sounding, and sirens approaching in the distance. Someone punched Leo in the head, knocking him off balance. It was enough force that he released me, but then I was caught by someone else as I stumbled backwards.

Leo bolted towards the open door of the building, a shot hitting his arm. "Damn it!" he yelled, as he disappeared inside the building.

"Cale!" I yelled. "Don't hit my son!"

"Your son's safe," said the officer who held onto me, while other officers arrived at the scene. "He's inside."

It was Mike who'd shot Leo. As he ran towards us pointing his gun at the officer who held me, he said, "Give me the lady or I'm gonna shoot."

The door to the building suddenly swung open and Leo fired at Mike, a perfectly aimed shot striking his forehead. He fell to the ground, a pool of blood forming around his head. And as quickly as Leo appeared, he was gone again, disappearing into the building. It bought just enough time for the combination of naval officers and the arriving police officers to overpower Richard's men. One of their vans sped away, while two other men fled on foot, the officers in pursuit.

"Let's get you out of here," said the naval officer who was holding me, as shock took over and I started to shake uncontrollably.

"I need my son, Cale. Where's my son?" I cried.

As we entered the building, Cale ran into my arms. "Mom!" I'd never hugged him tighter.

Chapter Forty-Two

"WHAT?" YELLED RICHARD INTO the satellite phone. "Cadence got away and Mike's dead? How could you guys *fuck up* this badly?" he asked.

"The naval base was teaming with officers. And Leo had her at gunpoint; he wouldn't let her go. Half of our team were shot down. We … we just couldn't get her without risking her life," explained Bob, who was Mike's right-hand man.

"Excuses. Nothing but excuses for a botched job. I want you to track her. The remaining team needs to get as much intel as possible, is that clear?"

"Yes, boss. We're on it." Truth be told, Bob was terrified. He'd heard rumours about what Richard was capable of. He swallowed, breathing rapidly, hoping that the sound wasn't audible through the phone connection.

"You had better figure out a way to get Cadence back here. If not, there *will* be consequences."

Bob felt like telling Richard off, and going into hiding, but there was no hiding from Richard White. He was shaken by the death of his closest friend, Mike, right in front of his eyes. He hated that he was trapped in the White Op. He'd talked to Mike about getting out last year, as he didn't feel right about abducting kids, but Mike's warning still rang in his ears: "Once you're in the White Op, you only quit if you're dead."

"Bob, are you still there?"

"Ah, yeah, boss. We're on it."

"There's no other choice. Get Cadence back. That's your top priority. And then you need to find Leo!" he shouted and hung up.

Peter stood there, terrified of Richard's wrath. Richard's eyes bore into his with a look of disgust. "You lost your bet. You bet your life on this, Peter, and here we are," he seethed.

"The naval base … it wasn't at all what any of us would've expected. A major curveball, boss."

"That team is world class and cost a fortune; handling major curveballs is part of their fucking job description. But the fact remains that Leo should never have been able to leave. And that falls on you, Peter," he said.

"I'll make up for it. I'll protect you and the girl. We'll figure out a way to get Mrs. White back; she'll want to see her girl again." Peter tried to sound as confident as possible, despite his mounting unease.

"It's actions that speak. Your words don't hold much weight now."

"Give me another chance, boss. I've been loyal to you for so long."

"It's only because of your years of loyal service that I am

giving you one last chance. We need to figure out a plan … and that plan *better* work, as I don't have the patience for any more mistakes."

Peter swallowed.

Sophie entered the office then and asked, "Did they land yet?"

"They did, Sophie," said Richard, taking in the sight of his sweet daughter; thankful that he didn't lose her last night. "Your mother and the boy are with the police."

Sophie was relieved, but knew enough not to show her joy. "They're not hurt?"

"It seems that they are just fine. Leo got away, though," Richard said.

"I hope he goes away forever," Sophie said.

"No, Sophie. I will find him and he will be punished. He does *not* deserve to live."

Sophie stared at her father, then at Peter, who looked visibly shaken. The whole scenario was just too much; all she wanted was to be back home in their apartment. She desperately missed her mom and dad, and brother. Yet she couldn't help feeling a tiny bit sorry for her father, with his bandaged head and shoulder, his scarred face, and worst of all feeling like the family he dreamed of was now torn apart.

"Christian?" I said into the phone, my voice cracking.

Christian felt a tidal wave of relief as he heard his wife's voice. "Cadence! Thank God, you're okay. And the kids?"

"It's so good to hear your voice. I love you so much. Cale's with me. Here—" I said, as I passed the receiver to Cale, who was sitting on my lap at the FBI's local field office in San Diego.

"Daddy!" Cale exclaimed.

"Cale, I'm so happy you're okay. Listen, you're a brave boy, son."

"Dad, where are you?"

"I'm out on a Navy ship that's been trying to track the yacht you were on. I wanted to be as close to you as I could. They're flying me back by helicopter soon, so I should be there in a couple of hours. Oh, God, I've missed you. Can I speak to Sophie?"

Cale handed me the phone and said, "Mom … Dad's asking for Sophie."

I took the receiver and said, "Christian, she's … she's …" and I started sobbing.

"Honey, it's okay. Calm down. I love you. It'll all be okay, Cadence," he soothed from miles away.

"She's with *him*," I blurted.

"WHAT? Our Sophie's out at sea with that lunatic! Oh my God, we need to get her back," Christian shouted so loudly that I cringed and started to cry.

"I know, Christian," I said, trying to fight back the tears that had already started rolling down my cheeks.

Christian, immediately regretting his outburst, said softly, "We'll get her back, honey. Don't worry, we'll have our family back soon. The FBI team on the case is outstanding, and I know they'll zero in on the yacht soon."

"Oh, Christian, I hope so," I said, never underestimating the power of Richard White.

"You both get some rest. You're safe now, but be very careful, Cadence, as there's no telling what that crazy bastard might do to get you back."

"I know. They're taking us to a safe house. We can't wait to see you, Christian. God, we've missed you," I said, my voice cracking again with a combination of relief and exhaustion. "But I doubt I'll sleep until we get Sophie back."

"Well, at least rest. I'll get to you as quickly as I can," said Christian. "Can you put me on speaker?"

I found the speaker button on the phone and pressed it. "You're on speaker," I said.

"I love you both very much, and it won't be long until we're together. Promise me you'll stay safe and both get some rest," he said, his now calm voice soothing us from a distance.

"We promise," we said, nearly in unison.

"Love you, dad," said Cale.

"Love you, Christian," I added.

"I love you guys too. Goodbye for now," he finished the call.

Leo ran faster than he could ever remember, his adrenaline-powered body navigating the maze inside the naval building, dodging voices as he traversed the dimly lit halls. He knew he was being pursued and it wouldn't be long before either an officer or a cop tracked him down. He could barely feel the headache lurking behind his eyes after the hard blow his head endured. And the bullet wound on his upper left arm felt like a mere cut, even though it splattered a trail of blood on the concrete floor.

He came to an exit and slowly opened the door, jumping as he came face-to-face with a young officer. "He's here!" the uniformed man yelled, while aiming his gun at Leo.

Leo's actions were automatic; programmed in his brain from so many similar incidents over the course of his dramatic CIA career. He lurched down and pulled the officer to the ground, the officer's shot firing wide at an awkward angle into the distance. Leo then knocked him out with a blow to the head and stripped him. Leo quickly put the uniform on over his sweat-drenched clothes, placing the hat firmly on his damp head. He tied the officer's socks tightly around the bleeding wound in his arm, to try and stop the bleeding so that it wouldn't seep through the white uniform and tip others off as to his true identity. Next, he slid the officer's wallet into his pocket, and took his weapon.

Leo took off towards another building, hearing the noises of other officers and cops zeroing in on his location. He slipped inside another door, just as they rounded the corner. He walked calmly through the building, passing other officers who obviously had been summoned to help outside, their eyes serious and focused. He ducked into a small meeting room, sitting in a chair and sighing with relief, feeling safe for the moment. Taking out the wallet, he studied the identity of Brent Burrows, memorizing his personal details and planning his exit off the base.

Agent Jack Kent stood with a small group of FBI agents at the naval base, taking in the details of what had just transpired. A base-wide search had been ordered for Leo. Jack's mind was racing, predicting what Richard White's next move might be. He had ordered that Cadence and Cale be taken to a safe house at a heavily guarded home in a gated community in La Jolla.

If they could catch Leo, they'd be one step closer to finding Richard White and Sophie. The mental energy he'd put into this case over the years had reached a boiling point, his mind brimming with information and potential strategies.

He cleared his throat and spoke to the team around him. "Fantastic job getting some of Richard's men, and running off the others. Those guys are ruthless, and it took great bravery to confront them. But make no mistake, there are more where they came from and they will be in full pursuit of Cadence Davidson. The key to solving the mystery of the yacht's location and where Sophie Davidson is being held, is to locate Leo. He's gotta still be somewhere on this base. He's ex-CIA and as stealthy as they come. He's likely disguised himself, maybe as a naval officer or a cop, but he was shot in the arm so blood spatter may give him away. All exits are being guarded, but we need every square inch of this base, including the entire fleet, searched," ordered Jack, as his team mobilized to aid the police and the Navy in the search for Leo.

Jack whispered to himself, "Richard White, your days of being free are nearing their end, of that I can assure you."

Chapter Forty-Three

I LAY ON THE king size bed, Cale sleeping fitfully in my arms. It was the middle of the night, and I tried to sleep, but my mind got in the way. Cale woke up from a nightmare. "Stop, stop!" he screamed, drenched in sweat and shaking as I soothed him back to sleep. The trauma had been too much for his young brain, and I wished he hadn't been taken captive with Sophie and me. How many years would he have nightmares about these last few days?

I heard voices in the house. I was hyper alert, imagining Richard's men breaking in and pulling me away from my freedom. The voices got closer, and I sat up, my heart racing. The door slowly opened, and there stood Christian, being careful not to wake us. I gently unwrapped my arms from Cale, jumped from the bed and ran into Christian's welcoming arms. He embraced me tightly. Protectively. His lips met mine, kissing me tenderly. I'd wondered if this moment would ever come when we were out on the ocean, yet here I was with my beloved husband.

But we couldn't celebrate yet. I pulled away and looked into his dark eyes. "I've been thinking about how they're going to find our Sophie," I said.

"I just spoke with Jack, and he can meet with us in the morning. His team is still at the naval base trying to catch Leo," he explained. "It won't be long until we get Sophie back, Cadence. I can feel this nightmare coming to an end. I'd give anything to be able to put a bullet through Richard White's warped head," he added, tensing up and emanating a level of hatred I'd never seen before.

"I just want her back safely. We can live under new identities. At this point I will do anything to be together as a family and not have to live in fear of being abducted again," I said.

"Did he hurt you?" asked Christian, holding my shoulders and gazing into my eyes, searching for clues as to what happened to me. His dark eyes showed both compassion and protectiveness.

"No, not really. I … I don't really want to talk about it now," I said, my mind flashing back to the master bedroom on the yacht. The hot tub on the deck. The rings, which I'd forgotten about until this moment; lifting my hands, I stared at the large diamond on my left hand, and the stunning ruby on my right ring finger.

"Oh my God," said Christian, taking my hands and staring at the impressive stones with disgust. "Where's our ring?" he asked, shaking his head as he knew the answer.

"He has it. Christian … I had no choice. I had to protect the kids," I said, alluding to how I'd agreed to be Richard's wife for those forty-eight hours.

Christian gently pulled the diamond off, followed by the ruby, and hurled them across the room. "Bastard! That crazy bastard, thinking he can have my wife! That he can steal my daughter and son! He may have billions, but he can't buy a family … *my* family," seethed Christian.

"I'm okay, Christian. Cale's physically fine but we'll need to deal with the mental trauma from being kidnapped. And we need Sophie back before we can all begin to heal," I said, hugging Christian tightly.

"We'll get through this. I love you so much, and it kills me that you had to go through this again," he said, embracing me for a few seconds. "Let's get a bit of rest and hear what the plan is from Jack first thing in the morning. I'll do anything it takes to make sure Richard White is never able to hurt my family again," he said. And I didn't doubt it.

Richard stood on the deck of the master suite, staring out at another picturesque sunrise over the ocean. Alone. Again. Sophie had finally fallen asleep in the last hour, safe in her room. Richard had watched her, much like he'd done from a distance so many times before. Her long, strawberry blonde hair splayed out on the pillow. He adored her. He couldn't imagine losing her. Ever. Yet he knew that if he didn't get Cadence back, he would face a very difficult decision. A decision that the voice in his head wouldn't let him forget.

You can't keep the girl apart from her mother. It's just plain evil. She will grow to hate every cell in your body. You can't raise her on your own. She'll turn out as warped as you are. A girl needs a mother, just like a boy needs a father.

"I'll get Cadence back. My men are good, very good. They

will get her back. Then I will have both of my ladies together again," Richard said, sounding as firm as he could, yet knowing that he had lost the complete control he thought he'd had.

Good luck with that. Now the FBI are protecting her. Half your team has been slaughtered. I'd say your chances of seeing Cadence again are extremely low to nil.

"I have faith. I do. And if I can't see Cadence again … then …" Richard's voice trailed off as he stared ahead, transfixed by the view, his mind clouded by the deep sense of loss he felt.

Then what*? Then what the fuck will you do?*

—

Like a rat successfully escaping a maze, Leo was finally out of the naval base, and inside an old car he'd jump started. He was heading towards his storage unit. It was a combination of being quick on his feet, both literally and figuratively, that had gotten him out of this bind. There were several close calls in that large naval base, but he'd navigated worse situations. His arm now throbbed in unison with his pounding headache, but he stayed focused on getting to his storage unit.

He hated that he was forced into this scenario. He would've done absolutely anything to protect Richard, yet that self-centered asshole had left Leo no choice but to shoot him. And now Leo would live out his days on the run, hiding from the cops, the FBI, and most challenging of all, from Richard White. The White Op would pursue Leo with a vengeance, but having been part of their team, he knew how to stay one step ahead.

He'd thought about ending it all, driving off a road and into the Pacific Ocean … maybe off one of the bridges. But the thought of Richard … his face … his green eyes … living on in this world seemed terribly wrong. If Leo was going to die, he was going to take Richard with him. Richard deserved to die. If Leo could go back in time, he would have left Richard to burn to death on that deck in Oregon. If he could only get back to the yacht, he would end Richard's life, once and for all.

He pulled into the secure lot in the early hours of the morning, showing his fake ID to the guard on duty, and pulling up to unit sixty-nine. He remembered being here months ago, setting up this storage unit just in case the abduction went south, and he needed to quickly disappear. He remembered chuckling at the number sixty-nine, allowing himself to imagine enacting that position with Richard. His momentary lust was replaced by intense loathing for Richard, and an intense drive to find him again and pay him back for the hurt and betrayal that Leo had suffered.

Inside the storage unit, Leo found his supplies. There were several bottles of water; he drank two immediately and poured another over his pounding head. He found his medical bag and swallowed a couple of painkillers. Then he stripped down and removed the socks tied around his wounded arm. He grimaced with pain and disgust as he removed the drenched socks, stained dark with his blood. He carefully cleaned the wound with antiseptic, swearing as the searing pain shot through his arm. Then he smeared the area with Polysporin, bandaged it, and got dressed in a clean set of clothes.

He powered on the disposable burner cell he'd left there. There was money, credit cards, a passport, and driver's license, all under the name of Patrick Hill. His new identity. He could answer any question thrown at him about good ol' Pat. And as Pat, his mission was simple … destroy Richard White.

Chapter Forty-Four

JACK SAT ACROSS FROM Christian, Cale and me in the kitchen at the safe house. He was buzzing with energy, even though his bloodshot eyes gave away his lack of sleep. "My team was able to zero in on a rough location of the yacht from the helicopter's satellite communications system, and we've now got a read on it. We're tracking it and the plan is to have the nearest Navy ship meet up with it, along with a secondary Coast Guard vessel. We are bringing in Air Force support as well. We aren't taking any chances, not knowing what type of weapons White might have onboard."

"I want to be on that ship," insisted Christian, his dark eyes serious as they looked from Jack to me and back.

"That's not possible, Christian. We barely allowed it last time, plus we need you safely here with Cadence and Cale at this juncture. And with emotions at play, we want to make sure we're thinking objectively about the best possible way to safely remove Sophie from the yacht," explained Jack.

"But I *need* to be there to meet her. I'm her dad, for God's sake, and I want to be there to comfort her after what she's been through."

"And I need to be there as well," I declared.

"I'm sorry, but it's too much of a risk, Cadence. I doubt anything would unravel for us, but if it did, you'd be at risk of being taken again," Jack said matter-of-factly. "That said, we will get Sophie to you quickly once we have her safely away," Jack explained. I knew it wasn't worth pushing any further.

"Good, cause I don't want my mom and dad to go," added Cale.

"We trust you, Jack, that after this, *Richard White* will *never* be in our lives again," Christian said. His tone when saying Richard's name had always been cold, but now it was full of rage and revenge, which I wasn't used to hearing from my sweet and calm husband.

Jack responded, "It's settled then. I will personally keep you posted every step of the way. I'll fly out this afternoon to join the ship. I have our best agents onboard, including my most trusted hostage negotiator, Agent Larissa Brody. By nightfall, we will have intercepted the yacht. We have the best team on board to ensure Sophie's safe release."

I shuddered, thinking of Sophie and the chaos aboard the Great White when this would all go down. I prayed that Richard would see the logic of giving her back to me. Of finally letting go.

Sophie woke up from a fitful, nightmare-filled sleep, and was startled to see her father standing in the doorway, arms crossed as he leaned against the doorframe. "What's going on?" she asked, her heart pounding.

"I was just checking on you, sweetheart. I'm glad you finally got some rest."

"What's going to happen? When can I see mom?" she asked, the question burning on her tongue since she learned that Cale and her mom were safe with the police.

"My men are trying to get her back, honey, so we can be a family again," Richard said, his eyes locked with hers. Although confident, he didn't sound as convincing as before.

"What about Cale, though?" Sophie asked.

"He's not coming back. He needs to be with his father, Sophie. I know now that I could never do justice to that role when it comes to him."

"Mom would never be happy without Cale. Father, you can't steal her again. It's wrong," Sophie said.

"There's nothing wrong with loving someone the way I love your mother, Sophie. But I fear she's slipping from me forever," he said, his voice edged with profound sadness.

Sophie studied his face. She once again felt sorry for this lost man. Was now the time to bring up her wish? Her idea?

"Father, I have a proposition," Sophie said, sounding hesitant, yet trying to remain strong.

"What is it, Sophie?" he asked.

"I want to see my mom and my brother. And my … dad. But I want to be with you, too. What if you let me go back home, but I promise to see you secretly? We could keep in touch, and I would never tell anyone."

Richard half smiled, but gently shook his head. "Oh,

Sophie. Your innocence is endearing, but that would be next to impossible. I live in hiding, and although I can reach out to you, it would be very difficult for me to spend any time with you. The FBI would be vigilant. I know how these things go. It took me twelve years to get you back … to have the right plan in place. And I'm *not* about to lose you so quickly now," he said, looking intently at his daughter.

"So, you're going to hold me hostage, and keep me from my family? That's not right!"

"It's neither right nor wrong, Sophie. It's just the way it needs to be right now. My heart is already broken from … from losing Cadence, and I can't endure another loss now." He ran his hand through his hair. Were those tears in his eyes? Sophie thought she spotted moisture in their familiar green depths, and again felt sorry for this man, along with anger for what he was saying and doing. "I'm going to keep hoping that they bring your mother back here, where she belongs," he said. "Speaking of which, I'm going to call my on-land security team for an update. Join me for breakfast when you're ready, sweetheart," he added, then gently closed the door and left.

Richard took the stairs two at a time, ending up in the security room where Peter was already engaged in a conversation on the satellite phone. "Give me the phone," ordered Richard.

"Do you have her?" demanded Richard.

"Not yet," said Bob. The FBI's got her well hidden, and there's no sign of Leo either. We're doing everything we possibly can. Even our inside connections aren't panning out this time," explained Bob in defeat.

"What a fucking disaster you guys are," Richard said. "Starting with you, Peter, for letting them get away in the first place!" he roared, turning towards Peter, his face red with rage. Turning his attention back to the phone, he said, "Keep up your efforts, Bob. You've got until nightfall, as I'm running out of patience." He abruptly ended the call.

Trying to maintain confidence, Peter said, "Boss, I know we—"

"You promised me on your life that we'd get them back," seethed Richard, grabbing Peter and throwing him down onto the wooden floor.

Peter looked up and implored, "Boss, I can—"

Richard kicked him hard in the head, not once, but twice, and Peter passed out without much struggle. Richard's younger age, size and strength, combined with his fury, were no match for the aged and exhausted older man. Richard opened the door to the deck just outside the security room, lifted Peter's limp body, and threw him overboard.

Chapter Forty-Five

"HELLO CADENCE AND CHRISTIAN, Jack here," said the familiar voice from the speaker phone at the safe house. "I've landed on the Navy ship and am heading towards the yacht. I'm with Agent Brody and the rest of the team. We just received an anonymous tip. A man just called the field office and gave us Richard's satellite phone number. We're guessing it was Leo. We're getting close to the yacht, and are going to call Richard to begin negotiations shortly."

"Please don't do anything to risk Sophie's safety … he's so unpredictable when provoked," I said, feeling Christian's arm trying to comfort me as I shook with anticipation and fear.

"We'll make sure that Sophie is safe. We've been doing this for a long time, Cadence. Just know that it could take hours. And it will be draining. But we *will* get Sophie back."

"I trust you," I said.

"We know you guys are pros, but Richard White is in a

league of his own. We can't take any risks when it comes to our daughter," added Christian.

"I know. Just trust me. We'll be in touch as soon as we have news."

—

Richard lay on his bed in the late afternoon as Owen tended to his stitches. "What were you doing, boss, to tear two of these?" he asked.

"Just moving around too much. I have always had trouble sitting still," Richard answered, the image of Peter's limp body hurling into the ocean playing repeatedly through his mind. He wondered how long it would be before anyone on board would notice his absence.

"You gotta get more rest, we can't risk an infection because—," Owen carefully lectured, but was cut off by Richard's satellite phone ringing.

Richard reached for it on his bedside table, dreading the latest report from Bob. "Yes?" he answered.

"Richard White?" a female voice asked.

Richard paused, knowing this was not good. He didn't recognize the voice on the other end of the line, but knew his signal was untraceable. "Who is this?"

"Mr. White, this is FBI Agent Larissa Brody. We're close to your yacht and we need to get Sophie safely back to her mother," the confident voice said.

Richard froze, automatically programmed to distrust what was being said, but a small part of him knowing this could be true. Could Leo have tipped the FBI off about how to find the

Great White's location? "How do I know that what you are saying is true?" Richard demanded.

"I can confirm your coordinates, they are …"

Richard listened to Agent Brody relay the information. He knew it was true, as he'd been on the bridge just a few minutes before. He'd been checking on their location and discussing their route with the second mate, Mitchell.

"Mr. White?"

Richard hurled the phone across the room, forgetting that Owen was still there. "Boss, is everything okay?"

"No!" yelled Richard. "Leave me alone," he ordered Owen, who looked concerned as he reminded Richard to radio him if a fever came on, then hastily left the room.

Pick up the phone, you coward, the voice abruptly started. *Deal with the disaster you've created. Your time is running out. Tick tock, tick tock!*

Richard winced in pain as he pulled himself off the bed, and walked towards the phone, inching down carefully to pick it up. The woman's voice was still there. "Mr. White?"

"Yes."

"We need an assurance that Sophie is safe."

"She's my daughter, of course I wouldn't let anything happen to her!"

"You need to give her back to her mother."

"I will give Sophie back, but only on one condition. I get the chance to see Cadence here on our yacht once more, and say a proper goodbye."

Larissa was caught off guard, not expecting Richard White to agree to give up Sophie this easily. And she was distrustful of his words. "Cadence is not here with us. She's back on the mainland, so that's not possible. But we could arrange for you to speak with her by phone to say goodbye," said Agent Brody.

"No. I want to see her one last time. Then I promise that I will return them both to you safely."

"Let me consult with my team for a minute. I'll be right back." Larissa muted the line to discuss it with Jack. "It's risky. Richard White is a master of hidden plans and has eluded us for years," she said.

"Let's see what Cadence thinks; it's ultimately up to her if he won't budge on his request," said Jack.

Larissa unmuted the line. "Mr. White, we'll need some time to contact Cadence and fly her out here, if she's willing."

"I know she'd want to be here to get Sophie. And if she wants Sophie, the least she can do is say goodbye to me in person," he said, his voice calm, yet with a hint of sadness.

"I'll call you back shortly."

"Fine."

Jack had already dialed the secure line to the safe house, and was immediately connected to Cadence and Christian.

"Cadence, it's Jack," he said through the speaker phone.

"What's happening? Is Sophie okay?" I asked.

"As far as we know, she's resting right now. Richard has agreed to return her safely to you, but in return for seeing you on his yacht one last time to say goodbye. But we need to understand your thoughts on this request. And to discuss the risks," Jack explained.

I was speechless, my throat tight with fear.

"That's too dangerous, he'll find a way to take Cadence away," blurted Christian, his dark eyes full of defiance.

"Any plan has its risks. Our only other option is to enter the Great White with force, but that's risky. We are worried that if Richard White is provoked or startled we are taking a greater risk than by going into a planned exchange. We can set the terms of you being there a short time, outside on the deck, and accompanied by our guards. You know Richard better than anyone, Cadence, so this needs to be your call," said Jack.

"I know Richard, he won't budge. If this is what he wants, then it's what I need to do to get Sophie back," I said, feeling calmer than I expected.

"Then I'm coming too," said Christian. "I can't let you go alone and risk never seeing you again, Cadence," he held both of my hands tightly, his eyes pleading with me to agree.

"That's not possible, it's too risky, Christian. We need you to stay with your son. We'll get your wife and daughter back safely, you can count on that," said Jack.

"He's right," I said. "Cale needs you." I looked at him, my eyes begging him, as I squeezed his hands in my shaking ones. "And I know that Richard won't hurt Sophie and me."

"I don't like this one bit," said Christian. "You can't go on there without a team of agents," he added.

"Of course, that will be one of our requirements," confirmed Jack. "There's no way he can harm Cadence or Sophie, nor would he be able to escape. We'll have naval, coast guard and air support all around the yacht. And the goodbye will be a short five minutes. That's it. Then this will all be over."

Christian ran his hands through his thick hair. "Let's just get it done quickly, so that we can have our family back," he said, surrendering to the situation.

"We will get it done as soon as we possibly can. I promise," said Jack.

"Then you'll blow Richard White's head off, I hope?" asked Christian, again his rage at a level that I was unaccustomed to.

"We'll arrest him, and he'll be tried for multiple murders and a litany of other crimes. You will see him get the punishment he deserves," promised Jack. "Agents will be bringing you to a chopper right away, Cadence. I'll see you in a few hours."

"Okay, thanks, Jack," I said, my body vibrating with anticipatory fear. The line disconnected. I hugged Christian tightly, both of us too emotional to speak. I was glad that Cale was playing a video game in another room, and had not heard our conversation with Jack.

Five minutes later I was at the backdoor of the safe house, clinging to Cale. "I'll be back with Sophie when you wake up tomorrow morning, sweetheart. Then this will all be over and we will never have to worry about Richard White again," I promised.

Larissa got the okay from Jack, and dialed Richard's number once more.

"Richard White here."

"Mr. White, this is Agent Brody. Cadence is being flown to our location and will be here in a few hours. When she arrives, a team of our agents will take her by helicopter to your helipad, where you will have five minutes to say your goodbye and handoff Sophie to her mother."

"Five minutes? That's too short," he said. Five minutes to say goodbye to the love of his life was unacceptable.

"That's all we can do, Mr. White. Do we have a deal?"

"Yes ..." he said, hanging up the phone.

Chapter Forty-Six

RICHARD SAT ACROSS FROM Sophie at the dining room table. Candles softly flickered in the center of the table as night fell over the Great White. His daughter looked lovely in a white dress, a red headband topping her hair. He wanted to savor this moment, to stretch it out, knowing this would likely be his last meal with her. Although he'd been able to spend some time with her today, he felt strained given how things were unraveling and the constant physical pain pulsing through his body only made things worse.

He had taken another painkiller before dinner in the hope that he could better enjoy their last meal together. "Sophie, you are so beautiful. So talented. So amazing," he said.

"Thank you, father," she replied. "Can we talk about what's happening? I need to know about mom," she said.

"She's being brought onto the ship in the next couple of hours. To get you … back," he said, his mask unable to hide the pain in his green eyes.

"And you'll ... let me ... go?" stammered Sophie.

He stared back at his daughter. He wanted nothing more than to get away from here with her on one of the lifeboats. To take her to one of his homes in Europe. Or Australia. Far away where no one would ever find them. But he knew he could never do that to her. He must let her go or risk her hating him forever. He wouldn't let himself be a father who was detested. He couldn't and *wouldn't* be like his own father. Without Cadence, his hope for having a family was annihilated. For the first time, he felt an utter lack of hope. And he could not come up with any viable plan. "Yes, Sophie. That's what they all want," he stated.

"But, I want to ... to see you again one day," she said, earnestly looking into her father's eyes. The eyes of an abductor, yet the eyes of a father who loved her. She felt torn.

"Sophie, I can't predict the future, but I want you to know that I love you and will always love your mother, too," he said. His sadness was palpable, and brought Sophie instinctively to her feet to go and hug him. He winced from the searing pain in his shoulder as her arms encircled him, but the pain was worth his daughter's warmth.

The voice came back as Richard was slowly making his way to the security room: *You have no more power. You're as powerless as you were at ten years old. And now your staff are going to pay for your stupidity. You're weak and pathetic—*

"Shut the fuck up," growled Richard, knowing that he

needed to take control, as he entered the security room and radioed Owen.

When Owen entered shortly after, Richard was sitting slumped in a chair, barely looking up as he addressed Owen. "Leo leaked our location to the FBI, and they are now an hour away. I will be releasing Sophie back to Cadence tonight, and will say my final goodbyes on the helipad. It will not be long until this yacht will be teeming with agents, and everyone will be interrogated. I don't want to alarm the staff, as there's nothing they can do to get away at this point," Richard said, finally making eye contact with a shocked Owen.

"Holy shit!" said Owen.

"I would have made arrangements for a helicopter to come get everyone, but there was no point. It would have been tracked and followed now that the FBI has our location," he explained. Owen had never seen or heard Richard so defeated. For once Richard didn't elicit fear and respect.

"We will all be charged as accessories to your crimes, including the abduction of kids," Owen stated, his voice trembling with fear.

"I would not use the word *abducted*. I was bringing my *family* together," said Richard, bending over with pain.

"Where's Peter?"

"I'm not sure; maybe he found a way to leave," said Richard.

"How could you do this to us?" asked Owen. "We trusted you."

"I did what I had to do to bring my family together. Leo is the one who committed a crime, a crime against all of us, which has put everyone here at risk. The blame rests with Leo, *not* me. I've told you the truth, but I do not want the staff to panic, so you are not to tell anyone. Now I need to spend my final hour with my daughter," said Richard, his tone clear and firm, as he turned abruptly and left.

Richard heard Sophie's beautiful voice as he entered her suite. She was singing in a beautiful, yet melancholy voice in her music studio. He stood in the entryway smiling, proud of her amazing voice. She continued to sing *Early One Morning* and ended with *I Dreamed a Dream* from *Les Misérables*, which was captivating. Richard discretely turned to wipe the tears from his cheeks, then clapped. "Bravo, darling. Bravo!" It took almost all his strength to show enthusiasm in his weakened state.

"If I can't see you, maybe you'll still come to my concerts like you used to?" Sophie asked, feeling strange about their impending separation; although, she couldn't wait to see her mom, dad and brother again, and have her life in New York back.

"If I can, I most certainly will, my dear," he said with a smile. How bittersweet this moment was; finally feeling a connection, a bond with his girl, only to have it imminently torn away.

"What will happen when we leave? How will *you* get away?" Sophie asked, now thinking beyond her own departure.

"I ... I'm not sure, Sophie. Let me worry about that once you are back with your mother," he said. "I would like you to take some things with you to remember me. I have packed some photos, including the ones of your mother and me from our wedding and her graduation. I also want you to take the jewelry I bought you, and anything else you would like from your room."

Just then his satellite phone rang. "Hello? Yes, we will be up there then," he said, ending the call. "Sophie, we have fifteen minutes until they get here. So please take whatever you'd like, sweetheart," he said. "I will be back shortly so that we can walk up together."

"Okay, father," she said. Was he just seeing things or were his daughter's eyes shiny with tears?

He felt sick with loss and despair, coupled with intense physical pain. He walked slowly to his bedroom, then entered his en suite and closed the door. "Why?" he yelled, and crumpled to the floor, sitting against the wall and sobbing like he had so many times before while growing up. Where was his drive to fight back? Why didn't he have an idea of what to do? He always knew what to do! There was always a way to get what he wanted given his wealth. But all he felt was weak and defeated, with the heat of a fever mounting in his body.

The voice suddenly piped up: *You should just end your life; it's going to be over after this anyway. If you have any courage left, you should finish yourself off and save your daughter the humiliation of a trial. So many people hate you anyway. What do you have left to live for?*

"My daughter loves me. She's what I have left!" he roared, forcing his weak body to stand and go back to say goodbye to Sophie.

The night didn't seem so dark as the stars shone brilliantly overhead. I'd been briefed several times on the flight here. When we landed on the naval ship I was transferred to another helicopter where Jack Kent, Larissa Brody, and a handful of other agents were waiting for me.

Jack spoke assuredly, "Cadence, you're going to do just fine.

Very soon we'll have your daughter back safely."

"I can't thank you all enough for putting yourselves at risk to free Sophie," I said, looking around at the intense faces of the agents who were strapped in beside me and eager to finally apprehend Richard White.

"You're a brave woman for dealing with that man, not once, but *twice*, and escaping both times," said Larissa Brody, her smile confident as her blue eyes stared at me with a look of admiration.

"I just did what I had to," I said, wondering what Richard would say to me in our final minutes together. Would he profess his love or his rage? In the back of my mind I couldn't help but wonder if he had another plan devised that would catch everyone off guard and risk Sophie and me being taken somewhere else.

Larissa interrupted my thoughts. "You acted bravely. You collaborated where you could and you navigated a brutally challenging scenario. When we land, we'll have your back," said Larissa.

—

Richard and Sophie sat on a bench next to the helipad, staring up at the stars, searching for planets and constellations in their final minutes together. Finding Sophie had been a greater joy than he ever thought possible. Oh, how he wished they could have had hundreds of these nights together.

The faint sound and light of a helicopter appeared in the distance and made its way across the night sky towards the Great White. Richard subdued his urge to grab Sophie and run … to speed off in one of the lifeboats. They would be followed anyway, and he simply didn't have the energy as the fever now burned even stronger, weakening his entire body. He felt as though he might collapse if he tried to go back downstairs.

"Father, you seem sick," Sophie observed, as Richard held his head in his hands.

"Just a fever, darling, from my shoulder wound."

She put an arm around him, then stretched up to kiss his cheek. "I hope you feel better soon, father. I'm going to … to miss you," she said.

Richard had a bag beside him and reached into it, pulling out a single red rose and handing it to Sophie. "This is for my lovely daughter. Red instead of pink, as you are growing into a beautiful young lady who will one day be an amazing woman. I have always loved you, Sophie, and will love you no matter what happens," he added.

Sophie wiped her tears, and gave him another hug, this time gentler, knowing how much pain he was in. "Oh, father, I love you," she said, as the helicopter began its descent towards the helipad.

Those words meant more to Richard than he could have ever imagined. Sophie's love gave him the final burst of strength he needed to say a proper goodbye and express his devotion one final time to Cadence. "I love you too, more than anything in the world," he said, as he stood up.

"Sophie, move back by the doorway, as the landing is not always smooth. The rotor creates a lot of turbulent air, and could knock you over. I don't want you to get hurt," he said, motioning her to move farther back towards the door.

He looked up at the helicopter, imagining Cadence on board, surrounded by agents. Like a rose surrounded by thorns, he thought. He noticed that his fever was making him less sharp, as he thought for a moment that he was seeing his own helicopter and not the FBI's. His fevered mind confused him further when he spotted a second helicopter coming from the other direction. This landing pad wasn't built for two.

He backed up as the helicopter positioned itself directly above them to land. Down. Down. Down. He wasn't imagining things, it *was* his helicopter. It landed roughly, the entire deck vibrating. Through a break in the window, a gun and a familiar face met his stare. "Sophie, run!" were Richard's last words, a second before a bullet blasted through his chest.

Sophie screamed as she ran through the door and down the metal staircase as fast as she could, nearly crashing into Owen who was on his way up. "Leo's back and he's got a gun!" she shouted.

"Go hide!" Owen pulled out his gun and ran up the stairs, expecting to shoot Leo on sight, and hoping not to be shot in return.

Owen cleared the doorway, and to his surprise, Leo's back was to him; he was sitting on the ground beside Richard. Another chopper was hovering closely over them, its noise cloaking Owen's steps as he made his way over to them with his gun aimed at Leo. What the fuck was going on? It looked like Leo was comforting Richard. Owen knew what he needed to do; he took a deep breath, aiming directly at Leo. As he was about to fire, Leo lifted his own gun and shot himself in the head, slumping to the ground beside Richard.

The chopper above was lowering down an agent, as Owen stared at the scene in shock. The agent landed on the helipad, her gun aimed at Owen. He dropped his weapon, putting his hands in the air. "Where's Sophie?" the agent yelled, as another agent was rappelling from the chopper.

"I passed her on the stairs. She told me that Leo was back, and that he had a gun, so I told her to hide. I'm Owen, the helicopter pilot and paramedic; if you want to land, I can fly this one off of here," he suggested, pointing to the helicopter on the deck.

"No way, one of our agents will fly it off of here. You're staying put," she commanded. "We have *lots* of questions." A second and then a third agent were rappelling from the chopper.

"I'm not the bad guy here. I was just doing my job. I was going to shoot Leo to protect Sophie, but he shot himself just as I got here," explained Owen, panicked about what lay ahead for him and wishing that he'd tried to make a run for it on one of the lifeboats.

Sophie hid under the bed in the isolation room. She guessed that this was one of the last places Leo would think she'd willingly go. When the door finally opened, a female voice called her name. "Sophie, are you in here?"

"Yes!" Sophie cried, crawling out from under the bed.

"Sophie, I'm Agent Larissa Brody. You're safe now. Leo is dead, and your mother is on the helipad waiting for you." The woman put her arm around Sophie, guiding her out of the room and upstairs towards freedom.

"Is my mother with my father?" asked Sophie, as they ascended the stairs.

"Yes. But I should tell you that Leo shot your father,"

explained Larissa, not knowing how the girl might react, given that he'd abducted her.

Sophie burst into tears. "Oh, nooo!" she cried, running as fast as she could up the stairwell.

I couldn't believe my eyes at the scene in front of me as I left the helicopter and stepped onto the helipad. Richard and Leo were both lying in pools of blood, and a paramedic from the team that just landed was examining them. I felt Jack's arm on my shoulder. "Up to you, Cadence, if you want to go over or wait for Sophie here. Larissa found her and they'll be up in a minute," he said, his strong hand and calm voice comforting me as my heart raced.

"Are they both … dead?" I asked, walking over to Richard and Leo.

"Leo was just pronounced dead. Richard White's still hanging on," said Jack.

The tears that sprang to my eyes surprised me, as I stood above where Richard lay. The paramedic who was with him looked up at us. "There's nothing I can do. He's lost too much blood and the bullet punctured his lung. He doesn't have long."

Just then Sophie burst through the door, followed closely by Agent Brody. "Mom!" she cried, sprinting over to me. I held out my arms and embraced her.

"Oh, Sophie, I'm so glad you're safe!" I said. We were both crying. Sophie pulled away and knelt beside Richard, in place of the paramedic who had just left his side. I knelt down beside her, the blood from the ground seeping into our clothes.

"Father, don't die!" begged Sophie, leaning down and kissing his cheek. His breathing was erratic and raspy.

Richard's eyes slowly opened, ever so slightly, revealing their green depths. "So … phie. C ... Cadence. I …" Blood gurgled from his mouth as he desperately tried to speak, "love you," he whispered.

We each reached for a hand, Sophie taking his gloved one and me the other. Our tears fell onto him in unison. I was crying for Sophie as much as I was crying to see Richard suffer. Despite all he'd done to me … to us … right now, he was just a man who was once a boy, someone I had once cared for, who needed love in his final moments.

"I love you, father. I'm glad you brought me here so that I could get to know you," Sophie said, "even if just for a little while," crying harder but trying to be brave.

I felt him squceze my hand. He tried to focus on us both, but was struggling to remain conscious. "Richard, I will take good care of our daughter," I said, softly touching his cheek. I felt a very weak squeeze from his hand as his eyes closed and he took his final breath.

Sophie hugged his body, sobbing, her face smeared with her dead father's blood.

"Goodbye, dad."

Epilogue

SOPHIE WAS BOTH NERVOUS and excited as she sat in the chair, the makeup artist doing the final touches around her eyes. Her bridesmaids were sitting in chairs nearby, sipping glasses of prosecco, chattering away while getting their hair and makeup done.

"Sophie, you look stunning," I said, taking a private moment with her. I smiled at my beautiful daughter who was marrying the love of her life, Brett, whom she had met three years ago while performing on Broadway.

"Thanks, mom," she said, smiling. Her vivid green eyes were luminous, set off by the makeup framing them. Those green eyes ... immediately bringing me back to the reality of the gift.

"I have something that I need to give you," I said, feeling an odd sense of being watched, yet knowing that this was no longer possible. It hadn't been possible for over sixteen years now.

Sophie became very still, her smile transforming into a

concerned look. "What is it, mom?" she whispered, not wanting to draw the attention of her friends.

I fished the pale blue box out of my purse. "It's … something that came in the trunk of items he left to us. His letter requested that you receive it on your wedding day," I explained, feeling like I was being controlled from another time and place.

"Mom, I thought we went through everything in there," Sophie said, recalling the trunk that had been delivered to them in New York, weeks after their rescue. It had been shipped by an attorney Richard had instructed to forward to us, should anything happen to him.

The trunk contained letters he'd written to Sophie and me, speaking of how much he loved us. About his childhood. About his dreams for our family. It had mementos he'd locked away for each of us, treasured bits and pieces from his bizarre and complicated life.

"We did go through everything, except this box that was marked as private for me. His instructions were clear that I would hold it for you until your wedding day," I explained, handing the light blue box to Sophie. I had peeked inside to make sure the contents wouldn't upset her in any way. I knew that she still felt Richard's loss, that in her own way she had grown to love Richard in the short time she had with him. Her tears at his simple funeral, with only the two of us in attendance, were heartfelt. She cried as much for the loss of him, as for how lonely of a life he had lived.

She gently pulled the lid off the box. Once it was off, she pulled out a small, folded note, revealing a sparkling necklace underneath. The necklace was comprised of a brilliant sapphire surrounded by diamonds on a simple, white gold chain. It was exquisite. "This is beautiful," whispered Sophie, not wanting to draw her friends' attention while she read. She carefully unfolded the note and started to read:

Dearest Sophie,

Today will be your wedding day, if this reaches you as planned. I wish I could be there to walk you down the aisle. I know you look beautiful, just like your mother did on our wedding day. Although I am not there in body, I am with you in spirit, and I very much wanted you to remember how proud I am of you, my daughter.

This gift was chosen for you with care for this special day. "Something old, something new, something borrowed, something blue," as the old saying goes, to bring you luck in the years ahead. Now let me explain. "Something old" is this note, written two months before you came aboard the Great White. I composed this in the event that things went awry and did not work out according to plan. "Something new" are these diamonds that I bought for you to signify your brilliance in so many ways. "Something borrowed" is the gold chain, which I gave to your mother and was left behind on White Island; I'm sure she'll let you 'borrow' it for as long as you want. Finally, "something blue" is the sapphire, which reminded me of the ocean and our time together.

I wish things could have been different, and that I could have been a true father to you. But I know that your mom has done an outstanding job of raising you. Sophie, may this day be everything you've dreamed and may your marriage bring you great joy.

Love always,

Your Dad

The End

Dear Reader,

Thank you for reading *Finding Sophie.* I really hope you enjoyed it, and that you'll consider leaving a review at one of your favorite online retailers and/or Goodreads.com. It's a great way to help other readers discover new books.

If you liked *Finding Sophie* and would like to find out more about upcoming events, contests, book signings and future releases, please feel free to follow me on:

- Facebook at Author.Laura.Lovett
- Instagram at authorlauralovett
- Goodreads at AuthorLauraLovett

You can also sign up for my newsletter, and view the book trailer for *Losing Cadence* and *Finding Sophie,* on my website at www.authorlauralovett.com.

Thanks,
Laura